De Remnant
Truth

De Remnant Truth
The Tales of Jake Mitchell and Robert Wilton Burton

Collected and with an Introduction by
Kathryn Sport and
Bert Hitchcock

THE UNIVERSITY OF ALABAMA PRESS
Tuscaloosa and London

∞

The paper on which this book is printed meets the minimum requirements of American National Standard for Information Science-Permanence of Paper for Printed Library Materials, ANSI Z39.48-1984.

Publication of this book has been assisted by a grant from the Auburn University Humanities Endowment Fund.

Library of Congress Cataloging-in-Publication Data

Burton, Robert Wilton, 1848–1917.
  De remnant truth : the tales of Jake Mitchell and Robert Wilton
Burton / collected and with an introduction by Kathryn Sport and Bert
Hitchcock.
      p.   cm.
  Includes Bibliographical references.
  ISBN 0-8173-0515-7 (pbk. : alk. paper) : $19.95 (est.)
  1. Afro-Americans—Alabama—Auburn—Fiction. 2. Afro-Americans—
Folklore—Fiction.   I. Mitchell, Jake.   II. Sport, Kathryn, 1958–
III. Hitchcock, Bert.   IV. Title.
PS1229.B62D4   1991
813'.40809761—dc20   91-27203

British Library Cataloguing-in-Publication Data available

We are a people. A people do not throw their geniuses away. If they do, it is our duty *as witnesses for the future* to collect them again for the sake of our children. If necessary, bone by bone.

—Alice Walker,
Foreword to *Zora Neale Hurston:*
A Literary Biography
by Robert E. Hemenway

Contents

Introduction   1

A Note on the Texts   21

The "Marengo Jake" Stories

M'renger   25

M'reener: How Uncle Jake Interviewed a
    "High-Drawin'" Ram   31

Marengo Mud: Old Jake's Story of
  the Bottomless Slough   38

Three Little Boys and Three Little Fishes   46

Marengo Jake Plays Another Trick on the Three Boys   52

Seismic Phenomena—Explained by a Marengo Scientist   59

Christmas in Marengo   64

Jake and Miss Emmer   71

Tripping Jake   77

The Marengo Prestidigitator   82

Marengo Jake: A Romance of Four-and-Twenty
  Blackbirds   87
Jake Cornered   94
A True Story: How Marengo Jake Elected Cleveland   98
Marengo Jake: He Tells About a Famous "Dry Drought"   105
Marengo Jake: An Incident of the Wet Drouth in
  M'ringer   110
A Marengo Runaway   116
Dick and the Devil   122
A M'ringer Rat Story   128
Old Time Christmas   134
A Pig Tale   142
An Ass in a Lion's Skin   147
Birmingham Dirt   152
Looking Backward   158
A Mule as Was a Mule   165
An Eating Match   171
Jake's New House   178
A Legend: How Clarke Played It on Marengo   183
Underground Farming   189
Jake's Senses   196
Jake Heard From   203
A Lesson in Natural History   208
Miss Mary; or, The Value of Education   214
A Model School   221
Mosquitoes of Marengo   228
Lightning   234
An Abridged Narrative   240

Introduction

De Remnant Truth: The Tales of Jake Mitchell and Robert Wilton Burton

 In Auburn, Alabama, in the late nineteenth century lived two unusually talented men. Except for residence in this small college town and the possession of extraordinary gifts for storytelling, the two had little in common. One was black; one white. One's literary medium was the spoken word; the other's was the written language. For different reasons neither would have called the other his collaborator, but that is exactly what these two individuals were. This uncontrived and heretofore almost unknown partnership produced the Alabama "Marengo Jake" stories, now rediscovered and published as a collection for the first time—and also for the first time granting full, deserved credit to the primary, black teller of these marvelous tales.

Who were the persons who gave life to Marengo Jake? And what exactly did they, and their characters, create? The white man was Robert Wilton Burton. The black man was

Jake Mitchell. Their social statuses and, relatedly, their motives and methods for storytelling differed tremendously. Together, however, with "Moss [Master] Wilbur" Burton recording the fabulous adventures and tall-tale yarns of "Marengo Jake" Mitchell, the two, in effect, co-authored thirty-six stories that appeared in major state newspapers from 1886 to 1891. These stories artfully presented the reality and the mythology of various Alabama social communities—and of the human community as a whole. If, as Burton's own testimony asserts, Jake Mitchell is to be credited with the tales themselves, it is to R. W. Burton that we owe their skillful preservation.

From one viewpoint, the Jake stories, whether considered individually or as a whole, are like a shapely tree of impressive natural growth: they provide an experience capable of untutored appreciation. Thus, one task of this Introduction is to expose a root system—to point out that while the shallow secondary roots of these stories are in the mixed topsoil of late nineteenth-century east Alabama, the primary root extends, through Europe and through centuries, deep into universal soil.

Exploring pertinent history of the local-color and tall-tale literary traditions will introduce the names of Thomas Nelson Page and Joel Chandler Harris through the American picture and that of Baron Munchausen via the European. Certain facts of post–Civil War social and cultural history must be acknowledged: that Wilton Burton and Jake Mitchell were not, and therefore are not now, co-equal co-authors; that the springs of Mitchell's imaginative genius were probably more negatively reactionary than creatively positive, more necessitated than voluntary; and that Burton's writing, part and parcel of his time and place, promoted a white supremacist stereotype. Such contextual and explanatory information should, however, deepen the intrinsic appeal, humor, and humane education that the Jake tales offer. Although in some sense extrinsic, such facts are integral. Understood as intended, they make these three-dozen memorable testimonies to the human spirit even more impressive.

Robert Wilton Burton

Robert Wilton Burton, 1848–1917. *(Courtesy, Special Collections, Ralph Brown Draughon Library, Auburn University)*

R. W. Burton moved to Auburn in 1878 in response to the request of the faculty of the prospering young college that he establish a bookstore there.[1] The Auburn venture was an extension of the bookselling business he and his brother had begun in nearby Opelika. Wilton Burton had assumed the occupation of bookseller after several years of teaching in various schools in Lee County, Alabama. Born in 1848 in Camden County, Georgia, he grew up in Lafayette, Alabama. Too young for regular army service when the Civil War broke out, Burton joined a youth militia whose members helped construct Fort Tyler near West Point, Georgia, in 1863. He enlisted in the Confederate army in March of 1865 and was assigned to Troop F of the Sixth Alabama Cavalry. Two days later he was captured on a troop train and held prisoner until the end of the war in May.

Thus legitimately if barely did he hold the distinction of being a Confederate veteran.

When Burton died on June 22, 1917, the *Montgomery Advertiser* reported that Auburn had lost the "educator, author, philanthropist" who had become its "best loved citizen." He had held numerous official positions—Presbyterian church elder, county superintendent of education, secretary of the town board of education, member and clerk of the city council, secretary to the college board of trustees. It was his unofficial offices, however, that most endeared Burton to his contemporaries. A participant in the N. T. Lupton Conversation Club, which met in members' homes to hear papers on literature, history, and current events, Burton was a well-read, genial, fun-loving individual. His bookstore was the natural gathering place for daily informal discussion of literature and life by the community's intellectual "lights." Burton's Bookstore, it was said, was "the Coffee House of the College City."

For Burton, "bookseller and stationer" (the designation that appears in the 1880 census), his retail store was a life's vocation, one to which he conscientiously devoted himself. Auburn's citizens looked forward each day to seeing what new rhyme or jingle the witty proprietor would compose for the advertising blackboard in front of his store. But Burton did not, he emphatically asserted, make "a business of literature." He did, though, confess that he had employed "some leisure moments" of a "busy life" in "writing."

Burton's writing was first published in 1875 and 1876 when the Lafayette *Clipper* printed several adventure stories, with touches of Gothic romance, by Trubon Townly (an anagram for "Burton [,] Wylton") and descriptive travel letters about the South by "Moses Primrose." In 1877, the West Point, Georgia, *Riverside Echo* published thirteen

Burton's Bookstore is in the two-story balconied building under the water tower in this view of Toomer's Corner, looking north down College Street, around 1910. *(Courtesy, Auburn University Archives)*

"Letters from a Farmer," humorous correspondence about agricultural and other local concerns that Burton had written under the pseudonym Haywood Oates. During the 1880s and 1890s, the first full decades of his long residence in Auburn, Burton produced writing of two different though not unrelated kinds and achieved two different, less local kinds of publication.

First, he contributed, in his words, "a good many stories to juvenile periodicals." These were serial adventure stories for boys, as well as some shorter local-color stories that appeared in magazines of national circulation. The most notable of these was *Golden Days for Boys and Girls,* which was among the best and more literary of the many popular American young people's magazines of the day. *Golden Days* was published in Philadelphia by James Elverson and in its comparatively long life (1880–1907) included among its contributors such well-known children's authors as C. A. Fosdick ("Harry Castlemon"), W. T. Adams ("Oliver Optic"), and Horatio Alger. Four of Burton's story contributions to *Golden Days* financed Auburn's only "four-story cottage," the author's jocular description of his residence at 315 East Magnolia Avenue.

His second kind of writing, according to Burton, was "many short sketches and verses in negro dialect." These, almost entirely, were published in regional metropolitan newspapers.

Between 1885 and 1894, newspapers in Montgomery, Birmingham, and New Orleans featured at least eighty humorous black-dialect tales and sketches by Burton. Between December 13, 1885, and November 13, 1887, his work appeared every week or so in the *Montgomery Advertiser*. The *Birmingham Age-Herald* ran his stories from March 3, 1889, to December 27, 1891. Only one story appeared in the *New Orleans Times-Democrat*—on August 12, 1894. Although he made a point of characterizing the production of these stories or sketches as not just a pastime but a "mere" pastime, Burton knew well it was by means of these pieces that he was known as a writer. (Of his juvenile tales Burton observed: "grown-up people don't read them, and young people don't remember who wrote them.") He probably also knew that in these newspaper sketches and tales lay his major achievement, that in them were grounds for any serious literary reputation he might gain.

Based, he said, on characters and events in the black community in Auburn, the tales were read and appreciated widely throughout the South. Burton was invited to appear, for example, on the 1897 program of the well-known Chautauqua in DeFuniak Springs, Florida. Like the many contemporary American local-color writers whose works he knew, Burton professed to have the dual objectives of amusement and historical preservation. Almost half, an even three dozen, of these newspaper sketches were stories about or by a character called "Marengo Jake."

Jake Mitchell

Facts are not easy to uncover about the second member of Auburn's creative duo, the person who needs to be recognized as Wilton Burton's collaborating co-author. Although actually named by Burton in one of the stories, the co-author's identification has not until now been acknowledged or confirmed. Marengo Jake was a real person named Jake Mitchell. Born in the mid-1840s in an Atlantic seaboard state, probably Virginia, Mitchell was brought to Alabama at an early age and spent most of his years in slavery on a plantation, perhaps the Drake family's, in Marengo County. Whoever his former owners may have been, the Drake connection probably accounts for Mitchell's relocation to Auburn. Dr. John Hodge Drake of that prominent west-Alabama family was for more than half a century the chief physician for Auburn, the village and the college. He came to be "an Auburn institution." Many black Drakes joined the likeable, respected white doctor in his postbellum Lee County residency and made Auburn something of a colony of black Marengo expatriates. Whatever other members of this contingent thought of the old days in Marengo, no one apparently discussed them so much nor expressed himself so distinctively as did Jake Mitchell, who himself became something of an Auburn institution as a result.

According to Burton, Mitchell's perennial theme, capable

in his hands of the most imaginative kind of evidencing, was the superiority, the supreme incomparability, of all things Marengo. Lee County, of course, was the standard, pitiful butt of specific comparison. The rats in Marengo County, for example, were the size of Lee County mules, claimed Marengo Jake. Burton asserts that Mitchell was more talkative around some white people than around others (notably, those most capable of supplying money, food, or tobacco), but all of Auburn's townspeople had heard or heard of the "whoppers" told by Jake Mitchell. He was, said Burton, "the most artistic liar, white or colored, illiterate or learned, I ever knew." Census records confirm that he was black and illiterate.

These two basic facts of Mitchell's life, reflected in his marvelous, artful tall tales, are in direct contrast to the racial and literacy status of R. W. Burton. In words attributed to Burton, Jake was "a typical old plantation negro" who possessed the "picturesque personality" of the "old-fashioned, unreconstructed" black. It is the familiar, hackneyed picture that was so dear to postbellum white memory in the South. Jake's speech and manner were that "of the untaught slave," Burton said, but through his proudest boast, that he had formerly belonged to a very wealthy planter in Marengo County, he adopted the pose of "a gentleman of decayed fortunes."

Mainstream Literary Roots

For his marvelous Marengo County stories Jake Mitchell drew unanalytically on the bountiful lore of oral folk tradition. Unknown to him, there was a printed tradition as well. R. W. Burton knew the precedent and called special attention to it: ingenious in "improvising wonderful tales," Jake, he said, was especially "given to relating stories of the Baron Munchausen type."

The *tall tale* has been so long and so closely associated with frontier America that it has come to seem a distinctively American genre. It is not, of course. Its beginnings go back to campfires thousands of years before there could be any contrast of the civilized and the primitive in North America. For the natural American development (or, at least, reporting) of the type, there is, moreover, a fascinating formal literary influence. According to a leading contemporary scholar of American humor, "an eighteenth-century German author who never visited the United States, and his immediate imitators, were the most important contributors to the plots, motifs, and techniques of American tall tale literature."[2] This German author was Rudolpf Erich Raspe (1737–94), university professor and internationally known scientist—also con man and thief. Raspe's *Baron Munchausen's Narrative of His Marvellous Travels and Campaigns in Russia* was published in London in 1785 when Raspe, as was usually the case, was in need of money. Success was immediate, and the popularity of his wildly extravagant tales has continued. By the end of the eighteenth century there had been not only an enlarged version with nine additional authorized or pirated editions, but at least two editions of a sequel—all this in England—and two augmented editions in Germany. Since then, in English or in German there have been close to 400 more editions, plus hundreds in other languages. In the United States, and especially in the territory that was yet to become part of the new nation, the fictitious Baron's fabulous tales were enthusiastically embraced.

The Munchausen tales include accounts of such exploits

as riding eagles and bridling giant seahorses (with the sling David used to kill Goliath, no less—a little Baronial family heirloom) and descriptions of such phenomena as a deer that grows a cherry tree out of its head and a horse that is sewn back together after being cut in two. In this last instance the Baron, astride the horse, discovers the latter half of his beast is missing when he seeks to learn why the horse's thirst can't be satisfied—the water was running out as fast as the horse could take it in.

Marengo Jake is easily a match for the Baron in what the Alabamian describes as "stretching the blanket." In Marengo County, for instance, the mud is so sticky that horses often pull their feet off trying to free themselves, then have to depend on wooden feet to carry them around for the rest of their days. A man walking to his neighbor's house has so much mud accumulate under his shoes that when he arrives at his destination he needs a ladder to climb down from the mud "posts." In Marengo the frogs grow as big as steers; crawfish cultivate and market cotton in their extensive underground world; rats meet to discuss grievances against farmers harvesting *their* corn; a snake stretching across a river disrupts steamboat traffic; four-story high pumpkins house fugitive slaves; and mules that stumble over watermelons drown in the juice. "A mule as was a mule" is so strong that it "humps" itself right out of its skin. A showman chops off a man's head; in his haste magically to mend the wound he sticks the head on wrong, and the victim has to "look backward" for the rest of his life.

Little wonder that Burton calls Jake Mitchell "a veritable Baron Munchausen in black." The similarities are impressive, down even to each taleteller's frequent insistence on the absolute veracity of his tales—in Jake's favorite phrase, the assertion that he's telling "de remmunt truf," the highest and only truth. Yet important differences exist between these narrators and between their tales. While Jake is not above personal aggrandizement, he is not the hero of his incredible narratives in the same way Munchausen is of his. The real hero of the Marengo Jake tales is Marengo County—a place, not a person. And this place is not, as is usual in the Munchausen tales, an exotic foreign setting to which the narrator has traveled; rather, it is where Jake has traveled *from*. It is *home*, and Marengo Jake's accounts of it include touching nostalgia, as well as entertaining braggadocio. Just how fondly, in actual fact and not in Burton's mind, Jake Mitchell remembered the place in which he was held in slavery may be open to question. Blacks frequently "wore the mask": of necessity they played the role demanded of them by whites. How better, too, to squeeze out a few more creature comforts than to flatter white patrons by recalling the days of slavery as a time of utopian contentment for all?

Place, especially regional place and distinctive localized characters, became very important in American literature in the late nineteenth century. Well read in both classic and contemporary authors, Wilton Burton knew exactly whose lead he was following in becoming a public purveyor of local-color, black-dialect tales in the United States in the mid-1880s. The use of dialect was certainly not new to the nation's literature. It had been a staple of Old Southwest humor before the Civil War and practically the stock-in-trade of the so-called literary comedians later. Black dialect entered the picture in a major way with the local-color movement, however, and Burton received high praise for his ability to represent this particular vernacular in print.

In the South, there quickly came to be two popular traditions in this new literary field, and Burton had praise for the founder of each. Thomas Nelson Page (1853–1922), nostalgic portrayer of the loyal old plantation "darky" remembering the "days befo' de wah," gained ample deference from Burton; but Page could be faulted, Burton thought, for idealizing black characters and making them more intelligent than reality justified. Joel Chandler Harris (1848–1908), on the other hand, secured Burton's unqualified praise. Making special use of black folklore from the plantation, especially the animal tale, and possessing greater skill with dialect, Harris had the genius to make those simple tales "immortal," Burton asserted.

Page, generally regarded as the most influential contributor to the old plantation school of Southern fiction, "owed his popularity to the local color movement, the interest of Northern readers in the defeated South following the Civil War, and the growth of the family magazine," according to Kimball King; the "civilization" he "eulogized," says King, was one "in which landlords abided by an almost medieval sense of *gentilesse,* women were exalted, and all the chivalric values prevailed."[3] Because of the editors' concern about so much of the narrative being in dialect, Page's first and most famous story, "Marse Chan," experienced a three-year wait between acceptance and publication. It finally appeared in *Century* magazine in 1884 and was featured, along with five other stories, in Page's first and best known book, *In Ole Virginia* (1887). Here, the Page trademark was established—what Lucinda H. MacKethan characterizes as "a totally sincere, elegaic, uncritical rendering of the plantation scene as prose idyll, presented by black narrators who were the 'chief 'pendence' of helpless owners and unable, in most cases, to survive their expulsion from Eden." Although, as MacKethan points out, Page "did not acknowledge his black narrators as individuals apart from their masters' interests, he yet depended on the vitality of their individualized voices to convey his vision." "They are," she rightly concludes, "his most memorable figures."[4]

Joel Chandler Harris, unlike Page, experienced Southern plantation life as a young employee rather than as the scion of an established aristocratic family. As early as 1876, Harris began making use of an old black character in sketches in the Atlanta *Constitution*. But Uncle Remus was firmly established in a new, now renowned guise by the time Harris's first book was published in 1880. *Uncle Remus: His Songs and His Sayings* (1880) was followed by four more Remus collections published during Harris's lifetime and then by several posthumous Remus publications. "However humorous it may be in effect, its intention is perfectly serious," said Harris of his original book. A main purpose was "to preserve . . . legends in their original simplicity and to wed them permanently to the quaint dialect," which he had tried to capture not merely in form but in essence. "Myth" and "fable" were words that Harris knowledgeably employed in his 1880 Introduction. What this self-described Georgia "cornfield journalist" achieved in the Remus stories was "a brilliant exploration of black dialect and folklore," Eric J. Sundquist believes. Not "whitewashing" the South with the absoluteness that Page's work did, the frame stories of Uncle Remus maintained "a taut balance between minstrel humor and a subversive critique of slavery and racism"; they "offer an instance of popular work grounded in local folklore that is more psychologically revealing than sophisticated narrative and speaks with an authentic and original American voice."[5]

Harris with his Uncle Remus stories remains incomparable, but it is he to whom Burton is closest both in what he attempts and, with Jake Mitchell's contribution, what he impressively achieves.

The Roots of Race

For the Marengo Jake tales published under the name of Wilton Burton, just as for the more famous Uncle Remus stories by Joel Chandler Harris, it is crucial to make a distinction between "the kernel and its husk," as Robert Bone phrases it. Readers need to be aware, says Bone, that the figure of Uncle Remus is "principally a figment of the white imagination," that a central question about these literary works is the extent to which a late nineteenth-century white Southerner imposed his own values and points of view in the process of writing down stories he had heard and providing them with a narrative frame.[6] We need to recognize, as Arthur Huff Fauset warned many years ago, that "the Harris [or Burton] variety of the Negro folk tale assumes to interpret Negro character instead of simply telling his stories," that the picturing of blacks in these works is dependent upon the stereotype of the contented plantation darky.[7] But we should remember, also, that the tales do get told, and, along with Robert Bone, recognize that although the "external wrappings" of white-reported black folktales may "function to perpetuate the plantation myth" about blacks, the tales themselves, the kernels, may remain unadulterated, their integrity respected and their recording accurate.[8]

If neither the Uncle Remus nor Marengo Jake stories directly verify the conclusion of historians that this period was the nadir of black-white racial relations in the U.S., the works of Harris and Burton do reflect the accuracy of another historical characterization of Southern racial relations at the time: "the new paternalism."[9] The "child," the black man of this relationship, was not, however, what the white "father" believed him to be. Generations of blacks had sung "Got one mind for white folks to see/'Nother for what I know is me/

He don't know, he don't know my mind."[10] For R. W.
Burton, Mitchell could provide direct reflection of Burton's
own preconceptions and desires about blacks. As Burton
pictures Marengo Jake in these stories, Jake is both the
source and the butt of humor. He is the stereotypical black
Rastus or Remus or Sambo character, the white man's
buffoon, a giver and grinner who was to occupy a dominant
place in American culture for almost a century.[11] "Clearly,"
says Joseph Boskin, "Sambo was accepted primarily because
both whites and blacks had created and needed him, the
former as an audience desperately demanding a perfor-
mance, the latter as the performer unable to escape from his
stage."[12] The key recognition that needs to be made is that
there were in fact two Sambos, one "the white man's con-
ception of the black man as Sambo" and the other "the black
man's utilization of Sambo," the latter a "complex role
involving a knowing act of pleasing and a manner of ma-
nipulating the relationship between him and his adver-
sary."[13]

Jake Mitchell's race and the roles he was consequently
called upon to play deeply influenced the tales that he spun.
Indeed it is not claiming too much to say that the tales were
the direct result of an intensely self-conscious black identity
in an oppressive white Southern universe. In the tales themselves, in their telling, and as a result of their being told in an
actual social world, black Jake Mitchell/Marengo Jake could
be and was master rather than underling. Defying political
reality, he could become a superior being in full control: the
man who always had the last word. Even the apparent irony
of Burton's, the white writer's, actually having the last
word—the final, printed word—turns to Mitchell's advan-
tage: this collection exists more to preserve Jake Mitchell's
tales than R. W. Burton's writing.

Charles Keil's assertion that "art of the 'put on' has of necessity been developed to an exceptionally high level in Negro culture"[14] takes on double meaning in view of the kinds of tales that Jake Mitchell told. "Full of folk wit and wisdom," the tales of slaves, say John F. Callahan, contained "some of the hyperbole of the tall tale, a tradition whose bravado both belies and confirms the slaves' defensive position."[15] With freedom came the development in black folk tales of the race's own Gargantuan figures, black tall-tale heroes to go with the ones white America had created.[16] Jake Mitchell was probably more the old school than the new, since he created no equivalent characters to, say, John Henry. But certainly he did exhibit the toughness and resiliency of black culture in his "ability to react creatively and responsively to the realities of a new situation."[17] His wonderful tales, in several respects, have "significance beyond . . . immediate entertainment."[18] Studied historically as ethnic folklore, they help us "to recapture the joys as well as the pains, to gain some sense of a people's angle of vision and world view, to better understand the inner dynamics of the group and the attitudes its members had toward each other as well as toward the outside world, to comprehend the mechanisms members of the group erected to guard their values, maintain their sense of worth, and retain their sanity."[19] What was entertainment for whites was ritual, drama, or dialectical catharsis for blacks. Sometimes, no one knew better than former slaves, folks have to laugh to keep from crying. Because they had to, talented black men became "specialists in changing the joke and slipping the yoke."[20]

The Fruits of Fantasy; Or,
How Far "Tall" Reaches

Not all of the Marengo Jake pieces contain Jake's tall tales of the Munchausen variety although these are by far the more memorable and amusing. Burton can, and does, provide reports about Jake without including narrative stories told by Jake. In this duality Burton is once more similar to Joel Chandler Harris, who, although it is seldom recognized, was the creator of two Uncle Remuses—one the beloved story-teller of the old plantation, the other a postbellum city-dweller who was the subject of amusement for adult white males and (in the opinion of those whites) the source of good counsel and deification for upstart younger members of his own race. The sketches Burton presents of Marengo Jake as a representative black resident of Auburn, a Jake who does not produce a wondrous tale about Marengo County, may be important as historical documents, but the unmitigated racial condescension of these pieces makes them much less appealing to readers today.

Burton characterized his writings as "illustrative of the humorous side of negro life and character." Actually they are illustrative of more than this, and Burton's claim of a "deeper purpose" than simple amusement is realized in the portrayal of more than a droll, good-natured old Southern black man. The Marengo Jake tales ultimately illustrate a humanity unrestricted by time or place, a universality unaffected by race. From them we get not only remnants of truth, but, as Jake claimed, "de remmunt truf" itself, the truth that is revealed only to a Chosen People. Scholars will be able to point out in these tales examples of timeless types and motifs of folk literature, mythic evidences of human beings trying to make sense of themselves and their worlds and, in the process, entertaining themselves and their worlds. What Jake Mitchell furnished his collaborator can, to cite Burton, be viewed as "crude material" that had to be worked up into "artistic forms." But Mitchell himself was undeniably an artist. His tales and R. W. Burtons's stories offer a double dose of the awesome capabilities, and opportunities, of human language—allowing us not only to transcend time and space but also, through the imagination, to break free from the painful, oppressive actualities of the material world.

In embodiments such as Marengo Jake, the Sambo figure, that "comic performer *par excellence,*" became the national American court-jester.[21] However, as Joseph Boskin has made clear, Sambo, unlike the traditional Jester or Fool, was "accorded the follies of foolishness" rather than "the beauty of wisdom"; unlike his honored predecessors, he was "denied wisdom and perspective, rationality and responsibility."[22] This reissue of the Marengo Jake stories is intended to revoke that denial, to grant to Jake Mitchell his rightful due. Providing deeply satisfying humor and a genuine aesthetic experience, these tales also have scholarly importance for American social and literary history. They represent, especially, a rediscovery of the black literary heritage of Alabama. Sherley Anne Williams wrote in the "Author's Note" to her novel *Dessa Rose:* "Afro-Americans, having survived by word of mouth—and made of that process a fine art—remain at the mercy of literature and writing; often these have betrayed us."[23] Because R. W. Burton did not, ultimately, betray Jake Mitchell, this collection, we believe, does not.

In one way at least, Jake Mitchell was highly fortunate to have R. W. Burton around. Wilton Burton was unquestionably lucky that he knew Jake Mitchell. But we, readers and a auditors well beyond their lifetimes, are the most fortunate of all.

—KATHRYN SPORT

BERT HITCHCOCK

Notes

1. The facts of Burton's life, and all subsequent direct quotations attributed to him, are drawn from Gladys Steadham Stewart, "Robert Wilton Burton: A Biographical Sketch, Including a Selection of His Writings" (M.S. thesis, Alabama Polytechnic Institute [Auburn University], 1932).

2. Walter Blair, "A German Connection: Raspe's Baron Munchausen," *Critical Essays on American Humor,* ed. William Bedford Clark and W. Craig Turner (Boston: G. K. Hall, 1984), 124.

3. Kimball King, "Thomas Nelson Page," in *Reference Guide to American Literature,* 2nd edition, ed. D. L. Kirkpatrick (Chicago: St. James Press, 1987), 427–28.

4. Lucinda H. MacKethan, "Plantation Fiction, 1865–1900," in *The History of Southern Literature,* ed. Louis D. Rubin, Jr., et al. (Baton Rouge: Louisiana State University Press, 1985), 212, 214.

5. Eric J. Sundquist, "Realism and Regionalism," in *Columbia Literary History of the United States,* ed. Emory Elliott et al. (New York: Columbia University Press, 1988), 514.

6. Robert Bone, *Down Home: A History of Afro-American Short Fiction from Its Beginnings to the End of the Harlem Renaissance* (New York: G. P. Putnam's Sons, 1975), 23, 20, 23.

7. Quoted in Robert E. Hemenway, *Zora Neale Hurston: A Literary Biography* (Urbana: University of Illinois Press, 1977), 90.

8. Bone, *Down Home,* 23.

9. "The New South and the New Paternalism, 1877–1890" is the title of chapter 7 of George M. Frederickson, *The Black Image in the White Mind: The Debate on Afro-American Character and Destiny, 1817–1914* (New York: Harper and Row, 1971).

10.   Lawrence W. Levine, *Black Culture and Black Consciousness: Afro-American Folk Thought from Slavery to Freedom* (New York: Oxford University Press, 1977), xiii.

11.   See Bernard Wolfe, "Uncle Remus and the Malevolent Rabbit," in *Slavery and Its Aftermath*, ed. Peter I. Rose (New York: Atherton Press, 1970), 200, 205.

12.   Joseph Boskin, "The Life and Death of Sambo: Overview of an Historical Hang-Up," in *Remus, Rastus, Revolution,* ed. Marshall Fishwick (Bowling Green, Ohio: Bowling Green University Popular Press, n.d.), 47.

13.   Boskin, "Life and Death of Sambo," 48, 49.

14.   Charles Keil, "Urban Blues," in *Slavery and Its Aftermath,* 285.

15.   John F. Callahan, *In the Afro-American Grain: The Pursuits of Voice in Twentieth-Century Black Fiction* (Urbana: University of Illinois Press, 1988), 32.

16.   Levine, *Black Culture,* 401.

17.   Levine, *Black Culture,* 5.

18.   Hemenway, *Hurston,* 172.

19.   Levine, *Black Culture,* 445.

20.   Keil, "Urban Blues," 287.

21.   Joseph Boskin, *Sambo: The Rise and Demise of an American Jester* (New York: Oxford University Press, 1986), 4.

22.   Boskin, *Sambo,* 15, 9–10.

23.   Quoted in Callahan, *Afro-American Grain,* 256.

A Note on the Texts

 The texts of the thirty-six Marengo Jake tales that follow are reproduced as they first appeared in newspapers; however, due to the poor condition and fading of some of the original copies, we have sometimes had to complete punctuation or missing words, or, in some cases, merely indicate the spaces where letters that once existed are now illegible. In any such instances we have placed brackets around the illegible or inserted items. In rare cases, we have also used brackets to correct blatant spelling errors, probably made by the newspaper typesetter. Some confusing inconsistencies in punctuation we have similarly rectified; and a few obvious punctuation errors, silently corrected. (Note: One set of brackets did appear originally— to indicate that the story "Looking Backward" is "After Edward Bellamy.") In no instance have we altered dialect representation.

The
"Marengo Jake"
Stories

M'renger

Jake is now a citizen of Auburn. He confesses as much, and he would not deny that his present estate is lowly. His clothes hang in picturesque tatters about his person; his wool rises in a grizz[l]y shock above his crownless hat; his walk is an apologetic shambling; his smile, though broad, discloses but a solitary tooth standing like a tombstone in memory of its departed fellows.

Not withstanding these tokens of present poverty and decay, Jake was once the petted child of fortune. His present condition is that of a man who has fallen from a great height—a broken down aristocrat whose most precious possession is the memory of a glorious past. Time can not efface that memory; adversity can not dim its splendor[.] On the contrary, as years and privations accumulate it grows brighter and brighter, and what once shone with the pale light of a star, now floods the chambers of memory with the strength and brilliance of a sun.

"You talks 'bout raisin' taters, Miss Purreleen," says Jake, puncturing the earth with his finger and inserting a sweet potato slip in the opening, "you des oughter seed de taters what we raised on ole Moster's plantation down in M'renger. D'aint no room in dis one-horse town for de sort o' tater patches ole Moster had. De littles' one he plant was fo' hunderd acres, an' dat warnt de onlies' one he had. Hit was des a little spot cloast to de house whar he raise yams an' de like o' dat. De patch whar he raise deze yer nigger chokers hit had more'n a thousan' acres in hit.

"What he want wid so many taters? Law! Miss Purreleen, ef you hadder knowed how many niggers ole Moster had you wouldn't a ax dat question. His niggers kiver de yeth wuss'n a swarm o' deze yer low cusses what I year de whi' folks readin' 'bout in de paper. He had three hunderd yaller gals an' three hunderd ginger-cake gals what was des 'bout grown, an' three hunderd fryin' size gals, sides de mens an' de ole womens. He use to make me wash all dem gals' fe[e]t ever' night de lawd sen'.

"Yas, ma'am, hit was a toler'ble big job to wash all dem nine hunderd gals' feets ever' night, but you see, Miss Purreleen, I had a monst'ous big tub for to wash 'em in. De tub hit was made out'n one o' dem big turnips what we raise down dar in M'renger, an' mighty nigh all dem gals could put dey feets in hit at de same time. Law! how dem sassy yaller gals love to slosh de water on me. Dey was likely gals, for a fack. I was ha'f dead to mar' one o' dem gals, but you neenter to tell Majane. I ax ole Moster for one of 'em, but he 'low' I was too black. I was de onlies' rale black nigger ole Moster had. Dat's how come I marr'd Majane. When folks can't git tater pooden dey has to take black ber' pie.

"Oh, yes, ma'am, de taters we raise was fine. Dey was so big we mos' in ginnerly had to cut 'em up wid a cross-cut saw

'fo' ever we could cook 'em, an' de folks use to come f'om
ten mile all roun' to git dat saw-dus' to make poodens out'n.
Sometimes dem gals'd buil' up a big fire in de fiel' an' roas'
one o' dem taters des for fun. Dey put one een in de fire an'
dey set down on de yuther een. You des oughter seed 'em,
Miss Purreleen—three hunderd yaller gals an' three hunderd
ginger-cake gals des 'bout grown, an' three hunderd fryin'
size gals, all settin' on de een o' one tater an' waitin' for de
yuther een to roas'.

   "Yas, ma'am, dey was plenty o' money down dar in
M'renger, an' I speck ef you was to go down dar now hit's
dar tell yit. Ole Moster had money in ever' pocket, an' he
had two banks of it in 'Moplis, an' ar one o' em was bigger'n
dat tater bank you had las' year. Ole Miss had 'fo' quilts
made out'n hunderd dollar bills, an' she had a gole walk
f'om de gate to de house, beca'se hit use to git mighty
muddy down dar in M'renger. Ole Moster use to trus' me
same es a w'te man. Many's de time I've tote his money back
an' forruds 'twix' his plantation an' 'Mop'lis. He used to say,
'Jake,' says 'e, 'yo' skin's black, but you can't hep dat, an' hit
don't make no different ef de black ain' but skin deep. I ain'
scared to trus' you,' says 'e. He gin me a fine pa'r britches
wonst, w'ich dey was pooty, streaked britches, an' I kep' 'em
for Sunday-go-to-meetin' britches. I war dem britches 'bout
six mont's, an' I never study 'bout puttin' my han' in de lef'
han' pocket, beca'se I mos' in ginnerly keeps my 'backer in
my right han' pocket. Well, ole Moster he come to me one
day atter I done been had dem britches six mont's, an' he
make inqui'ment 'bout 'em. He ax me whar dem britches
what he gin me, an' I 'lowed dey was hengin' up upsta'rs in
my house—all ole Moster's niggers' houses had upsta's to
'em. He 'low, 'Well, did you fine any money in 'em?' I says,
says I, 'No, sah, I [ne]ver partickler look for no money in

'em!' Wid dat ole Moster he tuck an' went up sta'rs in my house, an' he tuck an' tuck dem britches down off 'n de nail whar dey was hengin' an' he tuck an' turn dem pockets wrong-sided-outed, an' I aint yer dis minute ef he did'n fine a fifty dollar bill in de lef' han' pocket o' dem britches.

"Atter freedom come out I was des like all de yuther fool niggers: I des 'bleeged to go to town to live. I went to Uniontown, I did, an' I mad a contrack wid Mr. Black to he'p him run his libity stable. Well, Mr. Black he yeared ole moster talk 'bout me, an' he trus' me same es ole moster. He gin me fifty dollars a mont' an' my vittles an' cloze.

"You mighty right, Miss Purreleen, dat was big wedges, but dat was a big libity stable, an' hit tuck in a heap o' money. D'aint no stable like dat'n in dis po' country. D'aint no room for sich a stable in deze little towns like Aubu'n. You micy swell say hit was ha'f a mile long, be'ca'se hit was more'n a quarter an' a ha'f a quarter.

"No, ma'am, Uniontown ain't zackly in M'renger, but hit's so cloast hit's right smart hope up. De line pass thu de aidge o' town, an' hit cut dat stable right ha'f in two. One een was in M'renger, an' de yuther een was in Perry. Dem horses what staid in M'renger een dey was fat an' slick an' es sassy es dat yaller gal I wanted to marry. But dem what staid in de Perry een dey was sorter po' an' lazy, but dey was lots better'n deze yer Aubu'n hosses. Dey warnt nar horse in dat libity stable but what he was pearter'n ole George what b'long to moss Hodge. Ef moss Hodge had dat little sorrel filly what use to stay in de M'renger een he would'n hafter always be a clarn his throat an' a hollin' 'Gyup, gyup, George,' beca'se dat filly lif' her foot like she naich[e]rly spise de groun'. After I foun' out how peart she was I always rid her wid doom bits so I could hole her back, but de fus time I rid her I never had nuthin but common bits on her.

"Mr. Black he sont me down in M'renger to buy fo' thousan' bushels o' corn for de stable. No sooner I thowed my laig over dat filly's back she lit out es hard es she could t'ar. I fa'rly ra'red back on de bridle, but hit never done no good. Her foot hardly toch de groun'. De win' was blowin' de same way we was gwine, but we soon got 'head o' hit an' met another win' comin tother way. Hit po'd in my mouf so strong I could'n blow it out ag'in, an' I knowed ef I kep' on dat way I was 'bleeged to bu's' fo' 'long.

"W'en I got whar I was gwine I was dat full o' win dey hatter pump it out'n me 'fo' ever I could tell 'em what I com atter. Hit's de truth, an' I ain' gwine to tell you no lie. I cotch up wid a nigger on de road, an' he was ridin' of a mule. I hollered to him to cl'ar de track, but 'fo' he could move out[']n de way dat filly come 'long like a streak o' lightnin' an' pass right twix' him. I look roun' an' I seed one ha'f o' dat mule fall on one side de road an' de yuther ha'f on de tother side. His right yer an' his right fo' laig an' his right hine laig all fell on de right han' side de road an' lef' ones fell on de lef' side.

"No, madam, hit never kill de nigger, but hit split him up to his naick, an' atter dat he was de longes' laig nigger in M'renger.

"Dis yer's mightly slow wuck waterin' ever' one o' deze slips fas' es I set 'em out. We didn't hatter do dat in M'renger beca'se we always could git a rain when we 'bleeged to have it. Dey want no [r]ock[s] down dar neider. Deze yer rocks is what w'ar off my finger like it is.

"No, ma'am, hit never rained all de time in M'renger, but we never had no dry drought down dar. Hit warnt like it is up yer. Sometimes Mr. [']Fessor Mell hengs so many flags up on de college hit look like de cloze li[n]e at my house w'en Majane been a doin' a hard day washin' for deze yer caydets, an' heng out de cloze to dry, an' hit doant rain. Down dar in M'renger w'en we want it to rain we kill one o' dem big M'renger snakes an' den hang him up in a tree wid his belly up to de sun, an' hit sho rained. Ef Mr. 'Fessor Mell had one o' dem M'renger snakes he could make it rain all over Lee, beca'se hit'll retch f'om de top o' dat college to de tother een o' dis county.

"No, ma'am, nobody don't never see sich snakes es dem in dis country, cepin dey been a drinkin' too much licker, an' licker hit's 'bout es sca'ce es snakes 'bout yer.

"What made I lef't dat fine country fur to come up yer? Well, Miss Purreleen, I'll tell you. I'll tell you de remmunt truf, an' ain' gwine to tell you no lie. You see hit was sorter dis way: W'en freedom come out all dem niggers what b'long to po' w'ite folks dey come an' mix up wid us and soshate longer we all what b'long to rich folks, an' dey tuck to stealin' beca'se dey ain't never been had nothin' befo' in dey life, an' dey was a pow'ful big stealin' scrape atter w'ile, an' I never knowed who was gwine to be excuse o' doin' de stealin'. Mr. Black he 'low: 'Jake, I knows you is a hones' nigger, but ef I was you, guilty or infidel, I'd git up an' dus' way f'om yer, beca'use some o' deze yer low-down niggers aint too good to lay it on you.' Dat what make I lef' M'renger."

(The *Montgomery Advertiser,* February 21, 1886)

M'reener

How Uncle [Ja]ke Interviewed a "High-dr[a]win[']" [Ra]m

NEGRO DIALECT AS HEARD ON THE STREETS
OF LOVELY AUBURN—SOME HAPPY HITS
AT THE "SPEERIMENT" FARM

As Jake was shuffling along the street, carrying a spade and a hoe, he was accosted by the postmaster and informed that there was a letter in the office for him.

"Law! Moss Billy, I knowed you was gwine to tell me dat. Me an' Majane was a talkin' 'bout you las' night, an' Majane said ef dey was ar letter in de office for me you'd sho tell me 'bout it. I speck hit's a reddish letter, aint it, Moss Billy?"

The postmaster being new in the business, frankly confessed his ignorance of that species of epistle.

["]Don't you know what a reddish letter is, Moss Billy? Dey're dese yer letters what comes in a big amberlope what's got red streaks all roun' de aidges. Dey always has money in 'em, too, mon. When Moss Tom use ter stay in yer he gimme a reddish letter mos' ever' mont'."

The new postmaster was very sorry he could not be as accommodating as his predecessor. The letter that he handed out was in a plain white envelope and not registered.

While Jake was standing in front of the door vainly trying to read the superscription upside down, he was interrupted by the approach of Uncle Green Watkins.

"Hayo! Unk Green, is you been to see de high-drawin' ram yit?"

Something in the battered appearance of Uncle Green probably suggested the question. There was no answer. Uncle Green is an earnest man, and his means of locomotion are none of the best. He has no time to waste on the like of Jake.

However, the question aroused the curiosity of the postmaster who inquired what a high drawing ram was.

"De law! Moss Billy, aint you yeared tell o' dat high drawin' ram what Moss Cunnel Youman got out yander on de speeriment farm?"

"No. Tell me all about it."

"Well, sah, I done been yeared 'bout dat ram sence 'way back yander 'fo' Chris'mus, an' I laid off to go out dar an' see it de fus' chance. Las' Sundy evenin' I put on my best britches an' I tole Majane I was gwine off a wi'le to see Joe Eady. Joe he's my brer-in law, beca'se he marr'd Majanes sister, but his wife she tuck and quit him an' Joe he's a ole bachelder now. Dat's how come Joe an' Briscoe had dat fallin' out, beca'se Joe he went to chu'ch long o' Briscoe's wife. But I tole Briscoe dat warnt nothin,' beca'se dey aint nar marr'd 'oman in dis town but what she'd go to meetin' wid deze yer ole bachelder preachers. I been a tellin' Joe he better let yuther folks'—"

"What's all that got to do with the ram?"

"I was des a tellin' you, Moss Billy, how come I to go out dar to de speeriment farm. You see Joe he's sorter kin to we all—"

"I understand that. Tell about the ram."

"Gracious knows! Moss Billy, you aint gimme no time to git to de ram yit."

At this point the postmaster manifested symptoms of impatience so unmistakable that Jake decided to skip the rest of his preface.

"W'en I got out dar gin de woods lot fence," he continued, "I seed Joe up dar by de crib wid a basket in his han', look like he gwine to feed de hosses an' I hollewed, 'Hello, Joe!'

"Joe look all roun' an' he never seed nobody, beca'se no sooner I call 'im I drop behine a pos'.

"He low: 'Who dat take my name in vain?'"

The postmaster's impatience again manifesting itself, Jake hurried on with his narrative.

"I clum over de fence, an' w'en Joe seed who hit was he low: 'How you is, ole man?'"

"I says, says I, 'Tolerble. How you gittin on?'"

"'I'm toler'ble,' says 'e, 'how's yo' fambly?'"

"'Majane's toler'ble,' says I.

"'Whar you gwine?' says he.

"'I aint gwine nowhars,' says I, 'I des come out yer for to see ef all what I year's true. I year tell you an' Moss Cunnel Youman is doin' monsto'us big doin's out yer on dis speeriment farm.'

"You see, Moss Billy, I was sorter jubous 'bout makin' inqui'ment 'bout dat high-drawin' ram, beca'se folks tells sich big lies deze days you never knows what to 'pen' on.

"Joe naicherly love to brag, an' ef I had a tole him spotly what I come atter he'd a up an' a tole de whoppinest lie he could a made up. I says to myse'f, says I, 'Jake, you better keep yo' mouf shet ontell you kin see wher or no d'is ar ram out dar, beca'se folks might des a been a foolin you.'

"Joe he des stan' dar mighty jackandiffer like he aint a cairn wher he move or no. I speck he was sorter spicious I was gwine to ax him some mighty hard questions 'bout what happen twix' him an' Briscoe. He never said nothin; he des stan' dar on one laig, wid his mouf open, an' wait for me to injuce de subj[i]ck. He look at me, an' I look at him, an' nar one o' us never said nothin'. Atter w'ile I ups an' says:

["]'How y'll gittin' long a crappin' on de speeriment farm?' says I.

"Well, sah, dat gin him de chance he was hank'rin atter. He des everlastin'ly tu'n hisse'f loose. Seem like I aint never yeared no sich big tales 'bout farmin' befo'. He like to a bus' hisse'f open 'bout de crap dey made las' year an' de one what dey spectin to make dis year. Year him tell it, de crap what he made las' year was a buster, but dat'n what he spectin' to make dis year hit was gwine to be a outdacious sight bigger.

"Moss Billy, what make some folks love to tell sich big lies?"

"I don't know, Jake. It is strange."

"He [']lowed dey had a pile o' composes an' ever' kine o' cuis goanna, an' dey was gwine to make ten thousan' bushel o' corn an' five hundred bales o' cotton an' two thousan' gallon o' 'lasses sides de cow-peas.

"'You talkin' 'bout cow-peas,' says I, 'dat's in an' 'bout all you kin make on dis po' lan'. Down dar in M'renger,' says I, 'on ole morster's plantation, we all never use to fool long o' cow-peas.'

"'Oh yes,' he says, 'I knows all 'bout M'renger,' says [e], 'I done yeared Moss Lewis Youman read in de Abtise 'bout dem big lies you been a tellin Miss P[u]rleen.'

"I says, says I, 'How de name o' sense dat git in de paper? I aint been tole nobody 'bout what sort o' craps we use to raise in M'renger, cep'n Miss Purreleen an' Moss Hodge an' Moss Arthur an' Mr. Golat[e] an' dem folks what I wuck for down dar on Gay street, an' I never tole dem no big tales. W'enever I talks 'bout M'renger, I always teches it light, beca'se ef I was to tell it des like hit was, folks'd say I was stretchin' my blanket. You talks 'bout cow-peas,' says I, 'shoo!'

"He 'lowed dey never plant no common cow-peas. 'De sort we plants,' says 'e, 'we calls 'em crowders,' says 'e, 'an' dey is crowders, too. Ef you was to eat a bait o' dem,' says 'e, 'an' den take a drink o' water out'n de branch,' says 'e, 'dey'd show you how dey crowd. You'd be fuller'n you was dat time you rid de fast'filly,' says 'e."

"Me an' him kep' on [']scoursin,' an' I look ever' minute for him to say sumpn 'bout dat high-drawin' ram, beca'se I made sho w'ilst he was a braggin' he'd brag on dat some. But he got to usin' dem big words 'bout which kind o' minyo dey was gwine to use on dis an' dat, an' hit look like he never was gwine to quit. He talk 'bout ashes foshface an' proovin goanna an' a heap o' yuther kine o' fertilize,' an' atter w'ile he 'lowed dey was gwine to minyo some o' de cotton wid blood.

"When he out wid dat I knowed I had him in a cloze place. I ax him de question p'intly whar dey gwine to git so much blood f'om.

"Dat sorter got 'way wid him. He scratch his haid an' study. Atter w'ile he ups an' says:

"'Aint you yeared de news f'om Munggumry?' says 'e. 'Hit's nigger blood what we gwine to use,' says 'e, 'beca'se de Legislater done pass a law dat all deze yer niggers what tells big lies dey got to be kill an' dey blood goes to de speeriment farm to minyo cotton.'

"I says, says I, 'Umph—humph! Ef dat de case,' says I, 'you better be a humpin' way f'om yer. I speck you'll hatter foller Briscoe to Tallassee,' says I.

"I knowed I was gwine to trip him up on dat blood tale,

an' I says to myse'f says I, 'Hit's a good time to ax him 'bout dat high drawin' ram w'ilst he's down an' I got de egvantage of 'im. He dassent projick wid me now,' says I, so I ups an' says, says I:

"'I year tell y'all got a mighty fine ram out yer,' says I[.]

"'Yas,' 'says 'he, 'we is, too. Hits M'reener,' says 'he. 'Come on' an' I'll show 'im to you,' says 'e.

"Wid dat he walk down de hill an' call 'Coo, sheep!'

"De sheeps dey was down dar by de branch, an' w'en dey yeared Joe call 'em dey says 'Baa.' Joe call 'em agin, an' yer dey comes up de hill whar we was. W'en dey got toler'ble cloast to us dey stopped. De ram he come a leetle cloaster'n ar yuther one, an' he hilt up his haid an' look me right squar' in de eye.

"'Dar de ram,' Joe says. 'He's M'reener,' says 'e.

"I says, says I, 'Is dat hit?'

"He says, 'Yas, dat's hit, an' he's de fines' sheep in dis country. Moss Cunnel Youman wouldn' take five hunderd dollars for dat sheep.'

"Well, sah, I tuck a good look at dat sheep, an' I [']low:

"'Shucks! Dat aint nothin' but a common little spindle-laig sheep. How you make out he got so much strenk?' says I.

"Dat sorter non plush Joe. He looks like he didn' know what to say.

"He [']low: 'Who said anything 'bout his strenk?' says 'e.

"'Well,' says I, 'I been yearnin' lots o' folks talk 'bout him,' says I. 'I year tell he's a high drawin' ram,' says I, 'an' dey says he draws de water up f'om de pon' to water de gyarden sass an' de like o' dat,' says I. 'He don't look like he got de strenk to do dat,' says I.

"Joe laf an' he laf. He look like he was mos' tickll to death. He open his mouf big 'nough for a six mule waggin to be driv in, twarnt for runnin' gin de postes on bofe sides.

"Atter wile he sorter hole up a laffin, an' he ups an' says:

"'You ignunt fool nigger, I des now onnerstan' what you talkin' 'bout.' Den he laf some mo', and w'en he got thu he [']low:

"'Dat ain no common sheep. He's reg'lar M'reener. He's strong, I tell you. We des ties de rope to his haid an' he kin pull up fo' bar'ls o' water at one time. Ef you wants to see how strong he's built, you des tu'n yo' back to 'im an' stoop down an' look at 'im twix' yo' laigs,' says 'e, 'becca'se dat way you kin see 'im on a level wid yo' eyes,' says 'e, 'an' you'll see how strong he's built.'

"I done it. I tu'n my back to dat ram, an' I stoop over an' look twix' my laigs at 'im, an' des es I done dat Joe he motion his han' to de ram.

"Moss Billy, you've yeared deze yer school teachers say de worl tu'ns roun', aint yer?"

"Oh, yes."

"Well, sah, hit's a sho fack. No sooner Joe motion his han' to dat high-drawin' ram I yeared sumpn pop, an' dat minute de worl' 'mence to whirl round' an' roun', an' I seed 'bout fo' thousan' stars a dancin' in de ilements. I was layin' flat on de groun', but I had to hole on to de dirt wid bofe han's to keep f'om fallin' off 'n de worl'.

"Atter w'ile, w'en de worl' got sorter still, Joe up an says, says 'e:

"'Brer Jake,' says 'e, 'does you b'lieve dat ram got strenk to draw water?'"

(The *Montgomery Advertiser*, March 7, 1886)

[Note: The "high-drawing ram" of Jake's great interest is, of course, a hydraulic ram.]

Marengo Mud

Old Jake's Story of the Bottomless Slough

THE GREAT UNDERGROUND LAKE—
JINKS'S TURNING TO A NEGRO—
HIS TRIBULATIONS IN CUBA

 During the recent spell of rainy weather as Jake was perambulating the streets of Auburn and congratulating himself, per chance, on the solid footing that the sand and gravel afforded, he ran upon Moss Hodge sitting under an umbrella in his buggy, vainly waiting for the mails to come and as vainly trying to dry the atmosphere by burning tobacco.

The circumstances suited Jake exactly, for the weather afforded at once an excuse for stopping and a topic for conversation.

The usual compliments of a wet season having been exchanged, Jake continued the conversation by saying:

"Ef hit keep on a rainin' like hit have been, man, sah! hit won't be long 'fo' de boats 'll bring de mail up yer f 'om Munggumery."

"The water runs off too fast up here," remarked Moss Hodge. "It's not like Marengo."

"You mighty right, Moss Hodge, hit aint like M'rengo. Man, sah! ever' drap what fall down dar hit soak in de groun', an' hit go thoo de groun' an' make a roover under de groun'."

"I won't vouch for the underground river[,] but I know it gets very muddy down there."

"You's talkin' now, Moss Hodge. You knows what you 'scousin' 'bout, beca'se you'se to go down dar to yo' paw's plantation, but you didn't never stay down dar long 'nough to git good 'quainted wid dat mud."

"I've heard horses' feet pop like bottle corks when they pulled them out of the mud."

"You is dat. I knows you is. But you aint never seed air horse pull his foot boddaciously off trying to git hit out'n de de mud. But dey does, dough. I lay ef you was to go down dar now you'd fine lots an' cords o' hosses what's got one wood foot what de folks put on 'em place o' de one what de mud pull off. Hit's a plum' wonder hit don't pull a horse whole laig off, beca'se hit gits so deep de waggin hubs rolls on de groun'. Man, sah! hit takes ten o' dem big M'renger mules to pull a em'ty waggin an' den dey gits stallded on level groun'.

"Oh, yas, sah, de roads is fine in de summer time, cep'n hit rain a big rain an' den hit's mighty sticky. Hit's de bangines' stuff to stick I ever seed. De folks down dar cuts off de pigs' tails w'en dey little beca'se ef dey don't, de mud'll gether on 'em in a ball big es my haid, and de pigs can't tote dey own tails. Dat's de reason dey aint nothin' but bob-tail hogs in M'renger.

"Yas, sah, de folks walks wide-laiged beca'se de mud gether on dey feet, but dey got a way o' kickin' hit off what nobody up yer don't onnerstan'. Dey takes three or fo' steps, an' dey does dis way," and Jake threw one foot forward with a sudden jerk. Owing to certain favorable conditions, the illustration was better than was expected. Jake's shoe, being open behind, had travelled on ahead of his foot, and turned up at the toe in imitation of the fashion of two centuries ago. It aptly represented the mud in the case, and flew off his foot in a manner which did honor to itself and justice to the great Marengo kick.

Jake, having recovered his shoe, proceeded:

"Dey was a man use to live up dis way somewhars, by de name o' Rumpless—"

"Tom Humphrey?"

"Yas, sah, dat's de man. Well, him an' his wife dey went down dar to M'renger wonst to see dey kin-folks, You know, Moss Hodge, Mr. Rumpless he was a short, chunky man, an' his wife was a tall woman. She was always a crowin' over him, beca'se she could stan' flat-footed an' eat homly off 'n his haid.

"One night he lef' her at Mr. Peterses'[,] an' he went over an' staid all night wid Mr. White. Mr. White live 'bout two mile f 'om Mr. Peterses'. Hit was summer time, an' Mr. Rumpless walked, beca'se de road was hard es a rock. But hit rained a toler'ble hard rain dat night, an' nex' mornin' de road was sticky es 'lasses candy. Mr. White told Mr. Rumpless he'd loan him a mule to ride back to Mr. Peterses', but Mr. Rumpless said he ruther walk. He 'lowed he warnt 'feard o' mud. Wid dat he pitched out, an', man, sah! he never got no ways fo' de mud gether onder his feet, and he 'mence to grow taller. But dat never pester him. He want to grow taller. He growed taller an' taller de furder he went, an' twarnt long fo' he des knowed he was a haid taller'n his wife. He stop in de road an' laf, an' he fairly hollered, he was so tickle wid de idee o' bein' higher'n Miss Rumpless.

"Gin he got ha'f way to Mr. Peterses' he look des like deze yer boys what you sees walkin' on deze yer tom-walkers. Atter w'ile he 'mence to git oneasy, beca'se his haid was breshin' de tree tops. But de mud hit kep' on gethin', an' w'en he got to Mr. Peterses' gate his haid was way up in de ilements.

"He stopped at de gate, an' went to hellin' lo. He knowed ef he tried to stoop down and onlatch de gate he was 'bleege to fall an' bust hisse'f wide open. Miss Rumpless she yeard him, an' she run out on de po'ch, an' w'en she seed dat high, scary thing a stannin' out dar, she gin one holler, an' she drapped des like she was dead.

"Mr. Peterses' folks dey yeared de fuss, an' de run out dar an' po'd water on her face till she was 'bleege to come to or git drownded. She got up, she did, an' man, sah! w'en she seed dat curus thing she would a drop agin hadn't a been Mr. Rumpless he hollered loud es he could:

"Hit's me, ole lady. I'm up yer on dis everlastin' mud, an' I can't git down."

"Wen dey seed how hit was dey tuck an' fotch a high step-lather out dar, an' dey tole Mr. Rumpless to step on hit an' clam down. But he 'lowed he couldn't git his boots aloose f'om de mud, an' man, sah! he couldn't neither. He des had to leave his boots up dar an' come down in his stockin' feets.

"De sun shined out hot, an' man, sah! hit bake dem two mud postes hard es a brick, an' I reckon' dey'se stannin' dar tell yet.

"Miss White use to put flowers in dem boots ever' mornin', an' ever'body what come long de road to wonder de name o' sense she want wid sich high flowerpots in front o' her gate. But dem mud postes was mighty good to hitch hosses to."

"What about that underground river? I never heard of that down there."

"No wonder you never yeared o' hit, beca'se dem folks what knows 'bout it dey keeps it a secret. I wouldn't a knowed 'bout hit myse'f hadn't a been for a w'ite man by de name o' Jinks tryin' to cross Deep Sloo in de winter time. Dey say dat sloo ain't got no bottom to hit, an' sho 'nough hit aint. Hit's des like dat crawfish cut on yo' paw's plantation down dar. You recolleck dat, don't you, Moss Hodge? I knowed you would. You've seed de crawfishes run down in dey holes, an' you've yeard 'em drap in de water under de groun'.

"Folks says I tells big lies 'bout M'renger, but I tells 'em I kin prove enything I says by Moss Hodge.

"Well, es I was a sayin', Mr. Jinks he 'lowed de sloo what he couldn't cross warnt never made, an' lots o' folks gethered to see him try his han' on Deep Sloo.

"De folks was a stannin' up on de hill to watch him, beca'se dey dassent go no cloaster. He went in, he did, an' he jump f'om one piece o' wood to another, an' he got 'long toler'ble peart long es he could find a piece o' wood to jump on. Dey warnt air man in M'renger could beat Mr. Jinks a jumpin'. W'en he got to de een o' de pieces o' wood he clum a saplin', an' hit ben' over an' he got on another saplin'. Dat'n ben' over, an' he kep' on dat way tell he got to de las' saplin'. Dey was a block o' wood 'bout fifteen foot f'om dat'n, an' he 'lowed he was gwine to ben' de saplin' so es he could jump on de block. But de saplin' was 'mos' too big for him, an' hit never ben' fur 'nough, an' w'en he turn hit loose an' jump, man, sah! he lit right in de saftes' mud in Deep Sloo. He never had no time to say, 'Far you well, fren's,' de mud kiver him out'n sight so quick.

"Dem folks what was a watchin' him, dey couldn't do him no good, beca'se dey couldn't git to him, but dey 'lowed dey'd come back w'en de mud dried off'n him an' have his funal preached. Es for his berrin', he was done buried already.

"Dey went dar in de summer time, an dey dug in de groun', and hit warnt no time 'fo' dey found' Mr. Jinks' cloze, but dey never did fine air one o' his bones. Dey 'lowed hit was mighty cu'is mud what rot folkes' bones so quick, but dey tuck his cloze an' put 'em in a coffin, an' dey had des es big a funal es anybody want.

"'Bout a year atter dat a letter come to M'renger, an' hit come all de way f'om Cuber, an' de folks what got it dey read it, an' hit was f'om dat same Mr. Jinks what tried to cross Deep Sloo. He 'lowed Cuber was a mighty nice town for a w'ite man to live in, but he wouldn't 'vise none o' his fre'n's to come dar de way he went, beca'se niggers is niggers in Cuber tell yit, an' hit look like freedom aint never gwine to come out dar.

"He 'lowed w'en he drapped in dat mud in Deep Sloo he shot right thoo hit like a bow-an'-ower, an' he drapped into water what was a runnin' under de groun'. But de mud hilt on to his cloze es he was gwine thoo, an' w'en he toch de bottom he never had a thing on 'cep'n dat black sloo mud. But he warnt pestered 'bout de mud what was on his face an' in his ha'r an' all over him; he was studdin' 'bout how he was gwine to git back on top o' de dirt ag'in.

"Hit was mighty dark down dar, but atter w'ile w'en his eyes got sorter usened to de dark, he seed he was right on de aidge of a river 'bout twicet es big es de Bigby. He says, says 'e:

"'Hayo!' says 'e, 'dis yer roover's plenty big to run steamboats on.'

"Man, sah! he never hardly got dat word out'n his mouf 'fo' he yeared a steamboat w'istle: 'Toot—toot!'

"He looked up de roover, an' he seed de whoppines' bigges' steamboat he ever seed in his born days, comin' puffin' an' blowin' right todes him. He was dat scared he didn't know what to do, beca'se dey warnt nobody on dat boat cepin' black mens, an' dey was all naked. He made sho he was done got to de bad place, beca'se he knowed all de bad man's folks was black. Dem's de onliest rale niggers dey is, Moss Hodge.

"Mr. Jinks he let in to sayin' his pra'rs hard es ever he could, but all of a suddent he recoll[e]ck he always yeared tell dey warnt nair drap o' water in de bad place. Des es soon's he thought o' dat he stopped prayin', dat minute. Mr. Jinks was like a heap a folks I knows, Moss Hodge; he never would say his pra'rs cep'n [. . .] he hollered an' ax Mr. Jinks ef he want a job on de bes' boat he never cared, an' dey put out a plank, an' Mr. Jinks went on boa'd. De cap'n put him to wuck longer de yuther boat han's, an' dey tole him dey was all w'ite folks, but de mud an' smoke made 'em black. Hit was too warm to w'ar cloze down dar. De cap'n tole him dat boat an' all de yuther boats what run on de roover, was put on endurin' de war to cyar cotton to Cuber an' fetch back coffee an' sugar, an' atter de war dey tuck niggers down dar an' sole 'em, but dey soon got so black deyse'f dey couldn't tell de niggers f'om dey own mens. Den dey stop dat trade, but dey kep' on runnin' de boats, and he 'lowed dey was a right smart o' money in it yit, beca'se dey brung over seegyars an' whisky what de gov'rnment never even smell.

"Mr. Jinks he made fo' or five trips wid dat boat, an' he 'mence to git tired, an' he want to git on top side o' dirt an' wash his face in water what warnt so black, an' put on a bile shut an' a stannin' collar an' be like de yuther folks what he was raise wid. He baig de captin nex' time dey got to Cuber to let him go on de lan', an' de cap'n he sorter la'f, an' he 'lowed he was willin', but he speck Mr. Jinks was gwine to be sorry ef he done it.

"Mr. Jinks he never said nothin', but he spicion de cap'n was des a talkin' dat way to keep him f'om leavin' of de boat.

"W'en dey got to Cuber dat time an' dey was loadin' of de boat—"

"How did they load the boat?"

"You see, Moss Hodge, dey had a hole down thoo de groun' an' hit was box up wid plank, an' dey let a big tub down thoo hit.

"Well, Mr. Jinks he got in dat tub, an' dey drawed him up, an' man, sah! des de minute he put his foot on dry dirt de w'ite folks grabbed him.

"He tole 'em to turn him loose, but dey wouldn't do it. He ax 'em what dey rec-cog-nize him fur, an' dey 'lowed dey picked up ever' loose nigger dey fine. He 'lowed he warnt no nigger; he was a w'ite man. Dey laf' w'en dey yeared dan, an' dey 'lowed ef he was a w'ite man dey hoped to gracious dey'd never see a black un. Den dey showed him hisse'f in a lookin' glass, an', man, sah! he was black es de pot. Dat sloo mud was wucked into his hide an' hit had kink up his har des like mine.

"He 'lowed twarnt no use for him to say a word atter dat. He des let dem w'ite folks put him in slav'ry, an' he was wuckin' longer de yuther niggers. De onliest reason why he writ dat letter to M'renger he want to fine out ef dey was air new kind o' soap what'd make a w'ite man out'n a sho 'nough nigger. Ef dey was any what'd do dat, he want his fren's to sen' him some, but he 'lowed dey warnt no use o' sendin de common sort, beca'se any soap what'd wash dat mud off 'n him'd make de blackes' nigger in M'renger w'ite es snow."

(The *Montgomery Advertiser,* April 11, 1886)

Three Little Boys and Three Little Fishes

Grave-digging is one of Jake's avocations. It might be his vocation if his lot were cast in a less healthful region, where work in that line would be more abundant, for he has frequently been heard to express a de- cided preference for the employment of a sexton. But though gravedigging may justly be considered a serious and even solemn business, it has never seemed to exert a depressing influence on Jake's spirits. On the con- trary, Jake's heart never seems lighter than when he is engaged in preparing a last resting place for poor mortality. In this respect he differs not from the whole tribe of grave diggers and undertakers, for they have ever been noted for a jolly set.

Once upon a time, on a Saturday afternoon, just as Jake had finished a grave and was leaving the cemetery he espied three little white boys returning from a day's sport on the creek and bearing the trophies of their skill in the shape of three little fishes.

Jake being in excellent humor, accosted them, and with an arch look inquired[:]

"Whar y'll little boys cotch dem little bitty ole feesh at?"

"In Moore's pond," answered the little boys in chorus. Being new disciples of I[z]aak Walton, they were rather proud of their achievements.

Jake smiled.

"Lemme see 'em," said he, and he took the string out of the bearer's hand and examined each fish minutely.

"One little ole peerch an' one little ole silver-side an' one little ole honny-head," he said, disparagingly. "Is dem all de feesh y'all cotch to-day! Honey, aint ya'll scared dese yer feesh mammies 'll cry beca'se y'all done tuck 'way dey babies? What y'all gwine to do wid 'em?"

"Going to eat 'em," replied the little boys.

This thought was so ludicrous that Jake dropped his hoe and spade and laughed till the tears rolled down his cheeks, and the half dried clay fell from his clothes in a little shower around his feet.

"Aint they fit to eat?" asked the little boys in wonderment.

"Yes, honey, dey'se fit to eat, dat dey is, but gin y'all takes de eensides out'n 'em an' scrapes de scales off 'n 'em, dey won't be nothin' lef' but some thin skin an' dem sharp fins. Y'all kin swaller de skin, but de fins 'll stick in yo' th'oat an kill you.

"I knowed a man down in M'renger what was mighty hungry wonst, an' he eat some little bitty ole feesh des like dese yer, an' he got a fin stuck in his th'oat an' he aint never swaller nothin' f 'om dat day tell dis."

"Is he dead?"

"No, he aint dead, but he micy swell be. De doctor tuck an' bo'ed a hole in his breas' wid a inch auger, an' he stuck a piece o' cane in dar, an' w'enever dat man lows he's hongry somebody goes an po'es 'bout a quart o' soup in him. He gits fill up sometimes, but he don't never tas'e nothin,' an' he's mighty leaky, too. Ever' time he stoop over to pick up enything, de soup all runs out'n him, thoo dat reed, an' den he's got to be fill up agin.

"Ef I was y'all, I'd th'ow dem feesh in de fence cornder dar, an' let de anch eat 'em. D'is des 'bout a good bait for three or fo' o' dem littles' size anch."

The little boys regarded one another with looks of dejection, but they held on to the fish. They were shaken in their faith, but not entirely converted by Jake's argument.

"Didn't y'all know hit's pow'ful bad luck to cyar three feesh home? Well, hit is for a fack. I never is knowed but one man what ever 'spute dat. Dat man went a feeshin' wonst on Cottonwood creek, down dar in M'renger, an' de eas' win' was a blowin', an' ever'body he meet long de road tole him he couldn' have no luck feeshin' er co'tin' long es de' eas' win' was a blowin'. But he was a cu'is man, an' he said he be cust ef he b'lieve in luck. Well, sah, he went on, he did, an' he feeshed all day, an' he never cotch but three feesh. But dey warnt no little ole peerch like dem ar. Dey warnt none o' dem sort in Cottonwood creek. De feesh is bigger'n my han' w'en dey fus' born down dar in M'renger. Well, dat man start on home he did, an' ever'body he met lowed hit was bad luck to cyar three feesh home, but he kep' on, beca'se he never b'lieve in luck nohow. No sooner he got home one o' his little boys, des 'bout de size o' y'all, tuck an' got one o' dem feesh fins stuck in his han', an' his han' swell up big es my haid, an' de doctor had to saw it off.

"But de bad luck never stop dar. Hit kep' on, an' man, sah! hit's a keepin' on tell dis day. De nex' time dat man went a feeshin' he never got a bite, an' de eas' win' warnt a blowin' neither. He tried ever' way he could to git dem feesh to bite, but dey wouldn't. He put nasty fiddity on his hook, an' he

spit ambeer on it, but hit never done no good. He never got
nair bite dat day, an' he aint never got nair bite sence, cep'n
de time a copper-belly moggerson bit him on de heel.

"Ef he had a th'owed dem three fish away dat time, fo' he
got home, he'd a had good luck, beca'se anybody could
ketch feesh in Cottonwood w'en dey done right."

"Was that a good place to fish?" one of the little boys
ventured to ask.

"Which? Cottonwood creek?"

"Yes."

"You'se mighty right, honey. D'aint water 'nough
nowhars 'bout yer for to hole de feesh like dey was in
Cottonwood. Many's de time I've been a muddin'—"

"Muddying!" repeated the little boys, in astonishment.
"What's that?"

"Law! honey, don't y'all know? Taint no wonder y'all
never cotch nothin'; you aint 'quainted wid de way to feesh.
Ef you was, you wouldn't a been a cyan home dem three
little bitty ole peerch.

"Well, I'll tell you 'bout muddin'. Down dar in M'renger,
in de summer time, ef hit aint a wet drought, de creeks mos'
in ginnerly goes dry, cep'n 'bout in spots. De folks goes
down dar to one o' dem holes what's got water in 'em, an'
dey rolls dey britches up an' goes in an' stirs up de mud wid
dey feets.

"No sooner dey does dat, an' de water gits right muddy,
de feesh comes to de top. Dey des 'bleege to come to de top,
honey, beca'se dat M'renger mud hit's dat sticky ef hit git in
de feesh' gills hit'll stick 'em together des like hit was glue,
an' de feesh can't breethe.

"Well, w'en dey comes to de top you aint got nothin' to do
but des pick up es many es you want, an' 'vide 'em out
twix' de crowd, an' go home.

"Does y'all ever goes feeshin' on Sunday?"

"No," replied the three little boys in a breath. "We go to Sunday-school and to church[.]"

"Dat's right," said Jake, approvingly. "Three little boys des 'bout de size o' y'all went a feeshin down on Cottonwood one Sunday, an' dey'se settin' dar feeshin' tell yit."

"Why don't they get up and go home?"

"Beca'se dey can't, honey. Dey're stuck to de groun', an' dey han's is stuck to do feeshin' poles, an' nobody can't git 'em aloose. Folks tried to cut de poles, but de poles 'mence to bleed so fas, dey had to stop. Dey tried to pull de boys up off 'n de ground', but de groun' hit bled too, an' dem little boys fa'rly hollered, hit hurt 'em so bad. Dey des had to leave 'em dar, an' dey got to set dar tell Gab'el toot his horn, cep'n dey ever is 'nough feesh th'owed 'way what's been cotch on a weeky day, for to set 'em free[.]"

"I don't know what you mean."

"Law! don't you, honey? Well, hits dis way: 'Fo' dem little boys got stuck dey done caught nine feesh, an' for ever' one o' dem feesh what was cotch on Sunday, somebody what lives a fur ways off f'om M'renger is got to th'ow 'way three feesh what dey cotch on a weeky day.

"De las' time I yeared f'om M'renger dem boys was done got loose all but de seats o' dey britches, beca'se somebody somewhars 'way off yander done thowed 'way—lemme see—how much do three times eight make?"

"Twenty-four."

"Dat's right, honey[.] I was des a tryin' to see ef you knowed yo' jogfy lesson. An' you knowed it. You's a smart little boy, I 'clar. How you l'arn to count so fas'?

"Well, es I was a sayin', somebody somewhars 'way f'om M'renger is done thowed 'way twenty-six feesh what was cotch on a weeky day, an' dey don't like but three o' gitin' aloose.

"I speck ef y'all was to th'ow 'way dem three little bitty ole peerch, dem boy'd git de seat o' dey britches aloose dis evenin' an' dey'd be a gwine to Sunday school in de mornin' same es you.

"Well, I got to go back in de graveyard atter my pipe what I forgot," and having thus spoken, Jake retraced his steps into the cemetery, and squatted behind a bush to watch what the three little boys would do.

"Le's throw 'em away, Tom," said John.

"Well, if Jim's willing," said Tom.

"I don't care[,] if you all don't," said Jim. "They aint enough to divide out nohow."

With that the fishes were thrown into the fence corner, and the little boys wended their weary way home.

A few minutes later Jake again issued from the cemetery, stopped at the fence corner[,] found the fishes, brushed the ants off of them, crammed them into one pocket of his trousers, and humming a merry air, shuffled homeward.

(The *Montgomery Advertiser*, May 23, 1886)

Marengo Jake Plays Another Trick on the Three Boys

With a Marvelous Yarn of How a "M'renger" Dog Licked "M'renger" Mud till His Tongue Wore Off

 Early one morning, as Jake was going to work, he espied the same three little boys from whom he had obtained the fishes. Their faces were set toward the country, and appearances indicated that they were off for a day's sport.

"Hayo!" cried Jake, in friendly greeting. "Is y'all little boys gwine a feeshin' again?"

"No," was the answer, "we are going rabbit hunting."

"You is! I don't see nair dog ner nair gun y'all got. Is you gwine to run de rabbits down an' ketch 'em?"

"No, we've got a dog."

"War he at, honey?"

"He's coming on behind."

"What sort o' dog is he?"

"He's a little terrier."

This admission seemed to amuse Jake very much, and he laughed heartily.

"Honey, don't y'all know a little ole tarrier can't ketch a

rabbit? His laigs is too short. Rabbits 'll des take him to play wid. He'll run a rabbit all day in de shade o' one tree. Dey'll run all roun' an' roun' a tree des to scannelize him, becau'se dey knows w'en he git cloast to 'em dey kin des give one jump an' jump clean over his haid, an' w'ilst he's a turnin' roun' to follow 'em dey kin leave him cl'ar behine.

"Dats de way rabbits does a little dog. I knows all 'bout 'em, specially deze yer big swamp buck rabbits. Dey was lots o' dem kine down dar in M'renger."

"On Cottonwood creek where those boys went fishing on Sunday?"

"Yas, honey, dat's de ve'y place. How kin you guess so good? You's de bes' han' to guess ever I seed."

"Have you heard from those boys lately?"

"Yas, I is. I yeared f 'om 'em las' week. I seed a man what des come f 'om M'renger[,] an' he 'lowed somebody must a th'owed 'way three mo' feesh what was cotch on a weeky-day, beca'se dem little boys was done got plum aloose. But he 'lowed nobody never knowed who hit was th'owed de feesh 'way."

"Did you tell him?"

"Co'se I did. I sont word hit was y'all what thowed 'em 'way, an' I speck dem boys' paw'll sen' y'all a mighty nice present nex' Chris'mus, beca'se dey was mighty bad pestered 'bout dem boys.

"Whar y'all little ole fice at? I don't see 'm a comin'."

"I reckon he must have stopped somewhere. Here, Trip! Here! Here! Jim, you go back and get him."

Jim went, and returning presently, brought with him a small black-and-tan dog.

At sight of the dog Jake expressed his wonder in a prolonged exclamation uttered through his nose.

"Whar y'all got dat fice at? Dat's de fattes' fice I seed cep'n one what use to stay at a hotel down dar in M'renger. Man, sah! dat'n down dar 'n M'renger was de fattes' fice in dis newnited worl'.''

"What made him so fat?"

"Well, you see, honey, down dar in M'renger taint like hit is up yer on dis rocky lan'. W'en it rains down dar, ef you walk any ways, you'll sho get your feets muddy, an' ef hit's been a long dry drought, yo' shoes 'll be kivered wid dust tell dey look like deze yer ole yaller cow-belly brogans what we all use to wah fo' freedom come out.

"Well, dat was a mighty smart dog what stayed at dat hotel. He was des like folks. You could l'arn him to do mos' anything what you want him to do.

"An' man, sah! dat was a fine hotel what he stayed at, too, but dey was a ner hotel in dat town what was des 'bout es fine es hit. Sometimes de big qual'ty folks 'd put up at one o' dem hotels' an' sometimes at de yuther, beca'se nair one never had de egvantage. But dat was fo' ever dat man l'arn dat dog how to do.

"Atter he done l'arn him dat, de big qual'ty folks all put up at his hotel, an' de man what kep' de yuther hotel he like to a perish to death.''

Here Jake paused as if waiting to hear any comments his hearers might be disposed to offer.

"What did he teach his dog to do?'' inquired one of the boys.

"What did he l'arn dat dog to do?'' said Jake, as if he had not clearly heard the question. "Well, I bet nair one o' y'all can't guess.''

"How many guesses will you give us?''

"I ain't gwine to give y'll but one guess apiece, beca'se d' is three o' y'all to me one, an' dat way y'll got de egvantage o' me.

"Ef y'all guess hit right, all de rabbits what y'll ketch to-day 'll belong to y'all, but ef you don't guess hit right, all de rabbits 'll be mine. Dat's fair, ain't it?''

All the little boys agreed that this "turkey-and-buzzard" proposition was perfectly fair, and scratching their pates to stimulate their wits, they began to guess.

"I guess the dog toted people's valises up from the depot," said the first boy.

"I guess he went to the post-office after their mail," said the second boy. "I've read about a dog doing that in the second reader."

"I guess he laid down and rolled over when anybody come, to make 'em think he was glad to see 'em," said the third boy. "I use to know a dog that done that."

"Nair one o' y'all never guess hit right," said Jake, "an' all de rabbits what y'all ketch to-day b'longs to me. I'm gwine up yander to work in Miss [P]urreleen's garden, an' y'all kin fetch de rabbits dar to me ef y'all ketch air un," and he shouldered his hoe and started away.

"Hold on, Uncle Jake," cried the boys. "You haven't told us what that dog used to do."

"Dat warn't in de contrack, honey," replied Jake. "W'en I makes a contrack wid Miss Purreleen for to hoe her taters I don't hatter hoe her corn too—leas'ways not cep'n she pay me for it. I done done my part de contrack wid y'all an' I aint got no time to tarry. I got to wuck Miss Purreleen garden, beca'se Moss Ree's comin' home f'om offi'n de big water bum by, an' ef he don't fine no gardan sass dar he'll lay de blame on Jake."

"But we want to hear about the dog," pleaded the boys.

"Well, ef y'all so anxious to year 'bout dat dog, y'all hatter git aroun' peart an' ketch me a big fat rabbit to-day, an' den I'll tell y'all all 'bout him."

With these parting words Jake proceeded towards Miss Purreleen's. After he had turned the first corner, however, he stopped a few minutes, and then shielding the bulk of his form behind the fence, peeped furtively. The boys were going in a half run toward the country. Jake chuckled.

The little dog ran hares nearly all day without catching one. It was very much as Jake had predicted; the game easily eluded his pursuit. But the boys persevered. Unless they caught a hare, they could not hear about the trained dog. They did not stop for dinner nor anything else. They whooped and cheered on their dog until they were hoarse, but it did no good. The dog needed help, not encouragement. They perceived this by and by, and then they took an active part in the chase. They h[e]aded off a hare so many times that the little animal became frightened and confused, and took refuge in a hollow log.

Now the boys had the game just where they wanted it. They knew exactly what to do. They cut a long hickory rod, and thrusting it into the hollow, began to twist with all their might. But the hare, not relishing this kind of treatment, ran out at the other end of the log, and escaped.

Grievously disappointed, but not despairing, the boys set to work again, and fortune favoring them, they treed another hare. They were cautious this time, and left the game no avenue of escape.

After much twisting they got several bunches of fur and, finally, the half decorticated body of the hare.

It was now late in the afternoon, and they hastened back to town and stopped at Mrs. Purreleen's garden wall.

"Here's your rabbit, uncle Jake," they cried in chorus.

"Hey! What did you say?" came from the garden.

"Here's your rabbit, and we've come to hear about that dog," said the little boys.

"Well, sah! Gentemens!" exclaimed Jake, in feigned surprise. "Is y'all cotch a rabbit sho nough?" and he peeped through a crack. "Well, you is, for a fack! Go down yander whar de fence is low, an' clam over."

The little boys were soon at his side, and placed the game in his ready hand.

"Phew!" whistled Jake. "What a fine rabbit! Hit's a reg'lar swamp buck. Majane 'll be proud o' dis rabbit, I know. An' she won't have de trouble o' skinnin' of him, beca'se y'all done got mos' all his clo'es off 'n him.

"Aint he big! He look sorter like dem rabbits I use to ketch on Cottonwood, only, co'se he aint es big. M'renger rabbits is des 'bout dis big w'en dey two weeks ole.

"How y'all an' dat little ole fice cotch dis rabbit? I 'clar' to gracious, y'all is de smartes' little boys in dis yer town. I tole Miss Purreleen so. I tole her y'all was likely an' y'all was peart, an' she b'lieve me. She b'lieve ev'ything I tells her.

"Well, y'all wants to hear 'bout dat dog down dar in M'renger. An' I'm b'leege to tell y'all 'bout him, beca'se y'all done done y'all part de contrack.

"Well, sah, he was a little ole fice sorter like dis'n, only he was mighty po' at fus, but, man, sah! he had sense des like folks. He was a smart dog, an' his smartness done him a lots o' good for a w'ile, but atter dat hit done him harm. Hit made him fat, an' hit made him po'.

"Dat man what kep' de hotel he larn dat dog to set on de poach, an' wen any big folks come to de hotel he'd lick de mud or de dus' offin dey boots—"

"The dog or the man?"

"De dog, honey. He was des like folks. Man, sah! he had sense. But he never lick nobody boots cep'n de qual'ty folks. He never pay no 'tention to po' w'ite trash, but w'en a jedge er a colonel er a gov'nor come, he'd lick dey boots slick an' clean, an' dat what make de big qual'ty folks love to come to dat hotel."

"How could he tell quality folks from anybody else?"

"Law! honey, he could do dat easy 'nough. He knowed 'em by de smell. Ev'rybody don't smell alike, you know. Y'all don't smell like me. Dat dog he des smell one smell at a man an' he knowed all 'bout him.

"Well, de big folks was mighty tickle for to have dey boots clean dat way, an' dey was pow'ful please beca'se dat dog knowed dey was qual'ty, an' w'en dey come to dat town dey mos' in ginnerly put up at dat hotel. Dat dog he was allays in de dine room at eatin' time, an' he use to set up in a high cheer 'gin' de wall, so ev'rybody could see him, an' dem big qual'ty folks dey's give him chicken bones an' nice piece o' sheep meat wil'st dey was a eatin'. Dat what make him so fat. Man, sah! dat dog got so fat he couldn't curl his tail 'dout openin' of his mouf. His moster [']low he yarnt all dem nice victuals, beca'se de wah an' tah his tongue was wuf dat. Sho 'nough, his tongue wah off shorter an' shorter tell atter w'ile dey warnt much es a stub een o' hit lef '. Den he couldn't lick no mo' boots, an'—"

"How did he drink water then?"

"He drinks des like folks drinks, honey. Dat dog had ways des like folks, anyhow.

"Well, sah, he kep' on a tryin' to lick boots for a w'ile, beca'se dat was all his 'pen'ence for to git sump'n t'eat, but his tongue was wo' off too short, an' he des make dem colonels an' gov'nors mad, an' stidder givin him a bone, dey mos' in ginnerly gin him a kick, tell atter w'ile three o' his laigs was broke, an' his tail was knock skewonkle, an' haf ' his ribs was smash in, an' one o' his eye was put out, an' he got po' an' mangy. De hotel man he tuck an' driv' him off, an' he des hop roun' de town an' hunt for ole dry bones. Ev'rybody what meet him gin him a kick an' [']low:

"'Take dat, you ole slimkumpoke! Dat's what you git for bein' too smart an' tryin' to soshate long o' quality.'"

(The *Montgomery Advertiser,* June 27, 1886)

Seismic Phenomena

Explained by a Marengo Scientist

 A few days after the great earthquake Jake was seen armed with a scythe and on his way to a certain plat of grass which he had been engaged to mow. His blade bore tokens of long use and hard service, and was so stained and battered that it might have passed for an ancient relic—a chariot blade of the time of Scipio Africanus, for instance. But without any positive record to that effect, any observer, not an antiquary of the order of Monkbarns or Mr. Pickwick, would accept Jake's statement that the blade had never been used by any one but himself; that it was discolored by rust and not by Carthaginian blood, and that the numerous indentations came by contact with Lee county stones, and not with African skulls.

Jake and his scythe are old companions and understand each other perfectly. No other man could do such execution with so battered a weapon, and no other blade, not endowed with sentience, would so nicely accommodate its needs to its master's desires; for whenever Jake wishes to rest or talk his blade invariably needs whetting.

So it was at the time to which this narrative refers. Just as Jake was about to mount the fence behind which the imperiled grass was hiding, he espied Moss Wilbur approaching, and at the same moment he discovered that his scythe needed whetting for the fray.

Forth from his belt he snatched a wooden paddle, black with tar and gritty with sand, and drawing it rapidly along the curved blade, produced sounds which fell upon Moss Wilbur's ear like the tinkling of cow-bells, softened by distance.

Moss Wilbur drew near, and after an exchange of the usual civilities, Jake opened the conversation with the following inquiry:

"Did you year de yearthquake de yuther night, Moss Wilbur?"

"Yes," was the answer. "Didn't you?"

"Yas, sah, I yeard it. I did dat. I felt it, too, but I never knowed what it was at fus. I warnt a studdyin' 'bout no yearthquake in dis po' country. Seem like deyn't 'nough richness in dis country to make a man have a chill, let alone ob de worl' a shakin'."

"What did you think it was, Jake?"

"Well, sah, w'en I fus yeard it I was a settin' dar smokin' my pipe, an' toreckly I yeard a mighty rattlin', an' de house hit shuck. Majane she up an' [']lowed dat ole mule was done come back agin. D'is a ole mule what loaf roun' my oouse sometimes of a night, an' me an' her bofe thought hit was him a rubbin' hisse'f gin de cornder o' de house. But, man, sah! de house hit shuck wuss an' wuss, like hit was gwine to shake all to pieces. Den I got sorter ashy. I ris up, I did, an' I says, says I:

"'I'll show you who' house you makin' a scratchin' pose out'n.'

"Dis yer blade hit was layin' up on do jice. I retched up dar an' got it, an' I run out'n de do' purpozely to cut dat ole mule's haid offi'n 'im. Man, sah! W'en I got out dar dey warnt a huff o' dat mule nowhars 'bout.

"I stop an' study, an' toreckly I says to myse'f, says I:

"'Jake, whar you at? Is dis yer Firginny er is hit North Killeny? Mus' be you done move 'way f 'om whar you livin' at now, beca'se dis po' country hits weight down wid rocks tell hit can't shake! W'en I use to live in Firginny and North Killiny—'"

"I didn't know you had ever lived in Virginia and North Carolin[a]."

"Law! Moss Wilbur, didn't you know I was borned up dar?"

"No, I thought you were born in Marengo. When did you go to Marengo?"

"W'en did I fus went to M'renger? I dismember zackly w'en hit was, but hit was dat year de jewberry crap fail. Hit was a pow'ful long time ago, I tell you. W'en I fus went down dar Cottonwood creek was a little branch an' de Bigby warnt no bigger'n Mr. Mo's mill Creek."

"Do they have earthquakes in Virginia and North Carolina?"

"Yes, sah, dey does dat. Dey has 'em dar ever' time de moon change. Man, sah! ever' dog what you sees up dar he's a bob-tail dog, beca'se de yearthquake done shuck all de dogs' tails off 'n 'em.

"W'en I fus went to M'renger I looked all roun' ever' which-a-way, an' never seed no big hills an' neither no mountains, an' I made sho dey warnt no yearthquakes down dar. I says to myself, says I:

"'I'm in hopes I done got to a place whar I kin stan' stiddy on my laigs.'

"But, man, sah! twarnt long 'fo I foun' out diffunt. Stidder de worl' a shakin' down dar, hit's de folks what shakes. Yas, sah, dey does dat. I warnt dar no time fo' I seed a man a settin' on de fence in de hot sunshine—an' hit was a hot day, too, mon.

"I was dat stonish I didn't know what to do. I couldn' onnerstan' what dat man was gone to roos' for in sich a hot place. But toreckly de fence what he was a settin' on hit 'mence to shake an' de rails dey rattle down on de groun', an' dat man he was all over in a trimmle de like he was cole.

"I says, says I: 'Hayo! boss, does y'll have yearthquakes down yer?'

"He look down at me out'n de cornder o' his eyes, an' his teeth was a rattlin' des like Jess Jackson beatin' de drum for de caydets to go to bed. He 'low:

"'Whar you come f 'om, you old black crow? 'Case we has yearthquakes yer,' says he, 'only de folks has 'em eenside o' deyse'f stidder de yearth a havin' of 'em.'

"Hit was des so, too, Moss Wilbur. Dis yer worl' hit's des like folks. W'en hit git sump'n eenside o' hit what don't 'gree wid it, hit bleege to have de gripes er a chill, one or de yuther. Dat's what's de matter. Hit mine me of a nigger what's a pickin' cotton in de fall of de year. He got bofe han's a gwine stiddy, an' he got bofe eyes skin for ever' little watermillion what grow twix' de rows. De fus' thing anybody know dat nigger double up on de groun' an' got bofe han's on his stomach an hollin', 'Somebody go atter de doctor quick; my eensides is tied up in a double bow knot!'

"De w'ite folks gin 'im a doast o' cast' ile, an' dat sorter onlimber 'im for h wile, but he mighty poly yit. He too black complected to *look* pale, but he *feel* des es pale es a w'ite man.

De nex' thing, dat nigger got a ager, an' de house shake an' de winders rattle. I knows. I been all long dar myse'f.

"All my teeth was shuck out wid dem nasty chills. Dat's de only reason I takes so long to eat. Ma'jane she [']low hits caze I eats so much, but, Moss Wilbur, you know ef a man ain' got but two teeth, an' nair one o' dem don't hit de yuther one, you know he des bleege to take a a long time to eat."

"That's so, but you haven't told me what the earth has been eating that caused it to have a chill."

"Well, Moss Wilbur, you know hits been a rainin' a heap dis year, an' all dat wattr what fall out'n de ilements hit soak down into de eenside o' de worl' an' w'en de worl' turn over hit slosh bout des like watermillion juice in a nigger stomach, an' I speck dat what made de worl have a chill, but you neenter put dat in de Munggummery Appetizer nex' Sunday."

(The *Montgomery Advertiser*, October 31, 1886)

Christmas in Marengo

"Do you expect to have a good time Christmas, Jake?"

"I aint a studdin bout havin' no Chris'mas in dis yer Auburn, Moss Hodge. Hit aint in de back side o' my haid. Dese yer folks don't know nothin bout Chris'mas. Dey has what dey calls Chris'mas, but dey aint quainted wid Chris'mas. Ole Sandy Claus don't know whar Lee county lays. Ef he was to come up yer deze yer rocks ud w'ar out his waggin wheels toreckly.

"Yas, sah, I knows de w'ite boys always fixes deyse'f up in dey mammies' ole caliker frocks an' put on dough faces an borries yo' ole George an all de yuther horses in town to ride fantaskits. But dat aint nothin. Hit don't hole a candle side o' de Chris'mas we use to have down dar in Mrenger.

"Yas, sah, I'm talkin bout fo' freedom come out. De day fo' Chris'mas ole Moster always sont word out he want all his niggers to come up to de big house soon nex' mornin'. He 'low he want to git 'quainted wid 'em. He had so many niggers he never knowed all de grown ones, let 'lone all de babies what was born endurin' de year and de chilluns what was growed bigger sence de las' time he seed 'em. Man, sah! dey was a nigger baby born ever night in de year on de upper plantation, an hit was wuss'n dat on de lower plantation.

"Ole Moster had a piece o' lan' cleaned up front o' de big house for de niggers to gether in ever' Chris'mas mornin'. Hit had 'bout a hunderd acres in it, but we never called it nothin but a patch down dar in Mrenger.

"W'en all ole Moster's niggers gethered in dat patch dey was dat bad crowded some had to set on de fence all de way roun'.

"Ole Moster he was stannin fo' de big house do', and two big hoxits was stannin by him. Atter wile he toot a long tin trumpet, like a joanna h'on, an den de fun'al start. De niggers march roun' an' roun' des like deze college caydets, and ever time a nigger pass ole Moster he stop and injuce hisse'f to ole Moster. He low 'my entitlements is Ole Joe.' De nex' one low he's young Joe, and nex' one ud be Big Joe. Den atter dat ud come Little Joe an Bow-laiged Joe an Box-ankle Joe an Cotton-eyed Joe an Knok-knee Joe and Big-mouth Joe an Joe what could see ghoses beca'se he was borned wid caul.

"No, sah, dey warnt all name Joe, but a heap of 'em hatter have de same name beca'se dey warnt nough name in des Newnited worl to low one apiece for all o' ole Moster's niggers.

"Well, ever one what injuce hisse'f speckful to ole Moster, ole Moster gin him a goadful o' liquor out'n dem hoxits. Twarnt no little shot-goad neither; hit was des 'bout de size o' Majane's soap-goad. Hit hilt des bout es much es a common size nigger could tote. I aint a talkin 'bout deze yer

Aubun niggers. Dey couldn't tote a pint. But dem Mrenger niggers could tote it ef you gin 'em plenty o' han'roomance. Dey might not could walk in one o' deze yer norrow Lee county roads, but dey could keep eenside a hunderd acre fiel' tolerble easy. Wen a nigger had a goad-ful o' dat liquor he was des in de right fix to lay off fence rows. Wenever ole Moster want to buil' a new fence he always gin a nigger a goadful o' dat liquor an tole him whar he want de fence to start an whar he want de yuther een to be. Dat's de reason all ole Moster's fences tuck in so much lan'.

"Atter all de niggers done pass roun' ole Moster most in ginnerly low:

"'Well, all de horses done been watered now, I b'lieve I'll go to town an' hunt for Chris'mas.'

"Den he call Flat-nose Joe what drive de cyadge, an he low:

"'Hitch up a hunderd two-laiged black horses to de cyadge. Put Jake in de lead, beca'se he's de peartes' critter on deze stompin groun's, an hitch up a fine young filly side o' him for to make him feel proud. Step roun' lively now, you black rascal.'

"No sooner ole Moster said dat I 'mence to whicker and prance, an I prance up to de likeles' yaller gal on de plantation so ole Moster could see which'n I want hitch up side o' me. An he always pick out dat'n, too, mon.

"Wen we was all done hitched up ole Moster clammed up on de driver's seat an cracked his whoop. Man, sah! you ought to a seed de cyadge roll out'n de big gate. Yer we go down de big road, me and dat cream color filly workin in de lead, and all dem yuther black horses comin' on behine. Ever time we pass a house I gin a snort an a whicker, an de folks come a running out to see what was gwine pas'. Man, sah! dey look tonish an sprise wen dey see dat team, an' ever one norate 'bout what a fine black horse an what a likely cream color filly dat was, workin in de lead. W'en dey seed ole Moster a settin up on de cyadge dey [']low:

"'De Kernul mus' be on a reglar Chris'mas t'ar.'

"You know, Moss Hodge, hit's tolerble muddy down dar in M'renger. Sometimes wen we all come to a deep sloo we'd git stallded. Co'se we could a pull de cyadge ha'f in two, we didn't want to do dat. We did pull de tongue out'n it wonst, but atter dat ole Moster always made a whole drove o' niggers foller long behine de cyadge, an' w'en we come to a bad place he des made dem niggers lay down in two rows des wide 'nough part for de cyadge wheels to roll on 'em, an dat way we cross a sloo a mile wide sometimes.

"No, sah, hit never hurt de niggers, beca'se de mud was des es saf' es a feather-bed. But hit mash him so deep in de groun dey couldn't git up by deyse'f. We all des lef'' 'em layin dar tell de cyadge pass over 'em gwine back, an' den ole Moster ud sen' a gang o' han's to prize em up wid rails.

"De big time come wen we got to town. Man, sah! folks look out ever do' an ever winder. Hit was a sight to see dem hunderd horses jerkin dat cyadge, an dat peart black horse an dat likely cream color filly workin in de lead.

"Ole moster he driv' all over town des like a show waggin, an' ever'body stop what dey was doin to foller dat cyadge. Ole moster driv up on de squar; and dat team hit was so long hit wrop clean roun' de coat-house, an dat lead horse an dat cream color filly dey was right side de cyadge.

"Dat ar cream color filly she work mighty gentle in de big road, but wen she got in town she was skittish es a colt what aint never been had harness on her befo; she shy f'om everything what look yaller or blue, scusin de sign over de grocery do'.

"Wen ole moster hollered 'wo!' all de team stop. But dat

ar cream-color filly she was mighty onresless. She kep' on stompin her feet an th'owin up her haid, like she want to be biggity fo' all dem town niggers.

"Atter wile ole moster holler out to de man what keep de grocery, says he:

"'Bob, water dat filly what workin in de off lead.'

"Moss Bob he run in de house an toreckly he brung out a big tumiler full o' sump'n what look like branch water, wid some white san' in de bottom o' de tumiler an some trash an' grass floatin' on top o' de water.

"He put hit up to dat ar cream color filly's nose, but she r'ar back and snort like she don't want it. Den she smell at it agin, an she fiirt de water up wid her lip, an' she snort some mo'. She warnt gwine let dem town niggers know she was anxious to drink dat stuff. Man, sah! she put on a'rs. 'Bout haf de likely young nigger mens in de county des 'bout ha'f dead to trot in double harness wid dar ar filly.

"All dem town niggers dey [']low:

"'Don't she do pooty? Don't you wish you was in de place o' dat ar likely young lead horse?'

"Atter wile, atter she done show her raisin, dat ar filly put her mouf to de tum'ler an dreen hit dry.

"No sooner she swaller dat stuff de ole Scratch was in her big es a skin mule. She r'ared an she pitch, an she kicked clean aloose f'om de cyadge, an hit tuck fo' o' de likeles young nigger fellers in town to put her back, an den dey all got kick.

"Wen dey got her hitch up agin she was wuss'n ever. She was dat rambunckshus nobody couldn't no nothin' wid her. She done made up her mine to run way wid dat cyadge, and she done it too, mon.

"No, sah, she never had de strenk to des boddaciously pull all dem yuther hosses long wid her, but she cyad 'em des like you've seed a filly cyar a drove a mules out'n a paster, many a time.

"Ef somebody take de filly out dey des es well turn all de mules out too, becase dey des bleege to foller ef dey got to jump a stake-an-rider fence. You can't see no rope what de filly pull em wid, but she draw em right long des de same.

"Wen dat ar cream color filly made up her mine to run way she warnt a studdin bout dem yuther hosses hol'in' her back. An' dey never neither. Stidder dey doin dat, dey all tryin to see which one could keep de nighes' to her. Ever one gallin up hard es dey could go. Cose I kep' up right long side o' dat filly. Man, sah! we snatched dat cyad[g]e!

"Ole moster he went to hollin 'Wo!' but nobody wouldn't wo. All dem hosses had Chrismas in dey bones. Dat ar cream color filly fairly skim over de groun' like a rock skeet over de water. She never ax de mud no odds, becase she was a light built filly, an she look so much like a angel I wouldn' be supprise ef she didn't had wings what nobody couldn' see.

"Time we pass de two mile pose de cyadge was flyin thoo de a'r. Hit warnt so much es tech de groun. Ole moster he was holin on wid bofe han's to keep f 'om fallin off 'n de seat.

"W'en we was bout haf way home I yeard sump'n say 'Kerblom!' an I look back an I seed de cyadge done hit a tree, an we lef' it right dar.

"Wen ole Miss seed us comin she run to de do an holler:

"'Whar my ole man at?'

"We all couldn't do nothin but des whicker back at her. But Flat Nose Joe whar staid at home, he up an [']low:

"'I speck ole moster foun' mo' Chrismas 'n he could tote home. Here's de hosses done come home,' says he. 'Dat ar lead horse, Jake, he look fresh an peart like he des been a grazin in de paster,' says he, 'but de cream color filly done kick ever' scrap o' harness off 'n her. I speck you better sen' somebody to see what come o' de cyadge,' says 'e, 'because some o' de han's got to go an prize dem niggers out'n de mud anyhow.'

"Ole Miss she sont a gang o' hans, an, sho nough, dar dey foun de cyadge right gin dat same tree, hadn't move sence de hosses bus' loose f 'om it. But dey didn't see ole moster up dar on de seat whar we lef him, an hit look like he done gone on somewhar afoot. Hit dat way, but hit warnt dat way, because ole moster was too smart a man to try to walk thoo dat mud wid all dem groceries what he had to tote. Yas, sah, he had more sense'n dat.

"W'en he picked hisse'f up off 'n de groun whar de jolt thowed him he never stop to bresh his close yit fo' he crope in dat cyadge an quoil hisse'f up on dem saf ' cushions. Wen dem boys look in de cyadge dar he was layin, 'sleep, an he look des es peaceful es a infidel little chile.

"Dat's de sort o' Chrismus we all had down dar in M'renger."

(The *Montgomery Advertiser,* December 19, 1886)

Jake and Miss Emmer

When Jake is working in Miss Purreleen's garden his nostrils are often regaled with the most appetizing odors which are wafted from the Squire's kitchen just opposite. The odors have to cross a barbed wire fence, which is no great feat for an odor, good or bad; but what is no obstruction to an odor is an almost insuperable barrier to a man. It is in this respect that these odors exhibit wonderful powers by performing a superhuman feat, for they seize Jake by the nose and draw him to their source with such extraordinary energy that the barbed wires are fain to let the traveler pass, after exacting slight tribute in the shape of a portion of those little fluttering bannerets that adorn Jake's person and lend it the charm of picturesqueness. And so it often happens that Jake is found in the Squire's kitchen at the most interesting hour of the day. There is dinner at Mrs. Purreleen's for him, and he purposes to pay his respects to Miss Purreleen's cuisine in due season. Men of common mould are content with one dinner a day, but in Jake's composition there is a streak of Marengo mud which is noted for its swallowing capacity, and he is, therefore, not to be compared with persons that are formed of ordinary clay.

Had Jake lived in medieval time he would probably have figured as a strolling minstrel. His methods are much the same as used by those musical tramps whose "date is fled." When once he has effected an entrance into a castle he charms the inmates with some marvelous improvisation and is rewarded with the largess he most hungrily craves. If, however, his words should fall upon unappreciative ears; if he should fail to strike a responsive chord in the breasts of his entertainers; if the fingers be stiff, the harp out of tune or the fancy dull, the minstrel must resume his weary way, distending his stomach with generous draughts of air and water and tickling his palate with the hopes of better fare ahead.

Now the Squire's cook is a colored woman of unusual intelligence, and the tale that beguiles her and loosens the purse-strings of her generosity must be ingeniously conceived, and all its parts must be nicely dovetailed together, making a symmetrical whole in which no flaw can be picked. If she suggest a theme or furnish a motif, the improvisatore must take it up without hesitation and work out the details without blundering, else he cannot win her smiles or share her broiled chicken.

"Y'all up yer ain't much pestered wid mud, Miss Emmer," Jake began one day as the cook reproved a small boy for entering the kitchen without making use of the foot mat. "Ef you was down dar in Mrenger you wouldn't need no broom to sweep de flo'. Brooms aint no 'count down dar cep'n in de summer time. But you'd hatter keep a hoe an' spade in de kitchen to dig up de mud off 'n de flo'."

Miss Emmer didn't manifest much interest. She had a

surfeit of M'renger mud. Jake perceived that to gain her attention, it would be necessary to tax his powers of invention to the utmost.

"I tell you what's a fack, Miss Emmer," he said making another beginning. "I was gwine long down dar in M'renger one day, an' I seed sumpn black a layin right on top de mud in de middle o'de road. Cose I warnt walkin in de middle o' de road, because de mud was too deep. I was scared hit would a drownded me. I was slippin long der easy's I could on de side de road, and when it come handy I cooned de fence. But when I seed that black thing a layin in de road I says to mysef 'Hsays I, Hayo! wond' what dat is. Look like a hat.'

"Well, I tuck a rail offn de fence an' laid hit down so I could walk on it right up to dat black thing.

"Sho nough! wen I got to it hit was a hat, layin right on de mud. Hit was a good hat, too, man. Twarnt no old raggety nigger hat.

"I was mighty glad to fine dat hat, but I was sorter jubous bout techin it wid my han's. I was scared somebody done fix to trick me. I thought I'd kick it over fo' I pick it up, to see if they warnt nuthin under hit. Well, I drawed back one foot an' I giv it a kick, an' man, sah, no sooner I done dat somebody holler out:

"'Who dat aint got no better manners 'n to kick a gent'man in de face?'

"Sho nough! come to fine out, dey was a man's haid in dat hat. I axed him what he was a doin' down dar an' he [']lowed he was a ridin' long de road.

"I says, says I, 'Whar yo' critter at?'

"He says, says 'e, 'Hit's yer onder me, but seem like he aint a movin'. I speck we done stuck,' says he, 'Git up, Pete.'"

Jake watched Miss Emmer to observe the effect of this narrative on her, but she only sighed wearily when it was finished. In the current slang of the day, mud was a chestnut to her.

"I'm tired o' them big mud lies," she said presently. "There's stranger things happened than that. I heard of a shower o' frogs fallin' once, an' they fell out of a clear sky, too."

"Yes'm. Whar was dat at, Miss Emmer?"

"Lemme see. It was in Clark county, I believe."

"Yes'm, dat's right whar it was. I 'members hit des like hit was yistiddy."

"Well, maybe you kin tell how it was then. If you do— well, I'm goin' to have some mighty good dinner ready toreckly."

"Cose I kin tell you all about it Miss Emmer. Dem was M'renger frogs what fell down dar in Clark. You see Clark hit's jinin' M'renger, an' Clark never has nothin' no 'count 'cep'n hit come f 'om M'renger.

"Down dar in M'renger hit's de greates' place for snakes in de worl'. De snakes down dar dey're dat big an' long dey kin—"

"I don't care anything 'bout the snakes. You said you could tell all 'bout the frog shower in Clark, an' now you've got off on snakes in M'renger."

"Well, I'm gwine to tell you 'bout 'em, Miss Emmer. Seems like you mighty onres'less 'bout dem frogs. I was gwine long de road right todes 'em, but I never said I was gwine to jump right on 'em same es a duck jump on a june bug. But I say I'll git to 'em all de same.

"Well, es I was a sayin', dem snakes down dar in M'renger, dey're so long dey kin r'ar up boddaciously on dey tails an' stretch deyse'f clean crost de Bigby river. Hit's so, Miss

Emmer. One time one o' de bigges' mogsins dey was down dar, he tuck'n stretch hisse'f 'cross de river down dar b'low Moplis, an' he was dat proud w'en he foun' out he could do it, he des laid dar fo' or five days.

"Well, de steamboat what dey use to call de Betty Snipes, she come up de river atter w'ile. De Cap'n o' dat boat his name was Cap'n Bouncer, an' he could out-cuss air nother Cap'n on the river. When he seed dat snake lyin' crost de river, he thought hit was a big log. Wen he fust seed it he was so cloast he couldn't stop de boat, an' he des knowed in reason dat log was gwine to cyar off his smoke-stack an' all de top part o' his boat ef it didn't tar de whole boat all to pieces. He let in to cussin', he did, an' he cust so much de folks down at Mobile smelt de brimstone an' de smoke o' torment what come down on de water.

"Des de minute de Cap'n speck de stacks to hit de log[,] lo an' beholes! de log ris up in de middle an' let de boat pass thoo. Dat snake knowed what he was a doin'. Wen de boat come back he done de same way agin, an' he would a kep on a doin dat way hadn't a been for de frogs."

"The frogs! You haven't told anything about the frogs yet."

"I know I aint, but I'm comin to 'em now.

"You see, Miss Emmer, wen dat snake went to sleep his mout fell open[,] an' dem frogs thought hit was a big hole in de groun; an' dey der holler 'Eek!' an' jump right down. Yer dey com f'om all over M'renger, an' ever' frog what year bout dat big hole in de groun he norate bout it to ever yuther frog what he see.

"De snake he like it fus rate, becase, you know, Miss Emmer, snakes mostly lives on frogs.

"Man, sah! dat snake get dat full o' frogs he couldnt raise hissef up when de boat come up agin, an' w'en he boat hit him, man, sah! hit turned bottom side up an' drownded all de people what was in it, scusin o' de cap'n.

"De Cap'in he swum out an' went on up to Moplis to norate bout.

"Man, sah! You never did see sich a gettin' up es dey was 'bout dat time. All dem soldier compnies at Moplis an all dem yuther towns dey gethered on de river bank wid guns an' cannons, and dey loaded 'em all up an' dey aimed 'em all at de middle part o' dat snake an' wen Cap'in Bouncer gin de word, berlang! all dem guns an' cannons went off at wonst.

"Well, sah, wen de smoke cl'ared off dey warn't nothin' lef o' dat snake, but dey was 'bout fo' million frogs up in de iliments, flyin in' todes Clark."

(The *Montgomery Advertiser*, January 16, 1887)

Tripping Jake

 A gentlem[a]n recently had occasion to go to the depot to meet a train which reaches Auburn at a quarter past ten o'clock at night. There was a trunk to be brought up, and the services of Mr. Smith (of color) had been engaged for the purpose.

It wanted some minutes to train time when the gentleman reached the depot. There was no light about the place except that which the stars afforded. The little waiting room, which, during the day had been crowded with passengers of every shade of color, was now closed, and there was no place to rest except on the steps of the old dilapidated frog-stool, which, since the destruction of the railroad building by fire last year, does duty as a depot.

The gentleman had not been seated long before the sound of voices made him aware that he was not alone. The voices came from a pile of lumber hard by, and belonged to Mr. Smith (of color) and a blonde gentleman from Marengo.

The conversation, which the gentleman could hear distinctly, ran upon wonders of one sort and another and finally turned upon fishes.

"Well, Jake," quoth Mr. Smith (of color), "you is seed a heap o' cuis things, I know, but is you ever seed a rale sho nough big cat-fish?"

"Cose I is," returns Jake. "I seed a many a un down dar in M'renger.

"How big was he? Lemme see. De bigges one I ever seed his name was Tom."

"Yah! yah! yah!" laughed Mr. Smith (of color) "who ever yeard tell of a fish havin' of a name, cepin cat-fish an' pearch an' de like o' dat."

"Well, you see, dat'n whar I'm gwine to tell you 'bout he des laid roun de wof dar in Moplis so long till ever'body knowed him, an' dey tuck to callin' of him Tom. Dat's how come he had a name. Well, sah, dey tried to ketch dat feesh ten year er mo' fo' ever dey got 'im, an' w'en dey got him at las' dey cotch 'im wid a harpoon, becase he was too big to be cotch wid a hook. You aint never seed nair harpoon, is yer?"

"Naw. I dunno what dat is."

"Well, hit's a iron thing wid a beard on it. I aint talkin' bout har beard like dat what yo' wife pull out'n yo' chin."

"What make 'em calls it a har poon fer, den?"

"Hit's a sharp pinted thing an' hits got beard on it des like a feesh-hook. Don't you know ever you git a feesh-hook stuck in yo' britches de beard won't let it come out, dout cuttin' a piece o' de cloth out wid it? Well, dat's de same sort o' beard de harpoons has.

"Well, say, dey was some fellers a watchin' for dat feesh one day, an' w'en dey seed 'im dey tuck'n flung dat harpoon at 'im an' stuck t im 'im. Dat's de way dey cotch him."

"How big was he?"

"Man, sah! he was a buster. He was twenty foot long, an' big 'cordin'. Dey tuck an' drug him up town wid a six mule team, an' whar he drug 'long hit made a deep gully in de street, an' ef you go down dar to Moplis I speck you'll see dat gully tell yet."

"I spose everybody had fish to eat den."

"No, dey never."

"What's de reason dey never?"

"Becase."

"'Case what?"

"'Case folks warn't gwine to eat dat feesh. Dey warn't dat hongry for feesh."

"What was de matter wid him?"

"Dey warn't nothin' de matter wid him."

"What make dey never eat him den?"

"Becase dey knowed him too good. Dey knowed what he been a eatin' to make him grow so big."

"What he been a eatin'?"

"He been a eatin' dead folks. Ever'body what git drownded in de Bigby river, an' ef dey staid in de water long 'nough, dat cat-feesh eat 'em up boddaciously. Dat's reason dey use to couldn't never fine nobody whar git drownded in de Bigby. Man, sah! w'en dey cut dat feesh open dey foun' five er six gole an' silver watches in him."

"Oh, hush! Jake, you know dat aint so. Better mine what you say. I'll git you tangle up an' th'ow you fus' thing you know."

"W'en you git Jake tangle up on anything he tell you'll hatter git up fo' soon in de mornin'. Hit's de truth what I'm a tellin you."

"Well, how dem watches git in dat fish?"

"He swallowed 'em, man, des like you swallers biscuits. Dem watches was on men what got drownded, an' dat feesh eat 'em up. Some o' dem watches been in 'em fo' er five year, I reckon. Dey was all growed up 'bout in his meat, but, man, sah! ever one of 'em was a clicken. Dey hadn't lost nair minute sence de owners of 'em got drownded."

"Yah! yah! yah!" laughed Mr. Smith (of color). "I knowed you was a lyin' all de time. I was des givin' you rope so you could tangle yo'se'f up. Now I got you right whar I want you. You des like one o' deze yer little ole Texas mules what somebody got a long rope on him, an' des let 'im play roun' tell he git de rope all tangle roun' his feet. Den dey des gin de rope a jerk, an' de mule lying dar flat o' his back. Dat's de way I got you now."

"Well, jerk yo' rope den, an' crack yo' woop too. Jake 'll be dar, an' he wont be a layin' on his back neither. Jerk her. Jerk her."

"You said dat fish had five or six watches in [him]—"

"Lemme see. Did I say hit had five or six? Well, I made a mistake dar, sho. Hit was nine er ten I ought to a said."

"An' you said some o' dem watches been in 'im fo' or five year."

"Longer 'n dat. Some of em was in 'im ten year, becase some o' de folks whar seed em recolleck de time de owners of 'em got drownded."

"Well, now Sim gwine to trip you."

"Trip on, den."

"How dem watches kep' on a runnin' so long 'dout never bein' woun' up?"

"Fool you, de same time dat feesh swaller de watches he swaller de keys too. You ax me sumfin' hard next time. I don't like deze yer easy queshuns."

Jake went shuffling down the railroad track, and Mr. Smith (of color) stood scratching his head in great perplexity. Sombody had been tripped with a rope of yarn, but for the life of him Mr. Smith (of color) could not determine to which end of the rope himself had been attached.

(The *Montgomery Advertiser*, February 6, 1887)

The Marengo
Prestidigitator

"No, sah, dey never will."

Jake spoke with unusual energy and emphasis. He was thoroughly convinced of the correctness of the position he had taken. There was not a shadow of doubt on his mind—no more than there was in his tone or in the attitude he immediately assumed.

Jake seldom stands erect[.] It is his habit to walk or stand half bent in what might strike the observer as an apologetic or cringing atti[t]ude.

Such a posture is not without its advantages. It enables one to dodge more dexterously.

But on this occasion Jake stood so straight that, like the Indian's tree, he leaned the other way, and it looked as though there might be some danger that his spinal column would snap in two. However, the doctor was handy to promptly repair any damages that might be incurred.

He and Moss Hodge had been talking about the prospect of having a public hall in Auburn, and Jake had mildly expressed a doubt as to any first class show's coming to Auburn. Moss Hodge thought there was no foundation for such doubt, provided a hall was built, and so expressed himself. Jake then conceded that some tolerably good shows of a strictly one-horse variety might be induced to spend a rainy night in Auburn, but stou[tl]y contended that the people of this community would never, never see such a showman as once figured in Marengo.

"No, sah, dey never will!"

"Why, what sort of a showman was he?" inquired Moss Hodge, impressed by Jake's unwonted manner.

"He was a man des like you, only you sorter out favors him."

"I know, but I mean what did he do and what did he show?"

"I can't begin to tell you all what dat man done. He swallered swodes, an' eat fire an'—"

"Oh, he was a sleight-of-hand performer. Men will come here that can do all those things."

"Maybe dey will, but dey never is to do all dem things what dat man done."

"Tell some other things he did."

"Well, one night he axed somebody to come up dar on de stage an' he'p him, an' a young w'ite man name o' Mr. Hennigin went up dar an' hope him. De show man he put des a common hen aig down dar on de flo,' an' he turn a little ole box down over de aig, an he tole Mr. Hennegin to set down on de box. After wile de show man [']low:

"'Aint you done hatch yit?'

"Mr. Hennegin [']low he aint had no time to hatch; he

[']low hit take three weeks for a sho' nuff hen to hatch.

"'Lemme see,' says de showman, says 'e 'I speck you done hatch so long de chicken is fryin' size by now.'

"He raised up de box, he did, an' man, sah[!] out come a grown Shanghai rooster, an' cyowed.

"After dat de folks never called Mr. Hennegin nothin' but Mr. Roostergin."

"Is that all he did?"

"No, sah, dat ain't ha'f. He borrid all de watches he could git, an' he put 'em in a bag and stomped wid his feet. Den he took out all de pieces of 'em an' loaded up a big-mouf pistol wid 'em, an' he shot 'em at Mr. Hennegin. Man, sah! w'en de smoke cleared off all dem watches was hanin' by de chains on Mr. Hennegin's clo'es. I aint never seed n'air nother man wid so many watches strung round him."

"I've seen all those things do[ne repe]atedly."

"Maybe you is, Moss Hodge. I aint a 'sputin' but what you is, becase I knows you been a fur ways on' you's seed rights, but—"

"But what?"

"But dat man done one thing what you don't never seed nair nother man do."

"What was that?"

"I'm gwine to tell you 'bout dat man, an' I'm gwine to tell you de truth too. You know I always tells de truth, Moss Hodge."

"I don't know, you tell so much—"

"Well, dat's hit, sah. I tells all de truth. Some folks keeps back part o' de truth, and dat's des de same es tellin' a lie.

"I'm gwine to tell you all 'bout dat show man down dar in M'renger. He use to call up anybody what want to come up dar on de stage and let 'em shoot at him with a pistol.

Sometimes hit was Mr. Hennegin[,] an' sometimes hit was somebody else. Didn't make no difference so hit was somebody what could shoot good, because he want ever ball to hit him right squar in de forward. Well, sah[,] wen de bullet [hit] him he des lean his haid sorter so," suiting the action to the word, "and let de bullet drap out'n his haid on the flo. Co'se blood come too, an' some o' his brains fell out on de flo too. Den he tuck some shiny powder out'n his pocket an' put in dat hole whar de bullet went in his forward. After dat he tuck sump'n out'n his pocket what look like a gun wad an' he plug up de bullet hole wid dat. Den he po'ed sump'n out'n a bottle in his han' what look like mucinlage, an' he tuck an' smear some o' dat over de place, an', man, sah[!] in less'n a minute nobody couldn't a tole he ever been shot."

"Well, he wasn't shot. He just deceived you all."

"Yas, he was shot[.] Becase atter while he been shot in de haid so much all his brains was done spilt out, an' w'en he let de bullet drap out a speck o' brains come wid it—des some o' dat shiny stuff what he been a th'owin' in his haid. W'en hit come to dat pass he couldn't make nobody b'lieve he was shot sho' nough, an' he des hatter quit de sho business."

"If he had lost all h[is] brains he wouldn't have had any sense left."

"Dat's what folks said, but he was des es smart atter dat es he was befo', beca'se he had sump'n in his haid what do des es well es brains.

"Well, sah, w'en he foun' out he hatter quit de show business he low he was gwine to git him a office. He got on de kyars he did, an' he never stop till he got cl'ar to Washin'ton. W'en he got dar he went to see Ginal Grant, an' he lowed he come to ax Ginal Grant to 'pint him to a big office what 'I gin him plenty o' money an' nothin' to do.

Dem was de ve'y words what he told Ginal Grant.

"Ginal Grant he look at him right hard wid one eye shot, an' he [']low:

"'Aint you de show man what been down in M'renger?'

"De show man [']low: 'Yas.'

"Ginral Grant says, say he: 'Dey tells me all yo brains is done spilt out'n yo' haid.'

"'Yas,' de show man says, 'dat's so,' says he, 'but fas' es de brains spill out I put brass filin's in de place of 'em, an' now my haid's des es full o' brass es ever hit was o' brains,' says he.

"Man, sah! Ginal Grant never said another word. He des writ on a piece o' paper dat dat man was to have de bigges' office in de country."

(The *Montgomery Advertiser,* March 12, 1887)

Marengo Jake

A Romance of Four-and-Twenty Blackbirds

 "Whar y'all little boys gwine wid dat little bitty ole gun?"

The question was asked by Jake. It was addressed to his three little white friends who on former occasions had contributed somewhat [t]o his larder. The time was New Year's morning; the place on the outskirts of Auburn.

One of the little boys, Tom by name, had a small gun on his shoulder. The other two, John and Willie, were not armed unless in violation of the statute against carrying concealed weapons. Their pockets were stuffed with something—it might have been stones—which made them bulge as if they would burst.

The boys were setting out to enjoy the holiday in hunting, and they frankly ack[n]owledge[d] their purpose to Jake.

"What y'all gwine to hunt? I don't see y'all's little ole fice."

"Oh, we don't want a dog. We are going to hunt black birds."

"What y'all gwine to kill 'em wid?"

"With this gun," said Tom, bravely.

"I speck Willie and Johnnie gwine to kill 'em wid rocks, aint dey? Look like dey got dey pockets full o' rocks er sumpin."

"[']Taint rocks," cried Willie and John, in the same breath.

"'Taint? Well, maybe hit's Christmas what you got in yo' pockets."

"Something of that sort," said Tom.

"Hit look like oynges an' candy an' cake an' sich like."

"Yes," said John, "that's part of it, but we've got some bread and ham for our dinner too, because we expect to be gone all day."

"Well, honey, ain't y'all scared to go out mongst de blackbirds wid all dem things in yo' pockets an' nothin['] but one little bitty ole corn-stalk gun to perteck yo'se'f wid?"

By way of reply the three boys joined in a hearty laugh.

"Y'all neenter la'f. Blackbirds is dangious things. Ef they smell dem goodies dey'll fly down on you an' peck yo' eyes out an' eat all what's in yo' pockets. Better leave dem Chris'mas yer wid me."

The boys laughed immoderately now, and as soon as they could recover the control of their organs of speech they expressed their unbelief in the dangerous qualities of blackbirds.

"Y'all don't know blackbirds like I does. Down dar in M'renger dey use to be so many of 'em w'en dey come flyin' over hit darken de yeth so you couldn't see yo' han' befo' yo' face.

"Dey was a little boy down dar, name o' Tommie, an' he was des 'bout de size o' dis yer Tommie. He had a little gun des like dis yer'n—I 'clar to gracious! dis yer look like to ve'y gun he had. Hit do, for a fack!

"Dat boy yeared his pappy tell 'bout how many blackbirds he kill at one shoot, an' he thought he'd go out an' see ef he couldn't beat him.

"He knowed whar a mighty big drove use, an' he went right dar spotly.

"Sho' nough! w'en he got dar de groun' was kivered wid blackbirds, an' in some places dey was fo' deep.

"W'en he got close to 'em de nighes' ones begin to fly a little way an' light on top o' de yuthers tell atter w'ile dey was piled up higher'n Tommie's haid. Den Tommie begin to shoot, but dey was pack so tight dat little ole gun couldn't th'ow de shot into 'em, an' he never seed nair'n what he kill. He kep' on a shootin' till atter w'ile de ole King blackbird what was settin' up on a tree he turn his haid sorter sideways an' he look at dat boy out'n one eye, an' he low:

"'I wonder ef dat little ole boy 's a sassin' my folks.'"

"Blackbirds can't talk!" exclaimed the little boys, triumphantly.

"Dey can't talk like me an' y' all talks, honey, but dey kin talk to one an'er in blackbird talk.

"Dat King bird he watch dat boy aw'ile, an' he 'low:

"'I b'lieve in my soul dat sassy little rascal's tryin' to kill we' all wid his nasty little ole pop-gun.'

"Well, dat King bird he got so mad he fa'rly r'ared. Den he gin orders to all dem yuther birds same es a oberseer use to gin orders to a cotton fiel' full o' niggers.

"He hollered:

"'Ketch dat thing an' put out his eyes, an' pick him up an' cyar him clean 'way f'om dis country.'

"No sooner he said dat, 'bout fo' million blackbirds 'riz', an' dey kivered po' little Tommie f'om his years to his toes. Dey pecked out his eyes fo' you could say 'Jack Roberson.' Den all of 'em what could reach him cotch holt o' his clo'hes wid de bills, an' dey ris' in de a'r, same, as a b'loon. Hit was all done so quick po' little Tommie never had time to study 'bout nothin' 'fo' he was fifty miles f 'rom home.

"Dem birds flewed an' dey flewed tell dey got to de mountains 'way up yonder in de North. Den dey drapped po' little Tommie down in a hole up on top of a big mountain whar noboddy never go."

At this point in the narration Jake interrupted himself to draw one coat sleeve suggestively across his eyes.

"I can't he'p f 'om cryin' ever' time I studdies 'bout dat po' little boy," he continued.

"He would perish to death ef all dem birds had a went 'way an' lef ' him dar by his lone se'f. But two dozen of 'em staid dar to feed him, beca'se de king bird said dey mus' keep him 'live long es dey could, an' torment him.

"Well, dem two dozen black birds dey fed po' little Tommie reg'lar, an' dey brung him water, one drap at a time, in dey mouf.

"But dat little Tommie was a smart little boy. Mos' anybody 'll show some smartness, nough, w'en dey git in a sho' bad fix.

"He warn't in dat hole two days 'fo' he begin to study 'bout how he was gwine to git out o' dar. An' he fix up a smart trick. He tole dem birds dey'd look heap pootier ef dey had some w'ite paper tied to dey legs, an' he 'low ef dey'd tell him de nex' time any of 'em was gwine back down Souf, he'd fix 'em so fine all de hen blackbirds down dar in Mrenger 'd go 'stracted 'bout 'em.

"Dat tickle 'em mightily, an' twarnt ve'y long 'fo' two dozen new birds come up dar to take de place o' dem what was done got tired an' dem birds what been wid him all de time dey tole him dey was gwine back to M'renger, an' dey want him to fix 'em up so dey could cut a dash 'mongst de hen blackbirds down dar.

"Well, he fixed 'em. He had some ole paper in his pocket what he put in dar for gun waddin' an' he had some strings, too—little boys mos' always have strings in dey pockets, you know. An' he had a pencil.

"He tuck'n to' dat paper up in little pieces an' he writ a letter on 'em to his pappy—de same thing on ever' piece— an' he tied a piece to ever' bird's laigs. Dat letter hit tole his pappy right whar he was an' how he hatter come to fine him."

"How did Tommie know where he was?" interrupted Willie.

"He knowed by de way de seben stairs an' de helenyards stan'. He was a smart little boy.

"W'en dem birds was done fix up dat way dey was dat proud dey dis look at one an'er an' strut roun' an' say, 'Aint we fine?'

"Dat little boy kep' his mouf shot, an' dem birds flewed back to M'renger.

"Dey hadn't hardly to'ch de groun' down dar 'fo' Tommie's pappy kill some ob 'em, an' he read dem letters what was on dey laigs, an' he went right off an' brung Tommie home. But Tommie had to drink a lots o' Jooslem oak tea fo' he got well, becase he been a eatin' so many worrums, he was full of 'em."

A few moments of deep silence followed the narration of this rather remarkable story, and then Johnnie spoke.

"We a[r]e not afraid of finding enough blackbirds to carry us off."

"You're mighty right, honey. D'aint hardly any blackbirds 'bout yer, an' you can't kill none 'ceptin' you bait a place for 'em. Den you kin kill 'bout a hundred at one shoot."

"How do you do that?" was the eager inquiry.

"Ef y'all want me to, I'll bait a place for you."

"All right. Do it."

"Well, lemme see, to-morrow mornin'll be Sunday night ef it don't rain, won't it?"

In the excitement of the moment the boys gave assent to this preposterous proposition.

"Well, you can't shoot birds to-morrer, but I'll fix so you kill a thousand soon Monday mornin'. I'll bait a corn row over yander behine de branch, dis mornin', an' de birds 'll come dar to-morrrer mornin' an' feed. Den I'll bait it agin to-morrer, an' y'all must be dar by day Monday mornin' an' hide in de swamp right at de een 'o de ole corn row; den when de birds all gits in dar you'll have 'em in a row right befo' you, an' you kin des everlastin'ly go for 'em."

The boys were so delighted with this project that they insisted that Jake should begin it at once.

"Hole on," said Jake, cautiously. "Ef I do all dat for y'all, y'all's got to furnish de bait."

"All right. We'll furnish it. What do you want?"

"Dat Chris'mas what you got in yo' pockets 'll do. Birds loves oynges an' apples an' cake an' candy same es little boys does."

Regretfully, as when one parts with some cherished object, yet resignedly, as when one surrenders a present good to secure a greater in the future, the boys emptied the contents of their pockets into Jake's hat.

"I'll take dis an' strow it all long dat ole corn row. I ought to have some 'backer to put wid it, because birds kin smell 'backer a fur way off. Don't nair one o' y'll chaw 'backer, does yer?"

"I don't," said Willie.

"I don't," said John.

"Tommie don't say nothin'," said Jake.

"Tommie's got some tobacco in his pockets," said John.

"He said he was going to try to learn how to chew it to-day. Give it to him, Tom."

"Now, y'all go on home an' git yo' little ole fice an' go rabbit huntin', but don't come 'bout yer, beca'se you mought scare off de birds. Monday mornin', soon, y'all come out yer, an' I'll show you whar to go."

The annals of Auburn, in the record of that Monday, show forth no unusual slaughter of the feathered inhabitants of the field, and if a solitary blackbird came to a violent death that day, history is silent concerning the details of the tragedy.

(The *Montgomery Advertiser,* April 10, 1887)

Jake Cornered

"Moss Wilbur, I year tell Moss Frank done sont a letter up yer all de way f'om Greenville, an' he [']low he want to know how dat little boy what de blackbirds cyad off could see de seben stairs an' de helenyards wid bofe his eyes out.

"Moss Frank sorter like an'er man what I use to know down dar in M'renger. Dat man wan was cu'ises' w'ite man ever I seed. His name was Mr. Tom Thomas, but ef anybody had a tole him dat was his name he'd a up an' 'spute wid 'em 'bout it. He 'spute 'bout ever'thing what come 'long an' nobody aint dassent to tell him nothin' 'cep'n dey could cyar him right to de place an' show hit to him. An' den w'en you got him dar he'd ax so many foolish queshuns he'd mighty nigh make you b'lieve you done tole a lie."

"I've heard of 'doubting Thomas,' but I didn't know he lived in Marengo."

"Yas, sah, dat's right whar he live at, an' he raise up a pow'ful big fambly down dar, too.

"He had a nigger name o' Tobe. Tobe he was mighty bad

to stutter. He come a runnin' one day, an' he [']lowed:

"'Oh, M-Moss T-T-Tom, one o' yo' chilluns done cut his t-t—' an' dat was all he could git out 'fo' Mr. Thomas 'mence to ax queshuns so fas' nobody couldn't a answered him, let 'lone ole, stutterin' Tobe.

"Mr. Thomas [']low: 'Is he cut his throat? How you know he did? What did he cut it wid? How did he cut it? Is he dead? Which one is hit?'

"Ole Tobe he kep' on, 'T-t-t—' till atter w'ile he got it out—'toe.'

"Den stidder Mr. Thomas runnin' to see 'bout de fracas, he stan' dar an' ax queshuns. He want to know which one o' de chilluns hit was, like one was any better'n de yuther; an' he want to know which toe he cut off, like dat make any diffunce.

"Ole Tobe, sah, he kep' on a stuttin tell atter w'ile he got it all out—leas'ways, he got out 'nough to sassify de common run o' folks. He [']low hit was Jimmie what happen to de bad luck, an' hit was his lef' han' big toe what he done cut smack off wid de chop-ax.

"W'en he out wid dat Mr. Thomas he [']lowed he never b'lieve a word he said. He [']lowed he knowed Jimmie had mo' sense'n to be foolin' long o' de chop-ax. Ef hit had been Sam er Bill er John er Bob er Joe er Henry er dat little fo'-year-ole boy what warnt been name yit, he could b'lieve it, because some o' dem never had no sense, cep'n settle*ment* sense. Dey could l'arn how to go to mill an' sich like, but dey never knowed nothin' in de book.

"Tobe he sw'ar hit was Jimmie, but he couldn't make Mr. Thomas onnerstan' 'bout it. Mr. Thomas [']low:

"'Jimmie couldn't a cut off his lef' han' big toe ef he had a tried,' says he, 'beca'se he's de lef-handes' chile I got,' says he, 'an' nobody can't cut off dey own lef'-han' big-toe, cep'n dey hole de chop-ax in dey right han',' says he.

"He kep' on a 'sputin' an' axin' questions tell atter w'ile a wite man what live in de settlement come a runnin' up, an' soon's he yeared what Mr. Thomas was a-sayin' he up an' [']lowed:

"'Don't make no diffunce wher you b'lieve Tobe or no; I done been dar an' seed fer myse'f, an' you got to buy a lef '-han' coffin for Jimmie, beca'se he's done cut off his lef '-han' big toe an' his lef '-han' arm too, an' nobody never come an' hope him squench de blood, an' he's done bled to death,' says he.

"Moss Frank he's gittin' mighty nigh es bad es Mr. Tom Thomas. But dey's one what I speck Moss Frank'll b'lieve yit."

"Who is that?"

"Dat ar likely lady o' his'n."

"No doubt."

"But Moss Frank done got me in a cornder now, beca'se he's writ up yer, an' de word's got out Jake done tole a lie. Hit do look sorter spicious, don't it, Moss Wilbur."

"Rather so. You didn't e[x]plain how the blind boy could see the stars, but no doubt you could do so."

"Ef I had a said dat I could a-splain it, but I never said dat."

"Didn't you say the blind boy found out what part of the country he was in by the way the stars stood?"

"Yas, sah, dat was what I said. Hit come out dat way in de Appetizer, didn't hit?"

"Yes."

"Well, dat's right. Dat's de way de facks runs, an' I want you to write to de Appetizer an' tell 'em I never said dat bline boy seed de stairs."

"How am I to explain, then?"

"Daint on trouble 'bout dat. I never study 'bout nobody axin' sich queshuns es dat, let lone Mass Frank what kin read an' write. Don't you reccelleck I tole you 'bout dat boy talkin' wid de blackbirds 'bout puttin' papers on dey laigs? Well, dat boy he done been wid dem birds so long he done larnt how to talk blackbird des es good es he could talk M'renger. He ax dem birds, an' dey tole him whar de stairs stan at, and dat de way he foun' out whar he was at. I boun' Moss Ree would a knowed how it was."

(The *Montgomery Advertiser*, April 17, 1887)

A True Story

How Marengo Jake Elected Cleveland

 "Moss Hodge, dey tells dey gwine to have a big fa'r in Munggomry nex' week[.]"

"Yes: they're going to have the biggest fair they ever have had. Are you going?"

"I was des a stud'in' 'bout its sah. I yeared Pres'*dent* Cleveman's was gwine to be dar."

"Yes: he'll be there one day."

"Dey 'low his wife gwine to be dar, too."

"Yes, that's so."

"I'd like mighty well to see Pres'*dent* Clevemans an' Miss Frankie, beca'se I done seed dey picters hangin' up in de pos'-uffice, an' dey're de likelies' white folks ever I seed, cep'n to ole Moster an' ole Miss w'en dey was young."

"If you go to the fair next Thursday, you'll see them."

"Ef I sho' knowed dat, Moss Hodge, I'd go er bust a trace, but dey'll be sich a whoppin crowd dar I'm jubous I wont git to see 'em. I been to one fa'r in Munggomry wonst, an' I knows zackly how hit is. Hit was nigger day dat day what I was dar, an' hit look like ole slav'ry times on ole Moster's plantation down dar in M'renger. Dey darken de yeth tell hit seem like de sun was in de 'clipse. I never is seed sich an'er crowd o' *free* niggers but wonst."

"When was that?"

"Dat was at ole man Gabe's funal down dar in M'renger. Ole man Gabe was a mighty big man in his time, an' w'en word was sont he was sho' 'nough dead ever' nigger in M'renger went to his funal.

"I speck dey'll be des 'bout sich an'er crowd in Munggom'ry to see Pres'*dent* Clevemans an' Miss Frankie. Dat's what flustrate me 'bout gwine. I don't want to be dodgin' roun' de aidge o' de crowd like I done stole sump'n, an' I aint got no idee o' scrougin' myse'f in dat crowd an' git my liver an' my lights trample out'n me. Dat aint de sort o' place I wants to meet Pres'*dent* Clevemans and Miss Frankie."

"Where do you want to meet them, then?"

"I wants to meet 'em in a big open fiel wid nobody in it, so I kin walk right up to 'em an' tell em who I is."

"What do you suppose they'd care about you?"

"Ef dey was to see me des passin' 'bout in a big crowd dey wouldn't care nothin' impertickler 'bout me. Pres'*dent* Clevemans he'd up and low: 'Frankie, yonder go a mighty likely nigger feller.' He'd be bleege to nodis me dat much, but dat'd des ce 'bout all. But I lay ef I was to git a chance to pass a few comp'*ments* wid him, he'ed 'member me de longis' day he live, beca'se I was de casion o' him bein' 'lected pres'*dent*."

"You were! Well, what would you say to him?"

"I'd do him sorter like I use to do ole Mike. Ole Mike he was a ole one-eyed mule, an' nobody could'nt never ketch him cep'n dey crope up on him on the bline side, beca'se ole Mike was smart, mon!"

"Mr. Cleveland has two eyes, though, and they say he keeps them open."

"I aint a 'sputin but he's toler'ble peart, moss Hodge, but he ain't got no eyes in de back part o' his haid—nobody ain't. Dat what make I says what I does: ever'body got a blind side to 'em."

"Well, how would you approach him?"

"I wouldn't go too rushin' at him, Moss Hodge, beca'se anybody what ain't never been in dis country befo' dey're more'n ap' to be sorter bashful, you know. W'en I went to injuce de subjec' to his mine I'd take off my hat like whi' folks what never had but two or three niggers use to do w'en dey meet ole moster. Den de fus' word I'd say I'd 'low:

"'I'm hopes you won't excuse me o' consumption, sah,' says I, 'but w'en I seed Miss Frankie dar I couldn't he'p 'om makin' her a bow, beca'se she looks mor' zackly like ole Miss w'en ole Miss was a young gal down dar in M'renger, an' de young w'ite gent'mans use to crowd roun' her so thick tell she never had room to turn roun, dout knockin' 'em down, an' dey would a been glad for her to a wiped her feet on 'em, she was so likely, an' she owned two hundred stroppin' nigger fellers like me, scusin' womens an' chilluns.'"

"Hurrah! That would be a capital start. I think you'd get in on Mr. Cleveland's blind side with that sort of a speech. How would you then proceed?"

"I'd tell him I yeared he love to go feeshin—"

"That's so. He enjoys the sport very much."

"Do he? Well, I'd tell him ef he'd come an' go wid me dar down in M'renger, I'd show him some mighty good holes for feesh in Cottonwood creek an' de Bigby roover. He could catch heap bigger catfeesh down dar 'n he ever cotch in Washington. Well, w'en me an' him sorter got usened to one on'er, I'd tell him all 'bout ole man Gabe's funeal."

"Who was ole man Gabe?"

"He was a black man what use to live down dar M'renger.

He was smart, too, Mon. He was des a leetle bit too smart, ole Man Gabe was. He june der niggers 'roun' wuss 'n de overseers use to fo' de war, an' he made 'em ever' one vote de 'publican ticket ever' 'lection; beca'se he was des naicherly a publican an' a sinner.

"De fus 'lection ever I went to, ole man Gabe met me way out on de aidge o' town. He done norate all over M'renger dat de niggers mus' all come to town dat day.

"De fus word he say to me he ax me is I reddish. I never knowed wher I reddish or no. I never knowed what reddish was, but he larn 't me. He cyad me up to a winder whar a man was a settin' by a table wid a bottle o' ink an' a book on hit, an' he made me hole up my han' an' sw'ar my entitlements. Dat was reddish. After dat ole man Gabe gin me a ticket an' march me up to an'er winder, an' vote me. Hit was a publican ticket, too, Mon.

"Dat's de way ole man Gabe done ever' nigger what come to de 'lection dat day.

"After we was done all vote one time he tuck us out hine a house an' made us swap coats an' go back and reddish an' vote some mo'. Den he made us swap hats an' do it agin. Ever' time we reddish we hatter swear new entitle*ments,* tell atter w'ile I never knowed what my right name was. I done forgot it.

"Well, de publicans got 'lected dat 'lection, an' dey kep on gittin 'lected ever time long es ole man Gabe live, an' no wonder, becase dem niggers was scared not to do what ole man Gabe tole 'em to.

"De white folks naicherly 'spise ole man Gabe an' he had lots of fusses wid 'em. I wouldn't a been supprise ef dey hadn't a killed him mos' any time. Dey beat him wid sticks an' dey stabbed him wid knives, but ole man Gabe he overed it ever time. My ole moster he [']lowed he blieved ef anybody was to kill ole man Gabe he'd come to life again des for spite, he was dat obstroperlous. Shoo! my old moster had sense, mon.

"But atter wile de word come one day old man Gabe was sho dead. A wite man what he gin slack jaw to, tuck an' knocked him in de haid wid a rock, an' hit everlastinly mash dat rock.

"Dat what dey said, but nobody never believe it tell dey went to ole man Gabe's house an' seed him a layin' dar an' lookin like he was des 'bout es dead es a nigger eber git to be.

"A big crowd o' niggers gethered dar dat day. Dey put ole man Gabe in de coffin an' dey tole me go an' dig his grave.

"You know, Moss Hodge, I knows all 'bout diggin graves, becase I been at it, off'n an' on, all my born days.

"Well, I laid off to fix ole man Gabe's grave so he couldn't git out'n it no mo' tell Gabel toot his horn. I dug her deep, sar. I dug her ten foot deep, an' wen I got done I said to mysef, says I:

"'Ole man, ef you come to atter we git you in dar, you'll have a fur ways to grabble thoo de dirt!'

"Dey was a big crowd at ole man Gabe's funal, I tell you. Hit was a regular M'renger crowd. You know, Moss Hodge, niggers des naicherly loves to go to a funal, anyhow, and wen a big man like ole man Gabe die, de niggers 'll gether roun' his grave same es buzzard's roun' a dead horse.

"Ef dem many niggers goes to de fa'r in Munggomry, dey wont be stannin room for no white folks.

"Well, sar, dey laid two han'-spikes 'cross de grave, an' dey let de coffin res' on dem; den atter de preacher got thoo wid his prambles and revolutions dey put two ropes under de coffin to let her down.

"All dat time I was a stannin dar on de aidge o' de grave, des a watin'. I laid off to be ready w'en dey gin de word to let de dirt drap in. My foot was on de spade, an' de spade was driv ha'f way up in de dirt.

"De mens what had holt o' de ropes dey let de coffin down in de grave. But dem ropes warnt long 'nough to tech de bottom, an' de mens had to turn aloose an' let de coffin drap. De coffin hit de bottom kerblom.

"No sooner de coffin start down I shove my spade in de dirt an' got up a big spadeful. I laid off to drap dat dirt on de coffin time it hit de bottom.

"Man, sah! when I got up dat dirt an' turn roun' to th'ow it in de grave I seed a sight I aint gwine to forgit dis side o' jedgment. Ole man Gabe was done come to, des like ole Moster say, an' he was a settin' up dar in his coffin wid his mouf wide open.

"Ole man Gabe had a mouf des like a catfeesh, anyhow.

"You see, w'en dem niggers let de coffin drap it busted de led aloose, den ole man Gabe ris right up. I speck he been a layin' dar des a waitin' for sich a chance."

"Did you drop your spade and run?"

"Who? me? Ef I had a, Mr. Clevemans never would a been 'lected pres'*dent*, beca'se ole man Gabe he'd a got up out'n dat grave, an' w'en de lection day come he'd a made ever nigger in M'renger vote fo' times apiece fo' Mr. Blaines, an Mr. Clevemans he wouldn't a so much es knowed dey been any 'lection, beca'se de niggers is like blackbirds down dar in M'renger."

"Well, what did you do?"

"W'en I ris up wid de spadeful o' dirt I come round wid a whirl, I did, an' w'en I seed ole man Gabe a settin up down der in de grave, I des let him have de whole spadeful o' dirt right in his mouf.

"He had his mouf open, sah, but he never had no time to ax nobody ef dey reddish.

"Dat spadeful o' dirt knocked him back flat in his coffin, an' de led hit fell back on him, an' fo' ever old man Gabe could make a motion to raise up again, I had 'bout two waggin loads o' dirt on dat coffin led.

"You kin laf ef you want to, Moss Hodge, but hit was dat spadeful o' dirt what beat Mr. Blaines."

(The *Montgomery Advertiser*, October 21, 1887)

Marengo Jake

He Tells About a Famous "Dry Drought"

OLD TIMES ON A PLANTATION—
HOW JAKE TOTED WATERMILLIONS
FOR THE GINGER CAKE GALS AND
THE DISASTROUS EFFECTS

 Jake was making a great show of digging a hole in the ground for a fence post, but the earth was very dry and hard, and more than once as persons passed he manifested a disposition to stop and talk. But every one seemed intent on his own business, and hurried past, and, since he could find no one to whom he might address his remarks, he began to talk to himself.

"I clar to gracious!" he began, pausing in his work, "ef dis yer aint de hardest dirt ever I seed sence de big dry drought down dar in M'ringer—"

"What's that yarn about Marengo?" asked a voice at Jake's back.

Jake turned suddenly and discovered a white gentleman standing in arm's length.

"Law! Moss Tom, I didn't know you was anywhars 'bout," exclaimed Jake, making a profound bow and grinning from ear to ear. "You crope up on me, Moss Tom. I was des miratin' how dis yer crowbar bounce out'n de yeth ever I time I joog hit down."

"No, you were not, you old black rascal; you said something about the drought in Marengo."

"Did I, Moss Tom? Well I ax yo' pardon an' I grant yo' grace. I'm sorter forgitless dis mornin'. Y[e]s, sah, sence I come to reecolleck, I b'lieve dat dry drought did pass 'cross my mine. I never is to forgit dat time."

"Why?"

"Caze we all like to perish offer de yeth."

"Was it any drier than it is here now?"

"Moss Tom, you don't know nothin' 'bout dry times. You look at me. What does I favor?"

"A monkey more than anything else."

"Yah, yah, Moss Tom, you'd have yo' fun ef you was gwine to die. Well, I'm hopes I outfavor any monkey ever I seed in de show. I'm a black complected man, but w'en I was young down dar in M'ringer I was des es likely a nigger es ever put his foot on M'ringer dirt. Yas, sah; I was dat[.] My old moster had fo' hunderd ginger cake gals would a been glad to a cotch me, let lone de black uns, 'fo' dat dry drought come on."

"What did the drouth have to do with your personal pulchritude?"

"Hit had a lots to do wid it. Hit was de casion o' me havin' any. I use to be a tall sooply young man, des like a black snake stannin' upon de een o' his tail, an' I was a runner, too, man. Now I'm sorter stumpy, an' I don't speck I could jump a ten rail fence, cepin dey was somebody cloast behine me wid a double b[a]rrel gun. No, sah; and I couldn' crawl thoo a crack twix de rails neither, an' ef I was to fine a fat possum up a simmon tree, I'd des hatter stan' dar an' thow rocks at him, caze I know I couldn't reach him, an' I'm dat stumpy I couldn't clam de tree.

"Yas sah, dat was de driest drought ever been in dis Newnited state o' Alabama."

"Did the dry weather check your growth?"

"Who? Me? No, sah; I was done grown den; an' de idee o' gittin married was runnin' in my hed. I never is seed Majone yit, an' the onliest thing what bother me I couldn't make up my mine w'ich one o' dem ginger cake gals I want de wust. Yah! yah! yah—ee. Oh, dem likely gals! Dey use to honey 'roun' me, an' look pleasin' at me like I wus dat sweet dey nearly dead to buss me. But I knowed in reason ole master warnt gwine to 'gree for me to marry all fo' hundred o' dem gingercake gals, an' ef he had a, dem black complected gals dey would a raise de bigges' racket ever dey was on dat ar plantation. What I was studyin' 'bout was w'ich one o' dem gals I druther have. Dat was what was a pestin' me."

"Well, what's all that got to do with the drouth? I don't believe there ever was any drouth in Marengo. You are just working your jaws to give your arms a rest. I'll go on and then you'll have to go to work again."

"Hole on, Moss Tom; hole on. You's the most onresless pusson in dis yer Aubu'n town. You ain't gimme no chance yit to to tell 'bout no drought. I ain't but barly got on de aidge o' de subjick."

"Well, jump over your ten rail fence and get into the middle of your subject at once."

"I done tole you, Moss Tom, I'm out'n de jumpin' business now. I'm too stumpy an' squatty to jump deze days. I got to scratch under dat fence. Wonst dey was a time ef dey come long a wet drought, I could wade thoo de deepes' an' de slushier sloo down dar in M'ringer an' tote two gingercake gals cross at a time. But dat dry drought hit got way wid Jake. Man, sah! hit never rain a drop o' rain endurin' nine monts dat fall. All de creeks an' de branches dey went dry es a bone. Ole master he tuck an' had 200 waggin loads

'o fishes haul up out'n Cottonwood creek an' put on his lan'
for minyu. You know, Moss Tom, fishes kin stan' a wet
drought tolerble good, but dey natchelly spise a dry drought.
Man, sah, he kivered de groun' in de long black slipe bout
two foot deep wid fish[.]"

"Oh, what are you giving me?"

"Hit's a fack, sah, des like I tell you. All de fish in
Cottonwood perish, an' dey was pile up twix' de banks. Hit
made dat piece o' lan' mighty rich, too. Hit's rich tell yit, an'
you kin tell easy 'nough hit been had fish put on it, case ever
corn tossle is forked des like a fish tail, an' de shucks dey has
sumpn like fish fins stickin' out on ever side. Well, sah, hid't
make you hongry to meet a colored man whar been workin'
in dat slipe a hot day, caze he smell des like mak'rel. He do
dat."

"In the name of sense, how did the drouth reduce your
stature?"

"I des 'bout to injuce de subjeck, Moss Tom. You see w'en
water got dat sca'ce ole moster hatter send his ten-mule
waggins way down in Clarke atter hit. But atter w'ile de creeks
an' de pools dey all dried up, an' den he hatter sen' his
mules an' his cows off to stay whar dey was water, an' we
never had nothin' lef' to haul a drap wid."

"How did you keep alive then?"

"Ole moster he called me up to ax me what he better do.
I 'lowed dey was some water in de system yit, but de want
'nough for all de folks on de plantation. I tuck a stick, an' I
figgered an' I ciphered on de groun' an atter w'ile I an' tole
ole moster I done got de answer. De water in dat system was
'nough for all cep'n me an' dem fo' hunderd ginger-cake
gals, an' es for us, we all could live on watermillions tell hit
rain.

"Ole Moster he up and 'lowed we never had no teams to

haul de watermillions up, an' de patch was a fur ways f 'om de quarter. I tole him he neenter pester hisse'f 'bout dat; I could tote 'em up for dem gals ef he'd let me.

"He laf an' 'lowed dat was all right, but he would'n' be su[r]prise ef I hadn't bit off more'n I could c[h]aw.

"I went to wo[rk], I did, an' I toted dem big M'ringer wa[te]rmillions up on my haid fas as dem gals c[a]ll for 'em. Hit warn't no easy job, neithe[r] Moss Tom. Dem watermillions was hea[v]y. Dey warn't no little simlins like you see raised 'roun' Aubu'n. Some ob 'em weigh more'n a hundred poun's. An' dem gals—oh! dey was dev'lish gals—dey use' to make out like dey was thirsty des to make me trot. Seem like I never seed folks eat watermillions so fas'. I was on de trot all day, f 'om time de mornin' star 'pear in de ilements tell de seben stars was two hours high.

"Yes, sah, dat's how come me so stumpy."

"How?"

"Dem watermillions squushed me down[.]"

"Oh, pshaw! Get on with your work."

"Moss Tom, you ain't got nair' little piece o' backer 'bout yo' clo'es nowhars, is you?"

(The *Birmingham Age-Herald*, October 20, 1889)

Marengo Jake

An Incident of the Wet Drouth in M'ringer

THE COLORED PHILOSOPHER OF AUBURN PICTURES AN INCIDENT OF THE TIMES "BEFO DE WAH"

A Sketch from Real Life

 After "Moss Tom" had passed on Jake resumed his digging, but the earth was so dry and hard that the crowbar rebounded at every stoke as though it had struck a solid rock. Once it bounced so high that it struck his chin, for Jake is not a tall man.

No serious injury was inflicted by the collision—not even to the crowbar—but the incident gave Jake an excuse to stop and rub his chin a moment.

"Ef I was des a leetle taller, dat crowbar wouldn't a hit my chin," he soliloquized.

"Why ain't you a leetle taller, then?" inquired a gentleman who happened to be passing just as the words were uttered. "Did you forget to grow when you were young?"

"Naw, sah, I never, Moss Henry. I ax yo' pardon, sah. I never seed you comin'; ef I had a, I'd a said good mornin'. I warnt studin 'bout seein' of you yit. Naw, sah, I never forgot to grow w'en I was young. I growed same es a young chinyberry tree. I did dat. W'en I was a young man down dar in M'ringer I was mighty nigh seben foot tall. I was, sah, for a fack. You neenter whistle, Moss Henry, I'm tellin' you de naked tru[t]h."

"Well, Jake, I've always heard you were the biggest liar that ever wagged a tongue, but I didn't know you could tell as big a one as that."

"Moss Henry, don't you b'lieve what I [t]ole you?"

"What? That you were once seven feet high and now you are not more than five [f]eet five?"

"Yas, sah. No; lemme see. Did I say [s]eben foot?"

"That's exactly what you said."

"Well, hole on, Moss Henry, I made a [li]ttle mistake."

"Ah; I thought you did."

"Yas, sah; I made a mistake."

"Not a doubt of it. You meant to say [th]at when you were young and straight you [w]ere five feet six[.]"

"Folks will make mistakes sometimes, [y]ou know, Moss Henry, but I never made [da]t'n a purpose[.] I said seben, but I ought [to] a said eight[.]"

"Eight! You have the cheek to say you [w]ere once eight feet high?"

"Yas, sah; I used to been eight foot and [tw]o inches high w'en I was a young man."

"What's the reason you are not that tall [no]w, then? Just explain that, will you?"

"Well, sah, hit was all de 'count o' de [bi]g wet drouth what we had down dar in [M]'ringer 'fo' de war. Hit rain 'bout nine [or] ten mont's dat winter han' gwine. Ef [old] Norah had er been dar wid his ark, him [an]' all his fambly would a got drownded[.] [Da]t ark wouldn't a been no

more'n a com[mo]n washtub on de Bigby[.] De whole lan'
[wa]s a floatin in water. De mud was dat [de]ep nobody
dassent to go out o' do's for [no]thin'.

["]Moss Henry; hit soun' sorter cu'i's to talk [bo]ut so
much water endurin' sich a dry [spe]ll es dis, don't it?"

["]Rather; but it's still more curious to see [ho]w you are
trying to make me forget the [sub]ject. You set out to tell me
how you [had] your legs shortened, but when you found
[you]r invention was not equal to the task, [you] tried to
divert my mind with a discus[sion] of the weather."

["]Moss Henry, you talks same es hit reads [out]'n de
books. Ef I could talk dat way, [I'd] be a preacher an' live on
yaller-legged [chi]ckens, stidder diggin' holes in de groun'
[for] a livin'."

["]What about the process of shortening [tha]t you went
through with?"

["]I'm gwine to tell you 'bout dat, Moss [Hen]ry, but I
can't tell hit in a minute. Ef [I] [t]ell you how I got shorter,
I speck I [have]ter fus tell you how I got longer. Lem[me]
see. How high did I say I was?"

["]Eight feet two, you sable prevaricator."

["]Well, I made a mistake. I was nigh [bou]t nine foot
high, an' I was de likeliest [you]ng man on ole moster's
plantation. All [de] gals dey look up to me, an' old moster
[hiss]e'f he was dat proud o' me he used to [take] me 'roun'
to all de fa'rs to show me off. [Ef t]hings was like dey use to be,
I wouldn't [be s]upprise ef me an' ole moster wouldn't a
[still be] in Birmingham this minute at de big [stat]e fa'r. But
dat wet drouth, hit come [lon]g an' shorten me up[.]"

["]Well, how did it do it?"

["]I'm tellin' you 'bout dat now, Moss [Hen]ry[.] I des
tole Moss Tom 'bout it a [littl]e w'ile ago. Oh! hit was a wet
drouth [for a] fack. Hit never let up rainin' a min[ute

e]ndurin' 'bout ten mont's dat blessed [wint]er. Man, sir! I've yeared tell o' it [raini]n' down bull frogs, but dat winter hit [rained] down little niggers. Yas, sah, dey [was] more'n a thousand little niggers drapped [on] moster's plantation. Ole moster, he [ain']t a cairn. He 'lowed, 'Jake, let 'em [rain;] dey're des a makin' me richer an [riche]r.'

["W]ell, dey warn't nobody could go no[whar]s dat winter, cep'n me. I was dat tall [I coul]d wade thoo mos' any water, 'cep'n [de B]igby. One Sunday dey was 'bout fo' [hundr]ed o' old moster's gingercake com[plect]ed gals want to go broaden in de set[tlem]ent, but dey 'lowed dey couldn't git [nowh]ars on de 'count o' de mud an' de [wate]r. I tole 'em nemmine, I take 'em[.] [An I] did, too, moss. Toreckly we come to [a big] ditch, an' dey wan't no foot log cross [it.] Hit was 'bout 10 foot wide. I des [lay d]own cross dat ditch, an' dem gals dey [all wal]k over on me. Man, sah! seem like [I neve]r is had sich cu'is feelin's befo'[.] Look [like de]y was a streak o' lasses runnin' up [and down my ba]ckbone.

["Then] de rain hilt up one evenin' 'bout [setting] sun, an' hit mence to turn sorter [cold.] By de time hit was gittin dark de [Bigby] was froz' all over de top.

["I sa]ys to myself, says I, 'Hayo, w'en de [moon g]it up hit'll be amighty good night to [roam] bout some, caze de groun' 'll be hard [and there] won't be no patterolers out. But [I was not] a studyin' 'bout how I was gwine [to get s]horten up dat night.

["Wel]l, sah, I lit out, I did, an' lowed I'd [head] todes de Bigby an' see ef dey was [any] gal down dat a way grievin' her[self to] death caze she couldn't see me.

["D]e groun' hit walk mighty nice for a [while] but bymeby w'en I got down dar in [the mud] close to de roover, hit gin to git [mighty sa]ft, an' toreckly hit mence to [stick t]o my feet. Man, sah, de furder I [went the] mo' hit stuck to my feet, tell atter w'ile I feel myse'f raisin' up offa de ground. I walked on a little piece, an' I knowed I done growed two foot higher des by de mu' a gethin on my feet. I kep on a goin' an' twarnt long fo' my hed was up over de tree tops. I [']low, I aint a cairn ef I bump out a star or two, des so dey don't fall on none o' my gals.

"Sho 'nough, I kep' on a-reachin' up in de iliments tell I seed de man in de moon dat plain hit look like I could a rub my nose gin his'n.

"By dat time I was done got down dar cloast to de roover, an' w'en I seed how tall I was I change my mine 'bout gwine to see dat yaller gal. I was tooken wid a hankrin' atter a coal black gal wid lips same es ripe beets, whar live tother side o' de roover. I knowed in reason I could wade de Bigby, an' de water wouldn't so much es wet de bottom o' my feet.

"Well, sah, I gin 'bout two steps, an' I was on de roover bank. Hit was mighty full. I reckon hit was a mile wide, an' de water look mighty cole wid de moon a shinin' down in hit.

"I gin one mo' step an' I let one o' my mud laigs down bout a quarter cross de roover. I fetched up de yuther'n, I did, an' I drapt hit a lettle pass de middle o' de roover. I lowed to git out in one mo' step, an' I was a feelin' so good wid de idee o' seein' dat coal black gal what b'long to Mr[.] Rumpless, hit seem like I could tase her lips stannin' right dar in de roover.

"My foremos' foot hit was a stannin' right whar de water run mighty swif', an' wilst I was studyin' bout dem saf' red lips I reckon de water was tolerble busy washin' way my mud laig. Anyhow hit warnt more'n a minute fo' dey was a give'n way somewhar, an' I yeared a nigger drap ca[-]slush! right into de water. I yeared hit des es plain's I year you talkin' dis minute."

"Who was it?"

"Hit was a nigger des bout de size o' M'ringer Jake."

"You?"

"Yas, sah."

"How did you get out?"

"I swum out. Did you reckon I was gwine to turn to a black complected angel an' fly out, Moss Henry?"

"Well, go on with your marvelous tale."

"Dey ain't no mo' to tell, sah, cose I never got to see dat gal what I been talkin' 'bout."

"But you were going to tell me how you got shortened."

"Mass Henry, don't you ondastan' dat?"

"No; how should I?"

"You is a high-larnt man—"

"What if I am?"

"Hit look like you ought to a-knowed hit was dat cole water what swunk me up like you sees me now."

(The *Birmingham Age-Herald,* October 27, 1889)

A Marengo Runaway

Old Jake Recalls an Antebellum Incident

HOW CUDJO RAN AWAY AND HID AND FOOLED ALL THE HOUNDS AND THE WHITE FOLKS

 Jake took his pipe out of his mouth and laid it on the corner of the fence.

It was a small earthen pipe with a short reed stem. Both bowl and stem were black with nicotine, and the stem was partially chewed up also.

We are thus particular in describing the pipe, because some time or other Jake might lose it, and he would never cease to grieve if for any reason the finder should fail to return it to its rightful owner. It looks as though it had been his life-long companion, and he alleges that the stem is genuine "M'ringer" reed, superior in all respects to any that the canebrakes of the world contain. It has a local flavor which is delicious to Jake, reminding him at every whiff of the scenes of the good old days on "ole moster's plantation down dar in M'ringer."

But the pipe upon which we have wasted so many words, and upon which we had nearly grown eloquent, really has nothing to do with this story, except that it needed to be removed from contact with Jake's organs of speech before the story could go on.

"Talkin' 'bout runaway niggers, de wuss one ever I seed was named Cudjo. He use to b'long to my ole moster down dar in M'ringer. He was dat black de chickens went to roos' w'en he come roun'. 'Hits a sho fack, sah. I reckon he must a had some Af'kin blood in him what made him so bad. Anyhow, he come f'om ole Virginny. I yeard him say dat many's de time, an' he could talk Virginny des 'bout es good es I kin talk M'ringer.

"Well, dat nigger wouldn't wuck save nobody's life. Ef de overseer sen' him to de fiel' he'd keep on gwine, an' de man what cotch him 'ud hatter git up fo' soon in de mornin'.

"Dey warnt nair nother nigger on dat plantation but what spise Cudjo. Dey was scared o' him too, mon. He use to be all de time foolin' wid horse-ha'r an' lizzards an' all sich es dat to trick de yuther niggers wid. One mornin' dey was a 'oman name o' Nancy was tooken mighty poly, an' de doctor he couldn't tell what was de matter wid her. But I knowed, caze I done yeard Cudjo say he had a crow to pick wid her.

"I sarched roun, an' I sarched roun tell atter wile I foun' it."

"Found what?"

"Ole man Cudjo's cunjer stuff. Hit was right under dat 'oman's do' step."

"What was it?"

"Hit was a bottle."

"Did it have whisky in it?"

"Naw, sah. Ef hit had a had liquor in hit hit 'd a cyo'd her stiddier trickin her. Hit had some horse ha'r an' a lizzard an' a spider in hit.

"Well, des es soon es I norate what was de matter wid

Nancy de overseer he sont atter Cudjo, an' he 'lowed he was gwine to hit him 'bout a hunderd lashes. But ole Cudjo he was to smart for dat. He knowed in a minute what dat wite man want wid him, an' he lit out, he did. He 'lowed ef dat overseer want to see him bad he would hunt for him.

"Well, sah, dat was longes' runaway Cudjo ever tuck, caze nobody couldn't fine him nowhars on de top side o' de yeth, an' neither down on de groun', nowhars.

"Dat was a toler'ble good crop year down dar in M'ringer. Hit warn't de best crop year I ever seed down dar, but hit was toler'ble good. Dey was wuck plenty for all de han's to do pickin' cotton an' pullin' corn, let 'lone peas an' 'taters an' punkins. Dey was two bans out on de 'count o' ole Cudjo's cussedness; dat was him an' dat 'oman whar he done tricked.

"De overseer he [']lowed he was gwine to have Cudjo ef he hatter burn de woods an' sif ' de ashes an' strain Cottonwood. He sont atter a pack o' houn's an' he gether up all de young wite men in de settlement.

"Yer dey come, bookity, bookity, on dey fine M'ringer horses, an' de dogs dey ripped an' dey rarred like dey was ha'f dead to chaw nigger meat.

"Dey all rid down in de plantation, an' toreckly ole Loud (dat was de name o' de olest houn) he drapped his nose on de groun' an' he menced to wag his tail like he smell sumpin what tase like a runaway nigger track. Twant no time fo' he hilt up his haid an' he gin a yelp, like he was a sayin: 'All you yuther dogs, come on an' foller me ef you kin, caze I done struck ole Cudjo's track, an' I [']low to go a gillipin.'

"Sho nough hit was Cudjo's track. He been out somewhars dat night, an' he never put no conjure on his feet, caze he never spicion nothin bout 'em a running him wid dogs.

"Ole Loud he lit out, he did, an' dem yuther dogs dey tuck right atter him.

"De gemmen whar was on de horses, dey tuck atter de dogs, an' nobody ever is seed sich aner race. Ever'one was 'term'd he warn't gwine be lef' behine.

"Hit was a big cornfiel' whar dey fus' start de track. Hit run right down de middle o' one dem corn rows. De corn hit was stannin' dar yit, caze nobody ain't had no time to pull hit.

"Well, sah, fo' dem men got crost dat fiel' dey was fo' of 'em killed."

"How? Did their horses throw them?"

"Naw, sah, de horses never thowed nair' one o' 'em. Hit was a pity some o' dem nice gemmen never got thowed, fo' dey went ten steps, caze ef dey had a been thowed, maybe hit wouldn't a killed 'em. Dey might a got off wid des a arm or a laig broke, stiddier gittin' dey brains knock out an' scattered all 'long de corn rows."

"What knocked their brains out?"

"De yeas o' corn what hit gin em es dey wus ridin' so fas'. I done tole you hit was a tolerble good crap year dat year down dar in M'ringer, an' hit stan' to reason nobody couldn't ride a horse out'n a walk thoo one o' ole master's corn fiel's."

"Did the overseer get killed?"

"Naw, sah."

"How did he dodge the corn?"

"He never dodged hit, sah, but he was des natchelly a hard-haid man. Ever year he hit gin he busted hit all to flinders, an' de corn grains what he scattered dey come up thick es oats."

"Did they catch Cudjo?"

"Naw, sah, dey never, shoo! Ole Cudj he had too much sense to git cotch. He was des a settin' back in his arm cheer an' a laffin w'en he yeared dem dogs a barkin', caze he knowed dogs couldn't clam."

"Where was he?"

"Dat's des de same question dat overseer an' all dem gemmen was a axin.

"Dey ride on, dey did—"

"What! and left those dead men on the ground?"

"De niggers picked dem up, all but dey brains what was so bad scattered on de groun'. De punkins whar growed on dat groun' de year atter dat dey all had sumpin like a nose an' a mouf, an' dey was full o' brains stiddier punkin meat.

"Dem men rid on, dey did, tell atter 'w'ile dey got in ole moster's sho 'nough punkin patch, an' dar dey all got los', caze dem punkins was so thick on de groun' an' so big you couldn't see nowhars. Dey los' de dogs torectly. Dey could year em abarkin' but dey couldn't tell whar dey wus at no way dey could fix it. Dey soun' des like dey was barkin' way down in de groun', but dem men couldn't fine no hole in de groun' nowhars—dey couldn't fine nothin' but des punkins an' punkins[.] Some o' dem punkins was big es de Meth'dis' meetin' house, an' dey warnt nair middlin' size one but what hit was big es de Pistytalian or de Pre[ ]pyte'an meetin' house.

"Dem men, dey gin it up an' rid on home, and atter wile de dogs dey come on, too. De dogs dey was all kivered wid some sort o' yaller stuff. De overseer he lowed dey been wallin somewhars whar dey was one o' dem big punkins got busted."

"Where was Cudjo?"

"He was all right, and I reckon he'd a been dar tell yit, an' he never would a knowed 'bout freedom coming out ef he hadn't a tuck a fool notion to plant a crap o' corn in dat punkin."

"In a pumpkin!"

"Yas, sah, he was in a punkin. He was livin' an' enduin' in

a punkin all de time. He tuck an' cut a hole to git in at right under de vine, an' de dogs dey got in dar too. But shucks! dey couldn't git ter Cudjo, caze he was way up in de foth story o' dat punkin, an' dey wan't no way to git up dar cep'n dey clam a pole.

"Ole man Cudjo he like punkin mighty well, but he got sick o' havin' nothin' but punkin all de time, so wen spring o' de year come, he tuk an' crope out an' got him some corn to plant, so he could have a ashcake wonst in a wile.

"Well, sah, he had a right smart o' corn planted in dar, an' hit growed an' hit growed tell atter wile de stalks busted dat punkin open, an' ole man Cudjo hatter to gin hisse'f up, caze he never had nowhar to hide at an' nothin to live on."

"Did the overseer flog him?"

"Now, sah, I reckon ef dat overseer's livin' yit he dunno but what ole man Cudjo's dead. He never knowed nothin' bout him comin' back.

"W'en ole man Cudjo fus come to de quarter he nodis none o' de niggers knowed who he was, an' dat made him spicion sumpin. He tuck an' got him a piece o' lookin' glass to see hisse'f in, an' lo an' beholes! he been a eatin' punkin an' smellin' punkin an' sleepin' in punkin tell he done turn punkin color. He was done turn into a plum ginger-cake nigger.

"Well, sah, dey was heap o' ginger-cake-complected niggers on ole moster's plantation, an' dey warnt nobody in de worl' what knowed all of 'em.

"Ole man Cudjo he des went 'long wid 'em, an' he pass hisse'f off for a natchel born ginger-cake nigger, an' nobody never is knowed no difference."

(The *Birmingham Age-Herald*, November 17, 1889)

Dick and the Devil

 A hand-organ man appeared in Auburn the other day, and that set Jake talking about music and musicians.

"I don't see no fiddlers dese days, like I use to see down dar in M'ringer previous befo' de war," he began. "In dem days hit look like some niggers' arms des naicherly set to saw de fiddle, an' dey sawed her too, mon. Hit never sound like dese yer han'-organs whar mos' runs folks stracted wen dey starts. Shoo! Nobody never study 'bout givin' no fiddlers a dime to stop playin' an' move on. Stidder dat, dey mo'n apt to gin him a quarter to play some mo'.

"My ole moster he had a nigger name o' Dick whar was a fiddler f 'om Fiddlersville. Gentlemens! dat nigger could jerk a bow f 'om who laid de rail to who las de longes'. Des let him git his laig cross an' 'bout two drinks o' liquor under his shut, an' ef he didn't everlastin'ly make de chunes fly. Nobody couldn't stan' still wilst he was a playin', save dey

life. De worl'lans dey never tried to hold dey feet still. Dey des
let in to dancin', and dey mos' in ginnerly dance tell dey
heels fly up. Es for de chu'ch folks, dey couldn't stan' still no
mo'n nobody else, an' dey knowed it. Dey dance, too, but
dey never cross dey laigs ef dey could he'p it, an' ef de
preacher got atter 'em 'bout it, dey always 'low dey des been
a playin' twistification, dat was all. But a many an' a many o'
one got turn out o' de chu'ch on de count o' Dick. Yas, sah,
hit's a sho' fack. Ef you was to go down to de bad place right
now an' make inquiment 'bout M'ringer folks, de devil ud
show you des 'bout es likely a passel o' folks, black an' w'ite,
es ever you sot yo' eyes on. Ef you ax 'em how come 'em dar,
dey'll tell you dey yeared Dick a playin', and dey des bleege
ter dance, an' de fus thing dey knowed dey done cross dey
laigs.

"Dick he's dar, too. I knows he's dar des es well es ef I
done been dar an' seed him. Dat's how come I says some o'
dese yer folks what come thoo tells lies w'en dey gin dey
spe'unce in de meetin' house. Ever one of 'em says dey been
to hell an dey been to heben, an' dey seen all de folks in bofe
places. W'en dey come out'n de meetin' house I mos' in
ginnerly axes 'em is dey sho been to hell. Dey low hit's a sho
fack. Den I says, says, I:

"'Did you see de devil?' says I.

"Dey says: 'Yes, cose I seed him,' an' dey ups an' tells all
'bout which kine o' lookin' man de devil is.

"De next queshun I ax 'em hit gits 'way wid 'em, caze I
axes 'em ef dey seed Dick, de fiddler, what come f'om
M'ringer.

"Well, sah, I never is seed one yit what could answer dat
queshun. Some ob 'em makes out dey seed Dick, but nair
one can't tell how he look.

"Dick, he warn't no natchel born fiddler. W'en he first

growed up he use to be always tryin' to larn, but look like he couldn't larn save his life. He used to set up all night sawin' sometimes, but he never could strike nair chune. I use to git sorry for dat nigger, caze he was mightly nigh dead to larn, and he couldn't larn no way he could fix it[.] My ole marster, he got sorry for him, too, an' he bought him a bran new fiddle, an' he sont down to de lower plantation atter old man Sandy to come up an' larn Dick how to play.

"Ole man Sandy he staid dar a long time, an' he tried mighty hard to larn Dick, but he micy swell atried to a larn a mile pos'.

"Atter wile he up an' tole ole moster right to his face t'want no use to be chunkin' 'way time on Dick, caze Dick never had sense 'nough to larn nothin'.

"Wid dat ole man Sandy he lef, an' Dick he kep on, an' he kep on a sawin, tell, all of a suddent, Dick turn out de bes' fiddler in M'ringer. Everybody was stonish, caze Dick done larn how to play on de fiddle enduin one Sadday night, an' w'en Sunday mornin' come he could play 'Ole Molly Ha'r' an' 'Nigger on de Wood Pile' an' 'Soapsuds gin de Fence' an' 'Old Sally Gooden' an' 'Rockum bye de Baby' an' all dem yuther chunes same es ole man Sandy. Shucks! Ole man Sandy couldn't hole a can'le to him. He des beat de hine-sights off 'n all dem yuther fiddlers.

"Well, nobody never knowed how hit happen, but I could a tole 'em, caze I was sleep in Dick's cabin dat night[.] Leas'ways I was makin' out like I was sleep, but nobody couldn't a slep whil'st Dick was a makin' sich a ourighteous fuss wid his fiddle.

"Dick, he was a settin' dar a sawin' way by de fireplace, tryin' to strike a reel, but stidder strikin a reel he made sich a screakin' hit was 'nough to scarce all de rats off 'n de place. I yeard de clock up at de big house strike 12, an' I says to myself:

"'Hit's Sunday, an' dar's Dick a fiddlin' yit, but dat's all right, I don't reckon de good Lord 'll charge up nothin' gin a man for doin' sich fiddlin' es dat on Sunday.'

"Des bout dat time I yeard somebody draw de bow cross de fiddle, an' I knowed in a minute twant Dick, caze ole man Sandy hisse'f couldn't drawed a nastier draw den dat.

"I ris up on my elbow in de bed an' I looked.

"Dar sot Dick right befo' de fireplace, an' dey wan't nobody else dar. De fiddle hit was layin' on his lap, an' his mouf was open an' his eyes look like dey was 'about to pop out'n his haid.

"I kep' on a lookin', an' toreckly I seed sump'n pokin' down out'n de chimbley. Hit looked sorter like a big black snake, cep'n hit was forked at de een. I knowed hit was ole Scratch's tail time I laid my eyes on hit, but I dassent to say nothin'. I des laid dar an' watched.

"De tail hit kep' on comin' down, an' Dick he was dat bad scared he never move a foot. Toreckly de tail it curl out an' hit 'mence to saw backuds an' forruds on de fiddle strings, an' man, sah! de way dat tail played 'Sugar in de Gode' hit was 'nough to make a man cuss his mammy.

"Dick he des sot dar an' pat his foot. He couldn't a hope it, save his life.

"Toreckly de chune stop, an' I yeard somebody say:

"'Dick, does you want to knock 'em off like dat?'

"Dick 'lowed yes; dat was the onlies thing in dis worl' whar he sho want.

"'All right,' de devil says, says he, 'but ef I larn you how to scrape de fiddle dat way you'll b'long to me in dis worl' an' de nex' one too.'

"Dick he 'lowed he b'long to ole moster in dis worl', an' he didn't care ef he b'long to de devil in de nex' one, des so he could go thoo dis'n a fiddlin' like dat.

"Well, him an' de devil dey traded right dar.

"I've yeared tell de devil was a nigger, but I never knowed it befo' dat night. W'en he come a slidin down out'n dat chimbly I got a good look at him, an' ever whar de sut done toch him hit made a white mark on him.

"He tole Dick he'd larn him how to fiddle, an' den Dick ud hatter play on Sunday same es Monday, an' he hatter play for folks to dance by, an' he musn't never darken de do' o, de meetin' house.

"Dick he was dat anxious to larn how to fiddle he des promise ever'thing, an' sho' nough de devil he learn't him how to play.

"'Now, I got to fix some way to know you w'en I sees you agin,' de devil says, says he, 'caze d'is so many niggers yer on yo' ole moster's plantation I can't tell one f 'om de yuther, 'cep'n I got a mark on 'em. Bimeby, ef you don't do like I tell you, I'm gwine to come after you,' says he.

"Wid dat he tuck an' put his han' in Dick's mouf. I never knowed what he done dat for tell next mornin', an' I seed Dick grin es he was playin' de fiddle, an' lo an' behold! he done turn one o' Dick's teeth black es de back o' de chimbly.

"Well, Dick he had a big time a fiddlin' for all de white folks, an' de niggers tell way yander atter freedom come out. Ever' time he stop you could year de money whar he got for playin' des a jinglin' in his pocket. But atter wile Dick's daddy dide, an' he was bleeged to go in de meetin' house to year his daddy's fun'al preach. Man, sah! Dick was scart atter day. He knowed de devil was comin' atter him shotly, caze he done been in de chu'ch. He was des bleege to fix up some way so de devil wouldn't know him from de yuther niggers. He th'owed way dat ole fiddle, an' he lowed he never was gwine to hit her again. He rubbed dat ole black tooth ever' minit o' his life, ceptin w'en he war sleep. But de mo' he rubbed de blacker she got. W'en he foun' out dat, he made up his mine what he was gwine to do. He lit out for Moplis, an' w'en he got dar he went to de dentis' an' tole him to pull out dat black tooth, caze hit was achin' him all over.

"Well, sah, de dentis' he got his pullikins an' he sot 'em on dat tooth, but no sooner he done it he banish away, an' de pullikins dey turn into a black man wid a forked tail whar lif' Dick from dat cheer boddaciously by dat tooth an' flewed off wid him thoo de a'r.

"Nobody ain't never seed Dick sence. Ole mostar axed de dentis' about it, but de dentis' he made out like he never knowed nothin' 'bout it. He 'lowed he ain't seed Dick, but one day w'en he went in his office he smell a mighty smell o' sulphur an' brimstone, an' one o' his pa'r o' pullikins was missin'."

(The *Birmingham Age-Herald*, December 1, 1889)

A M'ringer Rat Story

Old Jake's Midnight Adventure in a Corn Field

A MEETING OF RATS TO CONSIDER IMAGINARY GRIEVANCES, WHICH WOUND UP IN A SAD CATASTROPHE

A party of cadets, dressed in gray uniforms with bright brass buttons, happened to pass the spot where Jake was at work.

"Umph-ph!" grunted Jake. "I never is seed sich a pooty passel o' young gentemens. I wouldn't be sprised ef dey aint got some backer or sumpin dey wants to give way."

"Rats!" cried the boys in chorus.

"Y'all talks a heap bout rats," observed Jake. "I years it constant. But y'all don't know nothin' bout rats, caze dey ain't no rats hardly in dis po country."

The boys stopped to listen, and Jake proceeded:

"Mr. Watlin'ton he could a tole y'all sumpin' bout rats, caze he come f'om down dar in M'ringer; but Mr. Watlin'ton he's done graduate and gone down in de piny woods, learnin' boys how to shoot de idee. Dat's what I yeared Mr. Wilk'son say."

"I don't believe there were any rats in Marengo," remarked one of the boys. "You never saw a rat in your life till you came up here."

"Yah! Yah! Yah!" laughed Jake, holding his sides, "ef dat aint de funnies' thing ever I yeard yet. I never would a come to dis town to see a rat. Dey's some things yer what dey call rats, but dey mighty nigh starve to death, an' dey look like dey never is ta'se corn in dey life. Rats aint gwine to stay whar dey can't git nothin to eat, an' I don't blame 'em. Ef dey gits any corn up yer dey hatter break open de crib do' wid a crow-bar, an' den dey got to sweep de flo' fo' dey'll fine air nubbin. Down dar in M'ringer de folks made so much corn dey never had nowhar to put it at. De cribs wouldn't hole it, an' dey des hatter pile hit up in de fiel an' buil' a boa'd shelter over hit. No wonder dey was so many rats down dar. An' dey got fat an' sassy, too, mon, des like a man what had a big office a'while. Dey use to do des like folks does. Dey hilt meetin's an' pass res'lutions an pint committy, an' dey had 'lections an' made speeches an tole lies des same es folks."

"How many rats did you ever see at one time?"

"Well, sah, I couldn't tell you how many dey was, coze I couldn't count 'em. Dey fa'rly kivered de yeth. Hit was one moonlight night in de fall o' de year, des about corn-pullin' time. I was a knockin' 'bout in de fiel', caze I had a idea o' gwine a cotin' dat night. De corn it was in piles all 'bout over de fiel'. Es I was walkin' 'long studyin' 'bout what I was gwine to tell de patterolers ef dey cotch me, all of a sudden I yeard somebody a talkin'. I looked up, I did, an' man, sah! I seed 2,000,000 rats gethered together roun' a big corn pile."

"Who was it talking?"

"Hit was dem rats. Rats kin talk good es anybody w'en dey mine to.

"I [']lowed I was gwine to year what dey had to say, caze

I knowed by de way so many ob 'em was gethered together dey was up to sump'n.

"I drapped down hine a little corn pile, an' I sot dar an' watch an' listen.

"Toreckly a big ole fat rat he tuck an' clam up on top o' de big corn pile, an' he let in an' made a speech. He 'lowed:

"'Gentemens an' feller-citizens: Whose lan' is dis?'

"All dem yuther rats hollered:

"'Hits we-all's!'

"'You's mighty right,' dat big rat says, says he: 'Hit blong to de horny-toed, long-tail grabblers whar work for dey livin' an' eats dey bread in de sweat o' de brow.'

"Wid dat dey all whooped an' yell same es a crowd o' folks at a free bobbycue.

"I tuck an' peeped roun' to see what kine o' rat dat was a talkin', an' man, sah! I ain't a stannin' yer ef he didn't have de cleanes', slickes' hide ever I see a rat tote. Hit shine same es my Sunday coat. Oh, he was dressed up plum drunk.

"Well, w'en dem rats all cheered him dat way hit made him feel dat good he fa'rly lumbered.

"'Whose corn is dis?' he says, says he[.] 'Hit b'longs to y' all, an' you knows it. Is you gwine to let dese yer niggers come down yer an' haul it out'n dis yer fiel'?'

"Dey all hollered, 'No, no!'

"'Dat's right,' he says, says he. 'We all done been 'posed 'pon too much now,' says he. 'Hit's time we was up an' doin'. Let ever man stan' to de rack, fodder or no fodder. Stan' up for yo' rights like rats,' says he. 'Who's afeard? Ef anybody's scared, let 'em git in dey holes an' pull de holes in atter 'em. I ain't afeared o' no nigger.'

"'How 'bout Jake?' one de yuther rats says, says he. 'He look like a dangious man, an' I nodis you always run in yo' hole w'en he come.'

"'You talkin' bout de head leader o' de niggers on dis

plantation?' says he. 'He's de maines' one I wants to git my claws on. Ef y'all des leck me gin'l I'll soon git yo' rights for you. I'll stan' up yer on dis yer corn pile whar I kin see all over de fiel, an' wen' I see Jake or air nother nigger comin' I'll give y'all de order, an' you'll be stonish how quick you kin eat him up. All y'all wants is a leader, an' I'm de boy for de money.'

"Wid dat he tuck an' sot down, an' a bobtail rat, wid a rusty hide, clum up on de corn pile.

"'Feller cit'zens,' he says, says he, 'I've yeard tell hit's better to let well 'nough 'lone. Hit 'pear like to me dey ain't none o' our rights trampled on. We git des es much corn to eat as our hides kin hole. 'Tain't no use to pester ourse'f 'bout what we ain't got no use for. An' lemme tell you an'er thing,' says he, 'niggers is dangious to fool wid[.] If you pay any 'tention to dat rattlehaid what been a lettin' off his gas, somebody'll be mo'n ap' to git hurt. Now, ef you'll des but 'leck me de head man, I'll promise you pease an' hom'ny, des like we got now; but, ef you 'leck dat rattlehaid, he'll sho' git you in trouble. De fus' news you knows dey'll be war an' tribulation a-gwine on yer, de country'll be all to' up, an' rats 'll starve to death. Dat dangious man Jake 'll plant his No[.] 11 foot on some o' y'all, an' he'll squelch de life out'n you[.] An' whar'll be Mr. Rattlehaid then? At fus' he'll be up on de corn pile, safe, des like he done tole you, but atter while, w'en he see dat dangious nigger Jake gettin' too cloast to him he'll scoot down in his hole, an' he'll grabble deeper an' d[e]eper, an' he ain't gwine to stop tell he git down to de bottom side o' de yeth whar dep makes dish war an' de folks walks upside down.'

"All de time dat rat was a-talkin' de whole crowd kep up a-groanin' an a-whistlin', an' de minute he tuck his seat dey call for dat yuthern.

"Well, sah, ole rattlehaid, es dey call him, he fa'rly rarred an' pitched, an' ever time he open his mouf, if hit was des but to take a chaw tobacco, all dem yuther rats hollered an' cheered.

"'Whar dat dangious nigger Jake?' he says, says he. 'Des trot him out an' lemme show you how quick I kin make sotched meat out'n him. Des let him show his haid ef he dar'.'

"Well, hit look like hit was bout time I was takin up dat dar'. I crope out, I did, des es easy es I could, an' I went to my cabin an' got my big ole cat whar went by de name o' Tom.

"I tuck Tom under my arm, I did, an' I crope back down dar in de fiel.

"Well, dem rats dey was gwine on wuss'n ever. Dat same rattlehaid he was up on de corn-pile des a braggin' what he was gwine to do to Jake.

"I crope a leetle cloaster an' a leetle cloaster, an' toreckly I ris up, I did, an' I pitched ole Tom right in de middle o' de crowd, an' I hollered, 'Rats!'"

"Then they all scattered, didn't they?"

"Who, de rats? Naw, sah; dey never scattered none cep'n rattlehaid. He scattered so bad I ain't seed him f 'om dat day to dis."

"Did all the other rats run?"

"Naw, sah; dey never run."

"Did they stand there and let the cat eat 'em up?"

"Naw, sah; de cat never eat 'em up."

"How did they get away from him, then?"

"Dey never got 'way f'om him."

"Well, what did they do?"

"Which? de cat?"

"No; the rats."

"Dey eat up dat cat so clean dey never lef' nothin' to make nair fiddle string out'n."

"Rats! Rats!" cried the cadets, hurrying away.

(The *Birmingham Age-Herald,* December 15, 1889)

[Note: College freshmen at Auburn were commonly known as "rats."]

Old Time Christmas

M'ringer Jake Recalls a Famous Celebration

THE DARKIES ALL A DANCIN'
AND OLE MASTER JINES IN—
FIDDLIN' ON A THREE-STRING FIDDLE

With a Glorious Wind Up

"Ole chrismus is a comin', but dat idee don't pester me," said Jake the other day. "Chrismus aint what hit use to be."

"I've been hearing that sort of talk all my life," said an elderly white gentleman. "All the old croakers like you are eternally lauding the past, decrying the present and prophesying evil for the future. It's all stuff."

"Well, I dunno how chrismus use to be yer in Aubu'n, but down dar in M'ringer—"

"Oh, everything must be referred to Marengo. Now I'll sit here on this log and patiently hear you describe an old-time christmas in Marengo, and if it's any jollier or better than we have these days, I'll give you a square of tobacco; but if it's not, I'll give you the big end of my cane. Now go on, but don't tell any of your big lies."

"All right, moster, I'll tell you 'bout one chrismus we had

down dar in M'ringer, an' I'm dat sartin o' gittin' yo' backer I kin tas'e hit now. I ain't gwine to tell you nothin' but de remmunt truth, nuther.

"Well, dat chrismus hit was des like all de yuther chrismus I ever seed down dar in M'ringer; hit las' two whole weeks.

"Dey can't be no good chrismus whar dey ain't no niggers. Niggers an' watermillions an' 'possums an' chrismus dey all goes long o' one aner, an' you'll mo'n ap' to find a mule to two dar. Dey aint nough niggers in Aubu'n.

"Hit was endurin' de war what I'm tellin' you 'bout. De chrismus fo' dat ole moster an' ole miss dey was mighty solemn an' sour, caze dat las' gone summer dey son Tom, whar was in de army, he got kill in a battle, an' dey ain' done grievin' bout him yit. Dey gin de niggers hollerday, but dey didn't low 'em to make no fuss ner have no fun in de yard. But dey was mos' done got over hit de time I'm tellin' you 'bout. Ole moster he been a-talkin' to ole miss all long, an' he tole her dey not ought to grieve atter Moss Tom, caze Moss Tom gin his life for his country, an' dat was right.

"Well, dey was gittin' usened to it, an' ole moster he ups an' lowed de niggers mus' have a jolly time dis chrismus.

"Dey was gwine to be a nigger weddin' on de home place, an' ole moster he lowed hit hatter be a chrismus day, and every nigger he hatter dance at dat weddin' ef he never dance before. So he sont word to all his yuther plantations for de niggers to come, an' dey come, too, mon. Some ob 'em rid in steer wagons and some driv mules, an' bout a thousan' walked. Wen all dem niggers got to the home place de chickens went to roos, caze hit look like night done come.

"Ole moster gethered 'em all together in a field by the house, an' he gin 'em all a drink o' red liquor apiece all 'roun'. Den he set ole Tobe up on top a bar'l wid his three-string fiddle, an' he tole him to strike up a chune an' not to miss nair' lick tell he tole him to stop.

"Den he hollered for all de mens to git pardners.

"Well, sah, dey done it. Some ob 'em 'lowed dey had de rheumatiz, but ole moster tole 'em dancin' 'ud cyo 'em; an' one man had a wooden laig, but ole moster made him go stumpin' 'roun' wid de res'. Ever' wonst in a w'ile ole moster 'ud holler to ole man Tobe to scrape livelier, an' ole man Tobe he'd do it. But some o' dem dev'lish chaps dey put a pack o' fire-crackers under dat bar'l whar ole man Tobe was a settin' on, an' toreckly, bang! bang! pop! pop! dey went right under ole man Tobe.

"Cose old man Tobe was scared, but he dassent to stop fiddlin'. Ever time a fire-cracker pop he jump. But he kep on a fiddlin' des de same. Atter wile a great big un bust, an ole man Tobe he gin sich a jump de bar'l haid fell in, and down he went. But he never stop fiddlin'. He dassent to. Dey want nothin' in sight 'cep'n de wool on de top o' his haid an his feet an' his arms. But he hilt de fiddle up an' kep a scrapin'. De fire-crackers dey kep a poppin', and de niggers dey was dat full o' laf dey couldn't keep time wid de fiddle.

"Twix de fiddlin' an de jumpin' f'om de fire-crackers, ole man Tobe turn de bar'l over toreckly, but he never stop fiddlin' for dat. He des laid dar on de groun' an' kep de fiddle agwine.

"Dem devlish chaps dey seed ole moster was a laffin, an' dey knowed he warn't gwine to git mad 'bout nothin'. Dey let in to rollin' dat bar'l on de groun'. Yer hit went rollin' over an' over f'om one een o' de reel to de yuther. But dat never pestered ole man Tobe. He des kep' on a fiddlin' an' he never miss nair lick.

"Man, sah! I've yeard a heap o' fiddlin' in my days; I've yeard Dick, whar de devil larn how to play, but I never has yeard no sich fiddlin' es dat Tobe done wilst dat ar bar'l was a rollin' over an' over. Dis yer common kine o' fiddlin' hit git in yo' years, an' sometimes hit make you feel right good, but dat ar fiddlin' whar Tobe done rollin' over in dat bar'l, hit never stop wid gittin' in yo' years; hit git in yo' laigs yit.

"De niggers was a laffin wen dat bar'l gin to roll, but dey hatter stop toreckly. Dey never felt like laffin. Dey warnt no foolishness bout dat fiddlin. Dey hatter dance, an' dey couldn't stop to laf. Ole Aint Peggy, whar was all double up wid de rheumatiz, she got out on de groun. She was a mighty ['] ligious ole woman, caze she never had de strenk to do devilment. She lowed she blieve de devil done got in her laigs, caze she couldn keep em still. An she knocked it off, mon, same ez a young gal. She farly made de dirt fly. She cut de pigeon wing, an she hoed taters tell she drapt in her tracks, an den she never stop a dancin. Her heels flew up in de ar, an ez she was a layin dar on her back, kickin up in de illements, hit look like she was tryin to dance on de sky.

"But de funnies' thing what happen, dat music got in ole moster's laigs bimeby. Ole moster he weighed mighty nigh fo' hunderd weight, but dat never made no diffunce; he was bleeged to dance. He cotch holt o' ole miss' arm an' he tole her to come on an' les trot a reel.

"Ole miss was de onliest one whar could keep her feet still. She was a studyin' 'bout dat boy o' hern whar got kill in de war. She tried to hole back, but ole moster he pull her on.

"'Ole man,' she hollered, says she, 'dis is all foolishness. Ef I was to dance I'd feel des like I was treadin' on my po' boy's grave.'

"But ole moster he pulled her on todes de clar groun' whar de niggers was a dancin', an' he 'low:

"'Don't let yo' feelins git way wid you, ole 'oman. Les dance while we in de notion,' says he, 'caze hit may be de las' time on de face o' de yeth. I feel cuis,' says he, 'I feels des like sump'n good gwine to happen. Hit may be bofe on us gwine to die tonight, but dat'll be all right, caze den we wont be yer to grieve 'bout our boy no mo'. So come on,' says he, an' he hollered to de niggers to clear de track, caze de bulgine was a comin'.

"De niggers dey got out'n de way an' made room for ole moster an' ole miss, but dey never stop dancin', caze dey couldn't.

"Ef ole moster hed a been a 2-year-ole colt he couldn't a cut up no friskier 'n he did. An' he cyad ole miss wid him, too, mon.

"Oh, hit was a putty sight, to see dem whi' folks gwine up an' down and sashayin' roun'. Ever' wonst in a wile ole moster'd stop an' knock off a double shuffle fo' ole miss, an' he weigh mighty nigh fo' hunderd poun'. Ole miss she'd look at him an' 'low: 'Ole man, I never knowed you had dat much nonsense in yo' bones.'

"'I don't for common,' ole moster says, says he, 'but I des feel like sump'n good's gwine to happen, an' hit's done got all in my bones.'

"Cose ole moster got out o' bref atter wile, an' he sot down flop! on de groun'. He was dat happy he couldn't speak. He des wave his han' to dem chaps to stop rollin' music out'n dat bar'l.

"Des soon's dey stopped ole moster got his bref nough to tell ole man Tobe he could res' a wile; but, man sah! ole man Tobe was cramped up in dat bar'l sich a way dat wen he breathe hit worked his arms an' played de fiddle. An' mo'n dat, he couldn't git out'n dat bar'l tell dey brung a axe an' chop hit open.

"D[e]s 'bout den de folks made room for de weddin' couple to come forruds, an' ole uncle Enoch, de bow-

laigged preacher, he tuck his stan' befo' em wid a shiny pair
specs on his nose an' a book in his han', des like he could
read, an' he never knowed B f 'om bull foot.

"He says, says he[:]

"'Ef anybody yer got any impedments to dis yer couple
bein' jine together in de holy boun's o' mattemony, let 'em
now speak it out or forever hole dey peaces es long es life
lastes.'

"No sooner he said dat, when up run little Billy, whar out
stutter air' nother nigger boy in M'ringer, an' he tuck his
stand right 'twix de parson and de couple, an' try to say
sumpin', but all he could git out was 'O—O—O—.'

"Everybody was dat stonish' dey couldn' say nair' word.
Dey was wondin' what jections dat boy had to dem two
niggers bein' jined. Nobody never knowed what business he
had a pokin' his mouf in no how, an' ole man Enoch he was
dat mad he could a bit his haid off.

"Aint Mandy she was Billy's mammy, an' w'ilst he was a
stannin', stuttin' 'O—O—O,' she run in an' grabbed him up
an' tuck him off 'hine de house to work on him wid a hickry
for not havin' no better manners.

"Well, de fust time de hickry hit his bar hide de words
come out'n his mouf:

"'Ole Towser an' all dem yuther dogs eatin' up de
bobbycue meat.'

"Hit turn out true, too, caze all de folks lef' de meat to
jine in de dance. But dey was 'nough lef' atter de dogs got
done, caze ole moster had two hunderd carcases killed for
dat bobbycue.

"Well, sah, de weddin' hit was over, an' de big dinner hit
was over, an' hit was a gittin night time o' day. De dark hit
was a comin' on, an' you couldn't see a man plain mo'n ten
steps. I yeard somebody hollin lo' at de gate, an' I went out

dar to see who hit was, caze I was de house boy dem days.

"A man was stannin' dar by de gate, an' he tole me to ax my mistis' ef she couldn't give a po fedric soldier a little sumpin t'eat. He [']lowed she mus' sen' hit out dar to him, caze he was to dirty to come in whi' folks' house, and he had de each, too.

"Ole miss [']lowed cose she'd give a soldier de las' moufful she had, but ole moster he want him to come in the house and set at de table. Ole miss lowed he was too dirty for dat, but ole moster he ups an' says:

"'I don't care how dirty he is; I reckon my boy used to git dirty too. Ef he's a Fredick soldier, he kin eat at my table ef we hatter hoe de dirt of [f]'n him.'

"'But, ole man, he might have some yease,' ole miss says, says she. 'Go out dar, Jake,['] says she, 'an ax him is he been anywhars 'bout de small pox.'

"I axed de soldier dat, an' he lowed he been pooty cloast 'bout whar folks had de small pox, an' he wouldn't say for sartain the wher he got it or no.

"I tole 'em dat, an' ole miss she fairly shudder; but ole moster he warnt sot back a bit. He says, says he.

"'Ef he had de small pox all busted out on him big es my two fistes, he could eat at my table,' says he:

"Den he put his arm roun' ole miss' shoulder, an' he says:

"['] Ole lady, member yo' po' boy what's dead an gone. Sposin he was dirty an' hungry an' had de small pox, would you a thanked anybody for fusin to let him eat wid whi' folks at de table?[']

"Dat was too much for ole miss, an' she gin right in an' tole me to fetch dat po' soldier in de house. De tears was des streamin' down her face.

"I fetched de soldier in an' I watched him mighty close, caze dey was sumpin' mighty cuis 'bout him. Soon's ever he got in de light I seed he warnt what I call a dirty man, an' I'm a tolerble good jedge o' dirt. He was des 'bout es likely a young soldier es ever I seed, only he need shavin' tolerble bad.

"'We are to had a soldier boy,' ole moster says, says he, ['Jan' he was des bout de age o' you, but he never had no whiskers yit. He got killed in a battle in ole Virginny a year ago dis las gone summer,' says he.

"'He never got killed,' dat soldier says, says he.

"'What dat you says?' ole moster an' ole miss bofe hollered.

"'I [']lowed he never got killed,' dat soldier says, des es quiet. 'He got bad wounded an' de yankees tuck him a prisner an' kep him tell de yuther day,' says he. 'I wouldn't be sprise ef he aint pooty cloast bout yer right now, caze I know he aint fur off.'

"Wid dat ole moster an' ole miss dey bofe jump up an' run to dat soldier an' look in his face cloast, an' toreckly ole miss hollered:

"'Oh Tommie! Tommie! my darlin' boy, is you done come back to yo' po' ole mudder?'"

Here the narrator paused. There was nothing more to tell, and the pathetic and the ludicrous were strongly blended as with one hand the elderly gentleman held out a piece of tobacco, and with the other brushed a tear from his cheek. He, too, had had a soldier boy, but his boy never returned. He was killed in a cavalry engagement, and though his horse and accoutrements were recovered, the spot where the young soldier found sepulture is unknown to this day.

"Hame cam the saddle all bluidy to see,
Hame cam the steed, but hame never cam he."

(The *Birmingham Age-Herald,* December 22, 1889)

A Pig Tale

 Jake is in fine spirits. He considers his reputation as a truthful man firmly established in Auburn. A great many persons, in times gone by, have questioned his veracity, have accused him of exaggeration, prevarication and downright mendacity because, forsooth, he has told some rather extravagant stories about Marengo; but now he can furnish occular demonstration of the truth of some of his most wonderful statements.

"Moss Wilbur, is you seed dat ar pig tail over yonder at de speerment station?"

"No, what about it?"

"Hit's a M'ringer pig tail.

"Las' fall wen Moss Wilson Youman was up yer to see his maw an' imparticlar dat young lady whar he so bad mashed on, he up an tole bout how dey hatter cut off de pig tails down dar in M'ringer caze de mud gether on 'em tell dey gits dat heavy de pig can't tote em. His maw she up and [']low:

"'Shucks! dat's too big a tale for me to swaller,' says she. 'You gittin des like Jake.'

"Moss Wilson he never spute long o' his maw. He larn better'n dat wen he was a spankin' sized chap. But wen he went back down dar to Uniontown he cut off a pig's tail an' wropped hit up in a piece o' paper an' sent hit to his maw, an' she got it now. Hit look sorter like a tater wen yo[u] fus git holt o' hit, but atter wile hit look like a cullud lady's bangs wropped up in mud. But dem bangs dey never come off 'n no [']oman; dey come off 'n de himos een of a pig.

"Ever middlin' size shoat you sees down dar in M'ringer he's bob-tail, caze folks cuts off dey tails wen dey little bits o' pigs to keep de mud fom weighten em down. Up yer, ef folks was to cut off de pigs tails an thow em way, bout haf de folks in dis country ud hatter go widout meat.

"I never is knowed but one man down dar in M'ringer what never cut off his pig tails. Dat was Mr. Rumpless down dar on Cottonwood. He des done it for contrary, caze he never would have nothin' like nobody else.

"Wen he fus' come down dar he had a ole sow by de name o' Trottin Bet. She had a back same es a cross-cut saw, and she never is pigged but one pig at a time in all her born life; but, man sah! des es soon's she got a taste o' dat M'ringer corn she drapped twenty pigs in one litter. An' dey was likely pigs, too, mon.

"One de neighbors in de settlement come long an' he see sich a nice chance o' pigs he let in to miratin 'bout 'em, an' fo' he lef' dar he tole Mr. Rumpless he better chop all dey tails off short wilst dey was little. But Mr. Rumpless he up an' lowed he warnt gwine to do no sich a dog-on thing.

"'You never will raise 'em den,' dat man says, says he, 'caze dey won't have de strenk to tote de mud what'll gether on dey tails.'

"'I'll show you,' Mr. Rumpless says, says he.

"Sho' 'nough, he 'fuse to bob off air tail. Hit des show what a contrady man'll do. Hit gin him heap o' trouble, but he raised all dem pigs wid dey tails on 'em, an' hit's a cu'is sarkumstance what I'm goin' to tell you, but hit's a sho' fack; dem pigs' tails dey was de mainest thing what made Mr. Rumpless rich.

"Well, sah, hit warnt but a mighty few days 'fore dem pigs' tails 'gin to gether mud, an' ever'body whar come 'long hatter stop an' ax Mr. Rumpless why in de name o' sense he didn't chop dem pigs' tails off 'n 'em. Dey tole him dat mud 'ud sho' ruin 'em.

"But de mo' dey devil Mr. Rumpless, de stubborner he git. He 'lowed M'ringer was de outdaciouses place ever he got in for folks to consarn deyse'f 'bout yuther folks' business. He 'lowed dem was his pigs, an' ef he mine to let 'em turn into mud all over, nobody never had no right to say nair word. He got dat stubborn he would a' let dem pigs' tails stay on 'em ef he had a knowed hit 'ud a killed ever last huff of 'em.

"All dem pigs was gilts cepin' to one. Hit was a borrer.

"Dat borrer was a tolerble good mud toter, but he couldn't tote de whole worl' an' de fus news Mr. Rumpless knowed his borrer was a callin' him in de fiel'.

"De borrer [']lowed, 'Quee! quee! quee-a!'

"Mr. Rumpless went down dar, he did, an' he foun' dat borrer done jine to de yeth by his tail. Yas, sah, he couldn't move a step cepin' he pull his tail off, an' he warnt man nough to do dat.

"Ef dat had a been air nother man but Mr. Rumpless, he'd a everlastinly whacked off dat borrer's tail; but Mr. Rumpless was a plum mule w'en he set his head. He done said he warnt gwine to bob nair pig to please nobody, an' he'd a died fust.

"He tried to pull dat pig aloose, but he micy swell try to

pull up a hickry saplin' by de roots. He may could a broke de tail off, but den folks would a said he was done gone back on his word.

"He lef' dat borrer a settin' right dar, an' he sot dar plum tell de nex' winter, an' den a cole spell come on, an' dat borrer died wid de so' thoat. Mr. Rumpless toted his victuals an' his water to him reg'lar, an' dat borrer made one o' de bigges' hogs ever was raised down dar in M'ringer. Wen Mr. Rumpless killed him he weighed seben hunderd an' ninety-seben poun', 'scusin' his tail.

"All dem yuther pigs dey was gilts. One night dey all laid down in a ring on de groun', an' wile dey was sleep dey come a light rain, an' hit saften de mud on dey tails. Dey tails was all a layin' in a pile together, an' wen dey waked up in de mornin', lo an' behole! all dey tails was fas' stuck together.

"Dey pull dis way, an' dey pull dat way, but dey couldn't git aloose f'om one an'er. Dey was jine together for better, for wusser, es de preachen says.

"Mr. Rumpless he des let 'em stay dat way, caze he was 'termed not to cut off nair hair off 'n nair pig tail. Dey got 'long all right, dough. Wen one ob 'em tuck up a notion to go anywhars, he des squeal out:

"'Les all th'ow in an' make up a crowd an' go down yonder to the sloo.'

"Den dey'd all 'gree, an' way dey'd go. Dat way, de one whar squeal fust ud be mo'n ap' to take de crowd his way.

"Well, sah, hit warnt so mighty long fo de bigges' gilt she pigged. She did dat. She drapped nineteen likely pigs, an' dey was all gilts cep'n to one, an' he was a borrer. All de gilts' tails dey was jine together, but hit warnt mud what jine 'em together; dey was des naickerly pigged dat way. De borrer he was de onlies one what was aloose an' could go whar he warnt to by hissef.

"Man, sah, w'en dat nex' size gilt seed what her sister done

done, she up an' pigged twenty pigs, an dey was all gilts cep'n to one; he was borrer. All de gilts dey was jine together des like de fus' litter, but de borrer he was aloose.

"Aner gilt she let in an' drapped twenty-one pigs, an' all o' dem was gilts but one. De nex' un she pigged twenty-two, an' dey was all gilts but one, an' hit went on dat way plum to de een, an' ever litter all de gilt's tails was jine together an' de borrers was loose.

"At de een o' de year Mr. Rumpless had 'nough borrers to meat him, scusin de sows.

"De folks come from all over de lan' to see dem cu'is breed o' hogs, an' dey devil Mr. Rumpless so he fenced 'em up in a big fiel' an' he wouldn't let nobody see 'em for less'n a quarter.

"Well, sir, he made fo' thousan' dollars dat away. Den everbody want to git in de stock o' dem ring hogs, as dey call 'em, an' dey was plum willin' to pay a thousan' dollars for one ring ob 'em.

"W'en I lef' M'ringer hit was twix' two suns, an' I never stopped to ax no foolish queshuns, but I reckon dey was a million o' dem ring hogs in M'ringer den. I reckon de stock's dar yit, an' I wouldn't be sprise ef Moss Wilson's got some ob 'em dar on de speerment station, caze Moss Wilson 's he's a sooner an' he's mo'n up to git de best o' what's gwine."

(The [Birmingham] *Weekly Age-Herald,* January 22, 1890)

An Ass in a Lion's Skin

 Not long since, as Jake was doing som[e] work in a garden, he espied a colored ma[n] of distinguished appearance walking in th[e] direction of the experiment station. Now Jake is quite accustomed to seeing farmer[s] from various parts of the state who come to Auburn to inform themselves on some ma[t]ter pertaining to their vocation, but suc[h] farmers are always Anglo Saxons, neve[r] negroes. Jake was therefore surprised, an[d] he at once resolved to lay down his hoe an[d] ascertain what business was taking to th[e] station a person too well dressed to pass f[or] a laborer seeking work, yet of a race whic[h] has never shown any desire for a knowledge of scientific agriculture.

The stranger was short of stature, middle-aged and black. He was dressed in a new business suit, a standing collar and a stove-pipe hat. He did not seem to be in a very great hurry, but walked like a gentleman of leisure, duly impressed with his own importance.

"Mornin'!" said Jake, raising his tattered hat in respectful salutation.

"Mornin'!" returned the stranger, halting.

"Pear like you gwine to de speerment station," said Jake.

"Way say," said the stranger, interrogatively.

"Dis lots o' folks goes out dar to larn how to make fine truck grow on po' lan," continued Jake. "You'll be mo'n ap to see sights you never is seed befo out dar at dat speerment station, vidin you gwine dar."

"Way him?" inquired the stranger.

"I reckon you knows de way, or you'd a axed me[.] You des keep on out dis yer straight-farrud street tell you git to de fus big gate, an' you turn in d[a]r ef you want to see all dem fine grape vines an' dat ar big plum orchud an' dat ar strawberry patch an' sich like."

"Ki!" exclaimed the stranger.

"What mought be yo entitlements?" inquired Jake.

"I lib Sawannah," said the stranger.

"You cum a fur ways, I speck," ventured Jake, unwilling to expose his ignorance of geography. "How did you git yer?"

"I been ride on de cyaz," said the stranger.

"I dunno what sort o' critter dat is," said Jake, "but I lay hit's perter 'n a mule. A mule he'll stop at ever house, an' he always wants to take de wrong road, an' dat way hit take anybody a long time to ride him anywhars[.]

"You see dat fus house up yonder mongst dem trees?"

"I shum," said the stranger.

"Ef you go in de gate des dis side o' dat house, you'll be mo'n ap to see Joe Eady in dar knockin bout de lot."

"Him buckra?" inquired the stranger.

"Joe, he's my brer-in-law," said Jake, "leasways he use to be fo his wife quit him. Well, Joe, he'll show you round de place. He'll take you down dar to de dairy—hit's dat little house a settin down dar at de foot o' de hill. Wen you go in dat house yo eyes'll open plum stonish."

"Hi!" exclaimed the stranger.

"You'll see mo milk an butter 'n you ever seed befo in all yo born days."

"Shum nuttin; git um him!" said the stranger in contemptuous tones.

"You'll see sumpn in dar what look like a big sotched grinder," continued Jake.

"Ki! for true," exclaimed the stranger.

"Dey calls hit de sep'rater," said Jake, "an' dey grines de milk in hit. Dey des po's de milk in hit an' turns de crank, same es you turns a grine rock, and de skim' milk hit spees out'n a little hole same es you see hit spee out'n a cow's titty, an' de rummunt cream hit run out'n aner' hole. You see hit grines de milk same ez you grines sotched meat, an' dat makes de cream come aloose f'om de skim' milk."

"Humph!" grunted the stranger.

By this time Jake was beginning to grow impatient. He had hoped to draw the stranger into conversation and thus learn the obj[e]ct of his visit to Auburn, but the man did not seem disposed to talk, and the little he said was wholly unintelligible to Jake.

"I reckon I better be knockin' long," said he, shouldering his hoe.

"You gwan day fer wuck for buckra man?" enquired the stranger.

"I don't work at the speerment station," said Jake. "Joe Eady, he stays out dar[.]"

"Enty woona day hab no obersher?" asked the stranger.

"You go on out dar, an' Joe he'll show you de brag oat patch an' de garden sass an' de cows, an' inperticklar dem fine fatnin' hogs dar cloast to de barn."

"Who ba'n?" inquired the stranger.

"D'e's five or six hogs dar, an' ever one he's in a pen by hisse'f. De fuss one what you come to—"

"Enty you do yerry me," interrupted the stranger.

"De fuss one," resumed Jake, irritated by the rudeness of the interruption, "dey'se feedin' him on buttermilk, an' dey weighs him ever mornin' to see how much he fatten dat night. De nex' one don't eat nuthin' but corn—"

"Ki!" exclaimed the stranger.

"An' de middle un 'll sho' 'stonish you, caze w'en you lays yo' eyes on him you'll sho' say he's a nigger. But he ain't, dough. He's des a common hog. He's de commonest kine o' hog[.] But he's shape des like a nigger. He's down on his all-fo's, and his number 'leben feet's a stickin' out behine him.

"He warn't raise in Auburn. Naw, sah; he come a fur ways, an' w'en he come I reckon he rid one o' dem ar critters what you 'lowed you come on.

"Moss Jim Clayton he was de fus one seed him. Moss Jim know de difference twix a hog an' a nigger. Nobody can't fool him. A hog might could talk, but he can't make hisse'f smell like a nigger.

"Moss Jim knowed dat was a hog in less'n no time, but all de yuther folks dey stuck to it hit was a nigger.

"Well, hit was tryin' to pass hitsef off for a nigger, an' ef hit des only would a talked, I wouldn't be sprise ef hit hadn't a been gwine roun wid cullud folks dis minute.

"W'en M[o]ss Jim Clayton fust seed hit, hit was stanin' up straight on hits hine laigs an' walkin' 'bout like hit own de town[.] Hit had on britches an' a coat des zactly like dem what you got on, an' look like hits stannin collar was gwine to saw hits years off. Hit had on a churn hat, too, man. Hit did for a fack, an' ef you don't believe me, you des but look in hits pen an' see ef dat churn hat ain't de onliest trough hits got to eat out'n.

"W'en Moss Jim seed hit he walked up cloast to hit, an' he ax hit ef hit didn't want to hire, case he want to hire a likely nigger to help Joe Eady.

"Well sah, Moss Jim stonish dat hog. Hit open hits mouf, but hit couldn't do nothin' but des grunt, same as any yuther hog. Hit [']low 'hi,' an' hit [']low 'ki,' an' hit [']low 'yi,' but hit couldn't say nair word what anybody could understan'. No wonder! Hit was des a common hog, an a stray one at dat. Moss Jim have picked up many [a] un des like hit.

"Well, sah, w'en Moss Jim see how de [la]n' lay he des flopped a rope roun dat hog's [ne]ck an' drug him out dar an' put him in [d]at pen, an' sot his chum hat befo him, an' [p]o'ed some slops in hit for him to eat, an' [h]e's been dar ever sence. If you go dar an [s]p[e]ak to him he'll des say 'hi' er 'ki.'

"Ef I couldn't talk nothin' but outlandish [ta]lk you wouldn't ketch me a pokin' roun' Auburn. No, sah! I'd hit de grit, an' I'd [hi]t her hard. Folks is too smart 'roun yer. You can't fool nobody by puttin' on a chun [ha]t an walkin' on yo' hine laigs—not cep'n [yo]u kin talk. I speck Moss Jim Clayton's [o]ut hog huntin' dis mornin', an' I wouldn't [b]e sprise ef he didn't come long dis way [m]os' any minute, an' imp[a]rticlar ef he [ye]ared anything what soun' like a hog a gruntin'. So long, mister."

(The [Birmingham] *Weekly Age-Herald*, January 29, 1890)

Birmingham Dirt

A Widespread Idea
Illustrated by Old Jake

HOW "MOSS RAIF" GOT RICH—
WHAT A "[M]RINGER" PIG'S TAIL
CAN DO WHEN IT TRIES

 "Moss Wilbur, is you yeard de news f'om Burnin'ham[?]" inquired Jake.

"No. What is it?"

"Moss Raif's done got plum rich up dar."

"I'm glad to hear that. How did he make his fortune?"

"On Burnin'ham dirt."

"That is not strange. A great many fortunes have been made by speculating in Birmingham real estate. Raif went up there to make money and he's a sharp fellow. I'm not surprised to hear that he has been successful[.]"

"You'se mighty right, boss[.] Moss Raif is des 'bout es sharp es dey ever makes 'em. He run agin some r[i]ght peart folks up dar, an' dey 'lowed dey'd clean him up fo' dey got done wid him, but man sah! he come out on top at las'. He's a sooner, Moss Raif is[.] Dem folks sorter got way wid him a little at fust, but nemmine dat, Moss Raif's all right now.

"Wen he fust got dar to Burnin'ham he had a right smart o' money, caze I never is seed de time w'en he didn't have de spons[.] He 'lowed he'd buy 'bout fo' hundred acres o' lan' right in de middle o' de town an' den set down an' res' tell dat lan' ud fetch 'bout five times es much es he gin for hit. Lots o' folks is done dat way in Burnin'ham."

"Not a doubt of it. Some people living in Auburn now have made a good deal of money that way."

"Yas, sah, dey is dat. But nair one's ever made es much es Moss Raif, caze none ob 'em ever study out es good a plan es him.

"W'en he went to make inqui'ment 'bout de price o' lan' up dar, he sot his eyes on some nice level lots right dar in de middle o' de city, an' he layed off to buy ever' one o' 'em ef de price was right. But w'en he ax de price o' dat lan' his eyes turn plum wrong-sided out, he was dat bad 'stonish[.] Dem folks tole him he'd hatter open his pocket-book ef he want any o' dat dirt—he'd hatter pull out dem ole gole pieces whar done got rusty caze dey ain't see'd de light so long— an' he'd hatter come down wid all de scads he got, caze dat lan' was wuf two hund'ed thousan' dollars a acre.

"W'en Moss Raif yeard dat word hit seem like he done change his mine, an' he don't want no lan', nohow.

"He went home an' he went to bed, sah, caze Moss Raif was sick, sah.

"But he overed dat in 'bout a week, an' he lit out to hunt lan' agin.

"Dis time he didn't want no dirt right in de middle o' de city. He want to go out a piece whar he could git fresh air ef anybody said anything to make a fellow sick.

"He went out 'bout two mile, an' den he stop an' 'mence to look 'roun.

"Hit was sorter in de aidge o' de woods, an' de frogs was

singin' tolerble lively, like dey might be a branch or a pon' somers 'bout dar.

"Moss Raif knowed lan' was gwine to be cheap 'nough dar. He was scared hit 'ud be mos' too cheap, and he'd hatter wait too long for hit to git high.

"He was des 'bout to start back an' go in 'bout a mile furder, but a man stopped him an' ax him don't he want to buy some mighty n[i]ce lan'.

"Moss Raif tole him yas, dat was de business he was on, ef de price warnt too high.

"Wid dat de man tuck him an' showed him roun'. He walked him better'n a mile fo' dey ever said air word 'bout de price.

"Moss Raif he was a gittin' sorter tired, an' he stopped an' axed dat man spotly what was de price of fifty acres o' dat lan'.

"Dat man he puckered his mouf same es he been eatin' a green 'simmon, an' he des whistle.

"'Who de name o' sense want to buy dat much?' he says, says he.

"Moss Raif he straighten hisse'f up an' he 'low:

"'Me.'

"Dat man looked at him up one side an' down de yuther, an' he sorter shade his eyes es he look at him, an' he sorter steady hisse'f 'gin a tree to keep f'om fallin' down.

"After wile he got breath so he could speak, an' he up an' says:

"'I ain't got nair slate big 'nough to make de figgers on,' says he, 'an' I hate to spile 'bout fo' acres o' lan' scratchin' hit up ciphrin on hit, but des to drap you a hint,' says he, shettin one o' his eyes mighty tight, 'dat lan' 'll cos' you sebenteen thousan' dollars a front foot.'

"Moss Raif he made out to git home, but he was mighty sick.

He was sicke 'n he was befo'. He was laid up 'bout two weeks.

"But he overed it an' he started out once mo'.

"Anybody might could thow Moss Raif, caze he ain't the stronges' man ever I seed, but de trouble is, nobody ever kin hole him down.

"Dis time he never stop tell he done seed de fo' mile pose.

"Dey warnt nothing roun' dar but des de remmunt woods. But dey was stakes driv in de groun' ever which a way.

"Moss Raif looked all roun' an' he never seed a livin' soul.

"But dey was a man a watchin' him. He was hid behine a pine tree.

"'Mos' too cheap, dis dirt is,' Moss Raif says to hisself, an' wid dat he turn roun' an start to go back home.

"Wen dat man seed him a makin' off, he come out f 'om hine dat tree in a hurry, an' he up [']lowed good-mornin' an' Moss Raif he howdied wid him.

"'I [']lowed maybe you was lookin' for dirt,' dat man says.

"'Yas,' Moss Raif says, sorter dry, 'but I'm scared dis yer dirt's too fur out o' town. What's de price you ax for one acre o' hit?' says he.

"'We don't sell hit by de acre dis nigh in town,' dat man says, 'but you come on an' lemme show you roun' some, an' we'll sho' an' to 'gree on de price,' says he.

"Well, dey went. Dey walked a right smart piece, and Moss Raif he was gittin' tired, caze heap o' dat groun' was boggy.

"He tuck and sot hisse'f down on a tussock to res'.

"'I wants to year yo' figgers, now,' he says.

"'All right,' says de man, 'I ain't no ways bashful 'bout tellin' my price, caze, gracious knows, hit's cheap 'nough.'

"'Hit out to be,' Moss Raif says, 'caze hit's sur 'nough out'n town.'

"'We sells it by de poun',' dat man says, 'caze den a man don't pay for nothin' but what he gits. Hit's $20 a poun',' says he.

"Moss Raif never said nair word. He bounce up off 'n' dat tussick same es a rattlesnake done bit him, an' he lit out for home.

"But dat man follered him.

"Moss Raif hit de grit; an' he hit her hard, caze he done felt one o' dem sick spells a comin' on him agin.

"Dat man broke into a plum run, and den he never cotch Moss Raif tell he done got back to town.

"'What you want?' Moss Raif says.

"'I want's you to pay me what you owes me,' dat man says.

"'I didn't know you charge me anything for des showin' me yo' dirt,' Moss Raif says.

"'I don't,' says dat man, 'but wen you come way you never bresh yo' britches whar you been a settin' down an' neither clean yo' shoes, an' you got 'bout haf a poun' o' my dirt, an' hits wuth $10,' says he.

"Moss Raif he 'fuse to pay. He never is yeard o' no sich sheecoonny sence de fust day he was borned into dis worl'.

"But dat man tuck him to cote, an' de j[e]dge made Moss Raif pay ten dollars for dat ha'f a poun' o' dirt. Yas, sah, he did dat, sho' es I'm a stannin' right yer.

"Moss Raif he paid it, an' he 'low:

"'Two kin play at dat game. Ef dat dirt'll fetch twenty dollars a poun', I'll sho' git rich,' says he. An' he did, too, man."

"How did he do it?"

"Well, de fus' thing he done he rented him a little house out dar whar de lan' was sole by de poun', an' he went out dar to live. Yas, sah, he staid right dar tell he got des es much money es he know w'at to do wid."

"Did he buy that dirt?"

"Naw, sah; he sole hit."

"How could he sell it without first buying it?"

"He got him a M'ringer pig, sah, an' ever' night he'd turn dat pig on dat man's lan', an' ever' mornin' dat pig 'ud come home an' fetch 'bout two poun' o' dat dirt on his tail.

"Lemme see, how much do dat make a day, Moss Wilbur?"

"Forty dollars."

"Well, dat's de way Moss Raif made de moes o' his money, but he never made it all dat way."

"How else, then?"

"Well, w'en he seed how things was gwine, he stopped washin' hisself."

(The *Birmingham Age-Herald,* February 16, 1890)

Looking Backward

[After Edward Bellamy]

 The half man was recently exhibited in Auburn, and every negro that could raise a quarter went to see the wonder. Ever since then the talk amongst the colored population has run largely on human monstrosities and deformities of one kind and another. Each vied with the other in telling wonderful stories, till at length the gentleman from Marengo gained the floor and told the following story, which eclipsed all the rest and silenced every tongue:

"Down dar in M'ringer dey was a man by de name o' Mr. Rumpless. Dey come long a showman an' he went to Mr. Rumpless an' tole him he dun foun' out a way to men' folkses bones an' meat same es you men's a plow or a hoe. He lowed he could cut a man's arm plum off 'n him an' den stick hit back, an' nobody wouldn' know hit ever been cut off.

"Mr. Rumpless he never pay much 'tention to dat show-

man at fus, caze he never b'lieve a word he said. He des
[']lowed dat showman was a lyin' des to hear hissef talk,
sorter like some o' deze Aubu'n niggers does[.] But, sah, dat
showman he kep on a devlin Mr. Rumpless. He tole him ef
he'd jine in wid him dey'd sho git rich. He [']lowed dey'd
take a nigger an' dey'd go 'bout all over de country an' give
a show; dey'd cut off dat nigger's arms an' his laigs, an' dey'd
stick em back on so quick de nigger wouldn't have time to
feel hit hurt him. Den w'en de folks see dat merricle 'form'
dey go an' norate 'bout hit all over de lan', an' everybody ud
des be bound to see dat show ef hit cos' em two dollars a
haid.

"Mr. Rumpless he tole dat showman dat'd be mighty nice
ef hit was des so, but he 'lowed he want him to try de fust
speerment on somebody else's nigger, caze he never had
nair'n to spar'.

"But de showman he never give it up. He kep' on a
dev'lin' Mr. Rumpless an' beggin' him to furnish a nigger
an' go in cahoots wid him, tell atter wile Mr. Rumpless he up
an' low:

"'Seem like ef you kin do folks dat way you kin do dogs,
too.'

"'I kin,' dat showman says.

"'Well, den, Mr. Rumpless,' says he, 'we'll try de fust
speerment on my ole yaller dog's tail, an' ef you can't stick
hit back all right I'll des have a bob-tail dog, an' a bob-tail
dog is des 'bout es good es a long-tail dog, 'cep'n' nobody
can't tell when dey're mad or when dey're pleasin'.

"Wid dat dey tuck an' called up ole Tige an' dat man
chopped his tail off, an' no sooner he done it he tuck an' rub
sumpin' on de stump whar look like dis yer sticky rozzum,
an' he stuck de tail on agin.

"Hit was all done dat sudden ole Tige didn't have time to howl fo' his tail was done stuck back on him, an' he never had nothin' to holler fer den.

"Mr. Rumpless was dat tickle he des laid back an' laf. He never is seed nothin' like dat befo' in all his born life.

"Dey waited a little wile to let dat stuff dry, an' den dat showman he tole Mr[.] Rumpless to see ef he could pull ole Tige's tail off.

"Mr[.] Rumpless he cotch ole Tige by de tail an' he drug him all over de plantation, but dat tail hit was struck des like hit growed dar f 'om a pup.

"Mr[.] Rumpless he wasn't zackly sati'fy yit. He 'lowed de showman might could stick de tail back on wid glue, but de dog couldn't use hit to fan off de flies an' to let folks know whe'r he was pleasin', or mad, or scared.

"Mr. Rumpless he got him a piece o' fat meat an' hilt hit up whar ole Tige could see hit.

"Man, sah! you des ought to a seed how ole Tige wagged his tail w'en he seed dat meat. Ef hit hadn't a been stuck on mighty tight hit' d a sho' drapt off. But hit staid dar, an' hit wagged, man!

"Atter dat de showman he use to cut off ole Tige's tail an' his laigs every day, an' he never fail to stick 'em back.

"Mr. Rumpless he was mighty set up wid de idee, but he axed dat showman what's de reason ole Tige wouldn't do des es well's a nigger, caze ole Tige never cos' nothin', an' a likely nigger was wuth $1000.

"But dat showman he wouldn't hear to no sich. He [']lowed he wanted sump'n whar could talk, an den folks ud see an b'lieve. He [']lowed ef dey tuck de dog, hit ud be des like de man whar stole de bob-tail cow an sewed a tail on her, an de owner cotch up wid de thief an lowed ef dat was ders a bob-tail cow he'd claim her; an de thief he cut off her tail an thowed hit in de roover an he want to know whose cow hit was den, an de owner he low he be ding ef he knowed, caze atter he done seed what he seed he never knowed nothin'.

"He kep on a dev'lin Mr. Rumpless, dat showman did, tell atter wile Mr. Rumpless he greed to let him try his han on Tobe.

"Tobe he was de toughes nigger down dar in M'ringer, an he warnt much account to work nohow.

"Well, at fust de showman des cut off Tobe's fingers an' his years, an' he stuck dem back on all right, an' Tobe [']lowed hit never hurt him a speck. But des es soon's dey mence to talk 'bout cuttin' off Tobe's arms Tobe he 'gin to grumble. He was scared to resk dat. He tuck an run 'way to keep 'em f 'om cuttin' off his arms, but dey cotch him. Dey runned him wid de dogs, an' ole Tige he had a han' it. Dey cotch him an' brung him back, dey did, an' ef ever you seed a scared nigger, ole Tobe was him.

"Dat showman he had a swode dat he done de cuttin' wid, an' man, sah! dat swode hit was sharper'n air shavin razor ever you seed, scusin' de fightin' razors! Hit cut off a man's arm same es my scythe blade cut a broom straw ha'f in two.

"Ole man Tobe he thought his time done come w'en he seed dat swode. He des good es died twenty times wilst dey was a gettin' everything ready. Dey tied him to keep him f 'om gittin' 'way agin, an' dey tuck an' propped up one o' his arms wid a forked stick, and dat showman whacked her. Yas, sah, he chopped off dat arm close up to ole Tobe's shoulder, but he stuck her back agin so quick ole Tobe never had no time to feel nair pain an' nair mis'ry.

"W'en Tobe foun' out hit warn't gwine to hurt him a bit, he 'lowed his was des fun, an' he didn't care ef dey whacked off his haid so dey stuck her back good es she was befo'.

"De showman he 'lowed he speck to chop off his haid bimeby, soon's he practice a little wid his swode.

"Well, sah, dey got ever'thing ready, an' Mr. Rumpless an'

dat ar showman dey tuck Tobe 'long an' dey travel. Dey gin shows at ever' little town, an' dey everlastin'ly tuck in de scads. Dat's how come Mr. Rumpless got so big rich, 'caze w'en he died he was de riches' man down dar in M'ringer, scusin' my ole moster.

"Dey showed, dey did, an' folks dey flocked dar to see dat show same es dey goes to a fun'al. Dat showman he'd whack off Tobe's years an' his arms an' laigs, an' he stick 'em back on des good's ever.

"Mr. Rumpless an' de showman dey'd vide de money out 'twixt 'em, ha'f an' ha'f. But Mr. Rumpless he warn't satisfy wid dat; he was plum anxious to l'arn how to make dat stuff to stick arms an' laigs back on wid. But dat showman he was too smart to tell anybody dat.

"Hit warn't so mighty long befo' dat showman fa'rly hone atter choppin' Tobe's haid off. Tobe he 'lowed chop away, he warn't afeard.

"De showman he made him a dummy des de size o' Tobe 'an he practise on her ever' day till he got so he could hit zackly in de same place ever' fire. Den he knowed he was all right.

"One night wilst de show was gwine on an' folks was des miratin' over him a choppin' off Tobe's arms an' stickin' 'em back agin, he up an' [']lowed he could do sump'n mo' cu'iser'n dat; he could do Tobe's haid dat a way yit.

"Wid dat a man out in de crowd he up an' bet him a thousan' dollars he couldn't.

"De showman tole him to put up de spons an' dey bofe put 'em up.

"De showman he drawed back his swode, an' ever'body in de house scringe, caze dey made sho' he wats gwine to kill de po' nigger[.] Twenty-seben haid o' women fainted right dar in dey tracks, an' fo' dey could come to agin de showman done had Tobe's haid cut off an' stuck back all right, an' he was puttin' all dat money in his pocket whar he done win.

"Dey kept on dat way, Mr. Rumpless an' de showman did, tell bimeby dey had mo money'n dey know what to do wid, caze ever time dey gin a show dey'd sho an' be some fool in de crowd what was willing to bet a thousan' dollars de showman couldn't cut off de nigger's haid an' stick hit back again. You couldn't git up a crowd but what dey'll be one fool in hit.

"Dey went on, dey did; dey went on, an' atter wile dat showman he was tooken sorter po'ly. One night he tole Mr[.] Rumpless he wouldn't be sprised ef he made a bust, he was feelin' dat non-plush an' po'ly.

"De show hit went on, dough. Tobe's arms an' laigs and years was chopped off, an' den de fool he come up wid his thousan' dollars. De showman gin a whack, an' off come Tobe[']s head. De haid hit fell on de flo', an' de showman he grabbed hit up like lightnin' an' stick hit back whar hit b'long. No sooner he got de haid stuck back, de showman he staggered roun' a little and drapt dead in his tracks.

"De doctors dey looked at him, an' dey [']lowed he died wid de heart zease or de appoplexion. De doctors dey always makes out like dey knows, an' ef dey don't know, dey des makes up a big word what nobody can't onderstan'.

"Well, ever'body was dat tuck wid lookin' at de showman nobody never nodis how Tobe's haid was stuck back on tell a right smart wile. Man, sah! ef hit wasn't stuck on backuds I hope I may turn to a nigger.

"Tobe he [']lowed he felt des as peart as ever, an' hit didn't hurt him a bit.

"Well, de showman he was dead, an' Mr. Rumpless he never had de leas' idee how to make dat stuff to stick wid, an' neither how to use hit ef he had hit. He was scared to cut off

Tobe[']s haid agin, caze he knowed hit 'ud kill Tobe, dead es a mackul. So he des had to let Tobe's haid stay like hit was.

"Mr. Rumpless he could a kep on havin' a show ef he want to, caze a man wid his haid set on hine part befo' was des as good a show es anybody want to see; but Mr. Rumpless he was tired o' de show business, an' mo'n dat he done got mo' money dan de banks could hole already. So he quit.

"Tobe he got long mighty well, only he couldn't look de way he was walkin' cep'n he turn his haid roun' same es a owel. But dey was one thing mighty cuis bout him; you know folks most in ginnerly totes dey brains behine dey eye, but Tobe had his'n befo his eyes, an dat's how hit was Tobe was always a studyin bout sump'in way yander ahaid o' anything he could see. He was lookin' backuds an studyin' forruds all de time, des zackly diffunt f'om de way yuther folks does. Ef he's a livin' yit, I wouldn't be sprised ef de tears aint des a tricklin' down his back dis minute on de count o' his great-great gran' son's great-great-great-gran' daughter's great[-]great-great-great-great gran' niece's wife's secon' son's got thowed off 'n a mule an got his front tooth knocked out."

(The *Birmingham Age-Herald,* March 2, 1890)

A Mule as Was a Mule

"'Pear like to me dese yer mules roun' Auburn gits littler an' littler," remarked Jake. "Dey was no count enough de fust time I ever seed 'em, but dey're no counter now 'an dey was den. I don't see how nobody kin make a crap wid 'em. Down dar in M'ringer we use to set wire traps an' ketch rats what ud outmatch air mule I sees roun' Aubu'n. Hit's bad enough for 'em to be dat little an' weak, but bad as hit is hit's wusser to have 'em loaded down wid morgins like dey is. I seed a rat de yuther day what had a so' place on his back big es my fryin' pan. I axed dat man whar had him what made hit, an' he 'lowed dat was whar a morgin done drawed a blister on him.

"Sometimes I sees folks roun' yer drivin' what dey calls a spike team. Dey has two steers at de wheel, an' a little ole rat mule by hisse'f in de lead. Dem steers dey always has long horns, an' hits a mighty good thing dey has, caze when dat little ole mule git stuck in de mud dey has to lif' him out.

"Ef dese yer Lee county folks ever was to make a sho' 'nough crap o' cotton, dey never could haul it to town wid de mules dey got. But dey ain't no danger o' nobody makin' a crap in Lee county, cep'n hit rain three rains a week an' a shower o' joa[n]na wonst a mont'. 'Twarnt for de joa[n]na de seeds wouldn't never come up, caze de lan' ain't got strenk 'nough by hitsef to lif ' em up out'n de dirt. Dey packs de cotton in mighty little bales to make hit go a fur ways an' so de mules kin pull it.

"I des but wonder what deze niggers roun' yer 'ud say ef dey was to see a M'ringer mule. Dey'd make sho hit was a long yeared elephint. Dey wouldn't want no sich critter es dat caze he'd eat up dey corn cribs, logs an' all, at one feed[.] Dey'd hatter git 'em a lather to clime up on him yit, an we'n dey want to go ter market dey'd des put de whole crap o' cotton on dat mule's back, stidder hitchin' up a wagon, an' dat'd make 'em shame.

"Oh, rats'll do tolerble well for Lee county, but down dar in M'ringer you got have mules what is mules.

"De mule whar I use to plow down dar on ole moster's plantation she could eat up bofe o' Monroe Tawce's rats at one moufful, an' she wouldn't a tas'e de mule tas'e yit. Man, sah! ole Kit was a mule[.] She was a mule what you read 'bout. She might not could a talked like dat'n de bible tell 'bout, but dat was de onliest thing she coul[d]n't do ef she set her haid. She had mo' sense 'n air nigger in Lee county, cepin dey got M'ringer blood in 'em. Man, sah! ole Kit was a mule what was a mule.

"De fus time ole Kit ever made a track on ole Moster's plantation I claimed her an' ole moster he let me have her, caze he never is fuse me nothin'. Many's de time he's tole me I could have anything I want ef I des but say de word, caze I was his right han' man.

"Ole Kit was a mouse color mar' mule, an' she was 'bout

twenty seben han's high. Her laigs dey was made out'n injy
rubber an' steel wire, and her back hit was cas'-iron. Dey aint
no use o' talking 'bout what she could pull, caze she could
pull everthing you could put behine her. She could pull de
hime sights off 'n las' year yit.

"She had a right sma't o' fun in her, too. She des naicherly
love to pile up de niggers on de groun'. I was de onliest one
what could ride her. I plowed her all de week, an' w'en
Sadday night come I'd ride her out in de settlement to see de
gals. Me an' her we was fas' pardners. She knowed me[.] She
knowed I'd 'vide de las' moufful I had wid her, an' ef I never
had but one bunnel o' fodder an' she was to ax me for hit, I'd
a gin hit to her ef I starve myse'f. As many times as I rid her
out Sadday nights, she never is tole ole master on me nair
time yit[.] Ole master he was in de habits o' gwine out to de
lot Sunday mornin' an' see how his mules look, an' ef dey
look like dey been rid de night befo', dey'd mo'n apt to be a
row raise' on dat plantation. But, man, sah! ole Kit never
gimme 'way nair time[.] She look des es fresh of a Sunday
mornin' es she look any yuther time, caze you couldn't make
her tired. But she was a puller, an' dat how come she ain't
down dar on de ole moster's plantation dis day an' time[.]"

"I suppose your man, Mr. Humphrey, fell in love with her
and bought her from your old master."

"Who? Mr[.] Rumples[s]? Mr. Rumpless never had
money 'nough to buy ole Kit; naw, sah; de way we got shet
o' her hit was jes by natchel hard pullin', an' hit happen in de
middle o' de winter time, and de mud was 'bout twenty foot
deep. But ole moster he yeared cotton done riz an' he was
des bleeged to git de egvantage o' de rise[.] Nobody warn't
tryin' to haul nothin' dem days caze de roads was dat rotten
six mules couldn't a pulled a empty waggin. I'm talkin' 'bout
six common M'ringer mules, 'scusin' Kit.

"Ole moster was bad pestered, but I up an' tole him he

neenter pester hisse'f, ef he des but gimme de word de cotton ud go to town.

"'How hit gwine?' says he.

"I says: 'Ole moster,' says I, 'is you ever knowed me to tell a lie?'

"Ole moster he looked at me up one side an' down the yuther, an' toreckly he slapped his han' on my back an' he says:

"'Jake, I don't b'lieve you could tell a lie ef you was to try,' says he. 'Hit des ain't in you. Stidder 'ceivin' anybody, you alays dat scared you'll say sump'n' what ain't zackly true, you don't tell things ha'f es big es dey is.'

"I says, 'Well, ole moster,' says I, 'you des' pen' pon me an' I'll git de cotton to market.'

"Ole moster 'greed to dat, an' I went to work an' got things ready. I hitched up six mules an' I loaded de waggin wid sebenteen bales o' cotton, an' ever' bale weighed a thousan' poun's. Dey warn't no little Lee county bales; dey was M'ringer bales.

"I hitched ole Kit in de lead befo' dem six mules, an' I put double trace chains on her, caze I knowed she was gwine to do some tall pullin'.

"We started, we did. I driv de waggin, an' ole moster he rid his horse on de hard bank side de road.

"We got long tolerble well aw'ile, but ole Kit kep' on a breakin' dem trace chains ontell I put 'em on her fo' double. You see, wen de yuther mules got bogged up she hatter pull mules an' waggin an' cotton an' nigger. An' she do it, too, man.

"Toreckly we got to de big sloo. Ole Kit she went in and de yuther mules followed her. Dey kept on gwine down, down tell time we got to de middle o' de sloo you couldn't see nair mule, and de wagon bed was flat on de mud.

"Toreckly ole moster hollered out:

"'Jake, you're stallded, an' you des es well gin hit up.'

"'No, I aint,' says I. 'Don't you see dat yander thing what look like a snake crawlin' on de mud?'

"Ole master 'lowed he seed hit, but he thought hit was a bobtail mogsin.

"'Dat's ole Kit's tail,' says I, 'an' long es you see dat a movin' you kin m[a]ke sho de mule an' de waggin's a follerin' long behine.'

"Sho nough! de waggin was a slidin' 'long on top o' de mud, an' hit warn't so mighty long fo' we seed ole Kit a risin' up on de dry groun' on de yuther side.

"Man, sah! hit'd a done you good to seed her heave an' set es she come out'n de sloo wid de mud a drappin' off 'n her.

"De yuther mules dey come on atter her, caze she pulled em an' dey couldn't he'p deyse'f.

"But de minute de hi'most mules got out de waggin wheels hit 'gin a log, or a ole bridge 'butment or sumpin' an' she stuck fast.

"'Dar, now!' ole moster says, 'dat waggin's good to spen' de winter in dat hole.'

"'Don't you be oneasy,' says I. 'Des wait tell I holler at old Kit.'

"I hollered, I did, and an' ole Kit she humped herse'f like she never is humped herse'f befo'.

"I knowed sump'n was bleeged to move, an' hit did too."

"Did the waggin and mules move out?"

"Dey did dat. You up an' guessed hit de first time. But dat warn't all what move. Ef nothin' else had a moved, ole Kit ud a been a good mule tell dis day.

"Laws o' mussy! I seed a sight dat day I never is seed befo' or sence.

"Dat Kit mule, sah, w'en she seed how things was, she des everlastingly laid hersef out[.]"

"Killed herself?"

"Naw, sah, she never zackly killed herse'f, but she pulled herse'f plum out'n her hide, an' her hide hit drapt in a pile on de groun'.

"Cose ole moster never had no use for a plum raw mule, an' he des hatter kill her[.]"

(The *Birmingham Age-Herald,* March 16, 1890)

An Eating Match

Long Tom Rumpless and Pervidin' Elder Hollerhorn

M'RINGER JAKE RECALLS AN INCIDENT
OF EARLY FREEDOM—A WONDERFUL
CLERICAL BATTLE AT THE TABLE

 Some one intimated that Jake had a phe-
nominal [sic] appetite, whereupon the
gentleman from Marengo defended himself in words as follows:

"'Tain't no wonder Auburn folks makes
a miration w'en dey sees me a eatin', caze I
was raised down dar in M'ringer whar d'is always plenty o'
'visions an' victuals layin' 'roun loose, an' folks do'nt hatter
go ha'f starved. No, sahree, de chillun down dar dey're
always fat and sassy. Dey looks like dey been wash in pot
liquor every day o' dey lives, dey're dat greasy. W'en dey
mammie's feeds em dey don't hatter run de yard stick down
dey thoats an' medger em [t]o fine out zackly what dey'll
hole. De folks up yer does dat way, and dey low dey're doin'
mighty well ef dey des but fill dey chillun ha'f full wonst a
day. Hit's a fack, sah. Dat's how come dey don't eat much.
Dey ain't usened to it. Ef a man's usened to anything he's
mo'n ap' to like it, caze he don't know no better. Ef dey was

to eat a good square meal dey stomachs 'ud be stonish, an' dey'd die wid de cramp colic. Down dar in M'ringer chillun larns how to eat, an' time dey're grown dey is some account. Dey got de strenk to do any kine o' work.

"I'm right smart swunk up sence I come up yer on dese old rocky hills. Dat's how come I can't eat no mo. Some o' dese yer locus preachers 'roun' yer kin outeat me yit, let lone of a circus rider. But den, you know, preachers always does eat mo'n yuther folks, caze dat's de main part o' dey business. Dey grub don't cos 'em nothin', an' dey goes for hit viegrous. You see 'em passin' 'bout an' knockin' 'roun', and dey always looks like dey're studyin' 'bout de sarment whar dey gwine to preach nex' Sunday. But don't you trus' dat. Dey look like dey got dey 'fections fix' up in heb'n all de time, but you des but let a yaller-laig chicken come 'long, an' I lay dey'll see it. Dey will dat, an dey'll 'member whar dat chicken stay at too. Dey calls me a big eater caze I kin wrop myself roun' a tolerble good size chunk o' middlin' meat an' 'bout sebenteeen biscuits an' a pot o' greens, but ef dey was to see a M'ringer preacher eat, dey'd wonder how I could live on dat little.

"Soon atter freedom come out dey was a man down dar in M'ringer name o' Tom whar use to b'long to Mr. Rumpless. Dey called him Long Tom Rumpless 'caze he was so tall. An he was holler plum to de een o' his toes, too, mon. Des soon's he foun' out he was free dat nigger up an' lowed he been to heb'n and he been to hell w'ilst he was sleep, an' he yeared a voice whar nobody else yeared callin' him. An' not only dat, he knowed he was called to preach 'caze de chickens was scared w'en he came 'bout.

"Well, sah, hit's a sho fack, de chickens on Mr. Rumpless' plantation did take to roostin' a right smart higher'n dey use to[.] Dey clum up to de highes' lim' ever' time dey year dat nigger holler. I knows, 'caze I was right dar. Tom was de feeder, an' I yeared him callin' de hogs ever evenin' o' dis worl'. I reckon dat how come I got so much aligion, I live so long right under de gospel soun'.

"Mr. Rumpless 'lowed he speck Tom ud make a good [pr]eacher, caze he was made right, he could holler loud ez de next un, an' nobody dassent try to eat 'gin him.

"Hit warn't long fo' Tom quit feedin' hogs an' 'mence to ride de circus. He rid her afoot mostly[.] Everywhars he went de price o' chickens r[i]z. He was a preacher f'om preacherville[.] He couldn't read an' write, but he could everlastingly holler, an' ef he des git up in de pulpit and call hogs, de sinners ud moan an' groan, an' fall an' come thoo, an' all de chickens in de settlement ud clam higher up de tree. Mr. Rumpless 'lowed Tom made soun' go for sense. I reckon he did, but hit done des ez well. I never did year him preach, but I yeared him callin' hogs, an' I got des ez much aligion as air 'nother nigger in Aubu'n.

"Heap o' folks b'lieved Tom could out eat air nother man in M'ringer, but some said he couldn't. De perviden elder down dar he was name Brer Hollerhorn, and he knowed sumpin 'bout eatin' hissef. He was a little stumpy man, sorter l[ik]e me, only he was a heap bigger roun'. Hi[t] ud take two plow-lines to reach roun' his bread basket. Dey was room in dar, too, mon. His hide was made out'n ingy-rubber; hit'd stretch to meet the casion. If he never had but one chicken and five or six biskits, he could make out on dat, but if you brung on a ten poun' pudden' to end up wid, dat ole hide ud stretch plenty big to hole hit.

"Well, folks got to sputin' which one o' dem preachers could eat de moest, an' dey quoiled an' fit 'bout it, an' dey was mo' niggers turn out'n de church 'bout dat an' ever dey was 'bout dancin'. At las', some worllians dey got up a bet[.]

Dey got me to hole de stakes, caze dey knowed I was plum honest[.] Hit was 'bout a thousand dollars.

"Dey sont a invite to dem two preachers to come to 'Mop'lis to a bobbycue. Dey never let on what dey want wid 'em, caze hit was de greement for de preachers to be onbeknownst.

"De yuther folks dey all eat dinner out o' do's, but dey put dat circus-rider an' dat pervidin' elder in a room by dey se'f. I was de onlies' one 'lowed to go in dar. Dey tole dem preachers I was deef an' dum, but I could wait on 'em.

"Well, w'en dinner was ready, dey went in an' tuck a seat an' sot down at de table. Hit was a long ole table, an' hit was loaden down wid 'visions. De pervidin' elder he sot down at one een an' de circus-rider he sot down at de yuther een.

"Time dey went in de room I nodis dey eyes sparkle an' dey mouf water.

"'Humph!' Brer Hollerhorn says, says [h]e, 'dey got us right smart o' comfo'ts yer [fo]r de inner man,' says he. 'Well, dey ain't [no] ladies yer, I reckon we can 'vour dese [']visions an' lick de plates ef we expose to,' says he.

"'Yas,' says Brer Long Tom Rumpless, 'we kin fill up ef dey's 'nough yer, caze dey aint nobody to make us 'fraid. Dis yer waiter, he's plum deef an' dum', an' ef we eat too much he can't tell nobody,' says he.

"Wid dat dey 'mence to 'spute about which one was gwine to ax de blessin'. Dey was mighty polite 'bout dat. Brer Rumpless he stuck it out he warnt gwine to ax her wilst ez big a preacher ez de pervidin' elder was dar. He lowed he had better manners 'an dat.

"Brer Hollerhorn, w'en he seed he hatter do it, he drapped his haid a leetle an' he ax de blessin'. But he kep' one eye open. He [']low:

"'Lord bless a reasonable potion o' dese 'visions to our

use, an' im particlar hab mussey on dat miser'ble sinner whar got his han' in de tater poodin'. Amen.'

"Brer Rumpless he never knowed Brer Hollerhorn had one o' his eyes open; had he, he wouldn't a went for de tater poodin' like he did.

"W'en de blessin' was over de manners dey was too. Dem preachers dey never knowed dey was put dar to eat 'gin one an'er; leasways not onless somebody tole 'em on de sly, but dey eat des like dey knowed it.

"Dey was fo' whole bobbycue carcases on de table, two cows an two sheep, sides de bread an cakes an nice things.

"Dey let in on de cows fust, and fo' you could a said Jack Roberson dey want nothin' but bones lef[.] Brer Rumpless he got done eatin' his cow des a minute sooner'n Brer Hollerhorn, an he up an 'low:

"'Thanky for de beef.'

"Brer Hollerhorn he des had one cow shank left, but he never passed dat to Brer Rumpless. No sooner he yeared de word he rammed dat shank down his th'oat, bone an all, an all he could say was:

"'Oogle google loogle.'

"De sheeps dey went. One eat one, an one eat de yuther.

"Dat fur dey was des 'bout eben."

"I hatter to keep count o' de biscuit's an' de pones o' bread, but nair one never had de egvantage o' de yuther'n. Dem biscuits an' poodens an' things dey slipped down dem preachers' th'oats same es peas down a rat hole. Dey kep dey eyes on one aner, an' Brer Rumpless he'd holler:

"'Tote fa'r, now, Brer Hollerhorn, caze ha'f o' dese yer victuals was put yer for me.'

"An' Brer Hollerhorn he'd answer back

"'Oogle google loogle.'

"'Twasn't no time fo' dat table was clarred, an' dey wasn't

nothin' on hit but de dishes an' de bigges' bones. Den Brer Hollerhorn he up an says:

"'How you feel, Brer Rumpless?'

"Brer Rumpless he 'low:

"'I feel toler'ble well sperityally, but I'm sorter hongry in de innard parts. How you feel, Brer Hollerhorn?'

"'I'm feelin' toler'ble,' Brer Hollerhorn says, says he, 'but I woosht to gracious we had sump'n' to crack dese yer bones an' git de morrer out. I'm pizen fon' o' morrer,' says he.

"Up to dat time I was bad pestered in my mine who to give dat money to, caze one o' dem preachers done eat 'bout es much es de yuther'n, ef not mo'. I stayed dar an' I looked at dem two men, an' I scratched my haid. I 'lowed to myse'f ef air one bust open I'd give de stakes to dem whar bet on de yuther'n, but dat was de onlies' way I could study how to 'cide dat bet.

"Dem two preachers dey sot dar lookin' at one a'ner. Nair one ain't dassent to try to git up.

"Toreckly Brer Rumpless he told Brer Hollerhorn to 'turn thanks.

"Brer Hollerhorn he done it. He never lean his haid down, 'caze I don't reckon he could. I speck dat cow shank done ris up in his th'oat. He 'turn thanks dough, but I never yeared nair word but des:

"'Oogle google loogle.'

"Brer Rumplesss he lean his haid down, an' he never tuck hit up atter Brer Hollerhorn got done 'turnin' thanks[.] He des helt it down and made out li[k]e he was wipin' his mouf on de tablecloth. But torec[k]ly I seed de tablecloth movin' long todes Brer Rumpless des like a serpent move on de face o' de yeth. Hit move on, hit did, an' de plates an' de dishes an' de knives an' forks dey gin to dance an' hop roun' like dey was live, an' some of 'em jumped off on be flo.'

"Hit didn't take me no time to see what was de matter. Dat tablecloth was crawlin' down Brer Rumpless' throat.

"Brer Hollerhorn's eyes was open big es sassers, but he was dat full he couldn't move. He never had de strenk to ketch holt o' de table cloth an' pull her back.

"I never wait to see no mo'. I stepped to de do', I did, an' I hollered to dem folks outside:

"'Brer Rumpless done won de bet[.]'

"De las' word I yeard, Brer Hollerhorn he drawed dat shank back outen his th'oat an' [']low:

"'Brer Rumpless, you ought to be shame. You're dat greedy dat it make de deef to year an' de dum' to speak.'"

(The *Birmingham Age-Herald,* March 30, 1890)

Jake's New House

"Moss Wilbur, is you yeard de news!"

"No; I can't say that I have. What is it?"

"I'm done move way f'om whar I'm livin' at now."

"That is news to me."

"Well, sah, I wants you to put it in dat Burninham paper, so when folks comes yer f'om a fur ways to see me dey wont take de wrong road an' git lost. I don't live down de railroad like I use to. I don't live down nowhars. I lives up[.] Dat's what de preacher tole me to do, and I'm a doin' it. He 'lowed we mus' all live up to our juty, and ef I ain't doin' dat dey ain't no use o' nobody tryin'. I'm livin' up de railroad todes Opelacker, and I'm livin' up on top o' de highes' hill in de town. E[f] dat don't satisfy de preacher I'll clam a tree an' roost in hit.

"I reckon you've yeard about somebody builn' a new house in Aubu'n, ain't you?"

"Well, yes; Mr. Gullatte, Mrs. Hurt, Mr. Thomas and several others."

"Mr. Golatte's house is gwine to be a tolerble fine un', so dey say. I reckon hit will, too, caze Mr. Golatte's got plenty o' money to built it wid. Ef you don't b'lieve it you des stan' at his sto' do' sometime an' listen at him talkin' to folks."

"Oh, he doesn't brag about what he has."

"I never said he did, sah. Dat ain't what I was talking 'bout. I'm talkin' 'bout dem winnin' ways he's got to sell goods, an' dat's how come he got so much money. Everybody whar go in his sto' 'bleege to buy sump'n. Dey des' can't git way f 'om him. Ef he ain't got what you want he'll sho' an' to have it tomorrow, caze he's got a car-load o' hit comin'.

"Mr. Golatte's house is gwine to be a fine 'un, an' I speck dese young ladies roun' yer is all of 'em a wond'in' which one o' dem he's gwine to ax to come dar an' keep house for him. But Mr. Golatte's house hit ain't hardly started yit. Es for Mrs. Hurt an' Mr. Thomas an' all o' dem, dey're mighty nice houses, an' de folks is livin' in 'em, but dey're in de valley o' de shadder, es de preacher says."

"What do you mean by that?"

"Well, sah, I means d'es been aner house built here in Aubu'n, an' hit settin' on a hill, es de preacher says, an hits shadder hit darken all dem yuther houses what sets down in de flat. Dat'n what I'm talkin' 'bout hit's fooled lots o' Aubu'n folks a'ready."

"How so?"

"Well, you see, sah, when dat 3 o'clock train come thoo in de night hit wakes up some folks, an' dey ginnerly goes to de do' to see ef day's a breakin'. Dey looks to de eas', an' lo an' behole! dey see sump'in what look des zackly like de sun a risin'.

"Ef you year anybody knockin' roun' way yonder fo' day, you neenter think hits somebody atter pullin' some o' yo' chickens off'n de roos'; hits somebody whar been fooled dat way."

"What is it they see that looks so much like the rising sun?"

"Hit's dat new house I been tellin' you 'bout."

"Is i[t] painted red?"

"Naw, sah; hit ain't painted 't all. Hit's des de natchel yaller color o' de weather-bodin' an' de shingles whar shines like de sun."

"Who is the owner of that wonderful new mansion?"

"De fus' two letters o' his name's M'ringer Jake."

"Oh, you!"

"Yas, sah; I tuck an' put up me a house. Hit's a house f'om houseville, too. Hit out shine air nother house in dis yer town. I 'lowed you'd yeared 'bout hit or either seed it, caze all de folks what passes in de train dey make a plum hullaballoo 'bout it. Hit's a setting right side o' de railroad cut, up dar on top o' dat hill beyant de ole londry place.

"I'm got a idee o' havin' me a sign painted an' stuck up over de do' todes de railroad, caze I'm gittin' mighty tired o' de train stoppin' dar so much."

"What does the train stop for?"

"Caze when de folks on bode sees my house dey always begs de conductor to stop an' let 'em take a good look at hit, caze hit's de fines house dey ever seed yit[.]"

"What do you intend to put on your sign?"

"I'm gwine to put, 'Dis yer's whar M'ringer Jake live at, an' he ain't deceivin' no comp'ny today!'"

"Ah, I see: you're bored by curious callers."

"You're mighty right, Moss Wilbur. W'en de train stops de folks des comes a tum'lin' out, an' dey all runs up todes my house like dey never seed a fine mansion befo'! Yer dey come, scram'lin' in de do' an' thoo de winder, an' I'm lookin' for somebody to let deyse'f down de chimbley, yit. W'en dey git in de house dey axes queshuns so fas' hit take

me an' Ma'jane an' all de chillun an' de yaller dog to answer.
De fus' thing, dey wants to fine out whose house hit is, an'
w'en I tells 'em hit b'longs to M'ringer Jake dey makes a
mighty miration. Dey all'ays says dey've hear'n tell o' me, an'
dey been a wantin' to see me, caze I'm de onles man, 'cep'n
George Warshin'ton, whar never could tell a lie. Wid dat, dey
pulls out dey pocket knives an' cuts chips off 'n de house an'
Ma'jane's bedstead an' de baby's cradle to take 'long wid
'em to 'member me by. Dat's de way day does. Long's dey're
in de house dey crowd out everybody else, an' de cat hatter
clam up on de rafters. Dat's what make me want a sign. But
I speck if had a sign bode some o' dese year caydets ud tote
it off, caze de preacher says a weeked an' dultous gineration
seekes' atter a sign."

"How many rooms has your house?"

"Hit ain't got but one. Hit ain't sich a mighty big house,
but hit's a fine un."

"Why don't you paint it?"

"Hit ain't de fashion to paint nothin' dese days. You go
and look in de new college, and you won't see nair spot o'
paint. Hit's all been rubbed wid ile. Dat's de way mine's
gwine to be. When de chillun eats meat, 'stid o' wasin' de
grease washin', I'm gwine to make em rub hit off on de
house[.] Dat way I'll git de whole house greased atter while,
cep'n meat git mighty sca'ce."

"Is your house plastered?"

"Naw, sah. I don't want no plastin' in my house, caze d'is
too many niggers knows how to write dese days. Dey'd git
fire-coals an' scrabble all over dem walls. Now, sah; I'm
gwine to let her stan' like she is tell de spiders hangs pooty
things all roun'. Hit wont take 'em long, caze Ma'jane ain't
gwine to pester 'em."

"Did you get your lumber from Marengo?"

"Naw, sah; hit come f'om de piney woods way down 'bout Little Texas. Hit's pine lumber. Dey don't have no pines down dar in M'ringer. When dey wants to buil' a house dey des cuts down a middlin' size cotton stalk an' hauls hit to de saw mill an' gits hit sawed up[.] Man, sah, dem cotton stalks makes strong houses, too."

"I fear your house will not be very strong."

"Hit ain't so mighty strong, sah, but gin we lives in it a year or two hit'll be strong es Mr. Anybody's house. Hit's got some M'ringer smell 'bout hit now, but de rozzum hit's dar yit. Oh, yas, sah, hit'll be de stronges' house in dis yer town. Ef air storm or slycone come 'long hit better take roundance on dat house, 'cep'n hit want to git boddaciously busted all to flinders. Dat house gwine to grow, too, man. Hit's young now. Hit's des de same size o' all de yuther Aubu'n nigger houses, but hit ain't gwine to stay dat size. I knows what keep dem f'om growin'—dey're weighted down wid morgins, dat's what's de matter wid dem. Tey ain't nair morgin on mine, an' dey ain't gwine to be nairn, 'cep'n folks stops dyin' an' I can't git to dig no graves. I'm hopes I ain't gwine to have no sich bad luck es dat.

"But d'is 'nother thing make me say dat house gwine to grow. I put goanna under ever' pillar, an' I built hit on de increase o' de moon[.] She's boun' to grow, an', ef she'll des hump herse'f an' grow fast es my fambly, I'll be plum satisfy."

(The [Birmingham] *Weekly Age-Herald,* April 30, 1890)

A Legend

How Clarke Played It on Marengo

"Moss Jimmie, yo' garden sas[s] is des a humpin' hitse'f sence de rain. Hit's a gittin' dar, s[h]o'. De dry drouth was a givin' dem English peas fits. I tole Majane so, but she would[n'] believe me. She 'lowed hit was my eyes what was a failin'. Dat what she been a sayin' ever sence I 'lowed dat was a likely gal what come down yer f'om Opelacker an' got me to tote her trunk un f'om de deepo. Majane natchelly 'spise dat gal. She 'spise de groun' dat gal walk on, an' hit's all 'cause I toted her trunk for her an' never charged her nothin'. I tole Majane dat she was de likelies' gal I ever seed dis side o' M'ringer, but Majane she up an' 'lowed my eyes gittin' dim wid ole age. She 'lowed gals was mighty 'ceivin' when dey was dressed up like dat'n was, an' imperticlar ef dey was a ole fool like me a lookin' at 'em. She axed me what de reason I never brought her nair mess o' peas f'om yo' house, an' I tole her de dry drought was mighty nigh done burnt 'em up.

She 'lowed she never b'lieved it; hit was my eyes was gittin' bline. But dem peas was bad scorched, Moss Jimmie, an' you knows it yo'se'f, but dey looks all right dis mornin'. Dey was des a wantin' a rain. Dey was sorter like I is when I aint got no tobacco; dey was all shrivel up. Dat's de way I feels dis mornin'—thanky, sah! Gin I light up my pipe I [']low I'll be renew an' substanchy same es yo' peas is dis mornin'.

"Dem beans is a lookin' right nice, too. Dey aint gwine to be de fines' beans ever I seed, 'caze, you know, I come f 'om down dar in M'ringer, but dey'll be de fines' beans in dis town.

"M'ringer's de bangines' place to make beans in dis newnited worl'. Man, sah, ef de M'ringer folks was des willin' to try, dey could make beans 'nough to do all de worl'. But dey aint gwine to do it, dough. Dey done larn a thing or two. Dey knows how hit 'ud be. Folks 'ud eat up dem beans an des cuss dem what raise 'em, 'caze de beans was too hard, or too saft, or too big. Dat's de way dis ole worl' is. I gin my boy my ole blue coat to be his'n, an' he grumble 'caze de tail o' hit drug de groun'. I des gin hit to him dry so. I lay ef I had a made him wuck for hit he wouldn't a foun' so much fault wid it.

"Folks use to think Clarke was de big bean county, but dey don't think so dese days. Dem folks down dar in Clarke dey use to sell 'bout a million barr'ls o' beans ever' winter. Dey waggins use to come up dar in M'ringer peddlin beans ever' which a way. Dey sole 'em by de quart or by de bushel or by de grab. Us use to have lots o' fun prizin' dem folkses waggins an' mules out'n de mud, case dey warn't usen to nothin' but san', an' time dem mules' feet stuck in de mud a time or two dey more'n ap' to lay down right dar an' quit.

"Well, hit was a plum wonder how dem Clarke folks sole dry beans. Cose de M'ringer folks could a raise de beans, too, but dey was rich an' dey wouldn't take de trouble to gether de beans. Hit look might cui's how Clarke could raise dem many beans, caze she never raise nothin' else es anybody ever yeared 'bout. Clarke was mighty nigh es po' es Lee.

"'Twarn't no trouble to raise beans in M'ringer. We didn't hatter put two bushel o' minyo under ever' vine. I never yeared tell o' goanna down dar. Nobody never knowed what goanna was. De lan' was des a leetle too rich. Dat was all de matter wid hit. De trouble was to gether the beans atter you raise 'em. Dey was so many an' so big, an' de vine hit run up so high nobody never tried to gether all dey raise.

"My ole moster's garden, hit was dat rich de groun' ud eat up a nigger's foot ef he went in dar bar' footed. He never did plant but one bean. Dat was nough, gracious knows. He use to plant dat bean on de lower side o' de garden, right gin de fence. When dat bean come up de fust thing hit done hit clam up on de fence and run long on de fence 'bout 10 foot, till hit got to a tall oak tree in de aidge o' de woods, an' den hit clammed hit.

"Dem beans whar growed on de fence, dey was more 'n any one fambly could 'stroy, an' my ole moster he never pestered de vine nowhars else. He [']lowed he never cared ever hit did clam up dat tree, an' he pester hisse'f ef hit run off thoo de woods, des so hit lef' 'nough beans for him on de fence.

"Dey was a man down dar in de settlement name o' Mr. Rumpless. One day in de summer time Mr. Rumpless he come dar to ole moster's house, an' he 'lowed he been down in Clarke, an' he nodis particlar dey warn't nair bean growin' in nair garden dar.

"Ole moster he up an' 'lowed dat was mighty cu'is, caze de talk was Clarke was de fines' kine o' bean lan', an' he's seed 'em hissef bringin' beans up in M'ringer by de waggin load.

"Mr. Rumpless he 'lowed he been studyin' 'bout dat, caze he been a buyin' dry beans from dem Clarke fellers ever winter. He 'lowed he b'lieve dey was some trick 'bout it; he was scared hit warn't beans he been a buyin' f'om 'em.

"My ole marster axed him what he reckon hit was ef hit warnt beans.

"Mr. Rumpless he 'lowed he 'spicion hit was ox vomit, caze ox vomit look sorter like beans, an' dey was lots o' steers down dar in Clarke.

"My ole marster he des 'lowed, 'Shucks!' much ez to say dat was all nonsense, an' de onlies' reason Mr. Rumpless never seed no beans in dem Clarke gardens hit was caze his eyes was givin' out.

"Anyhow, Mr. Rumpless 'lowed ef he live to see nex' fall he was gwine down dar in Clarke, an' he was gwine to see whar dem folks gethered all dem beans f'om.

"An' he went, too.

"I rickerleck de day he come back mighty well. Hit was in de fall o' de year, an' dey aint nair bean waggin come fo'm Clarke yit. Ole moster he was a settin' out on his pieazer when Mr. Rumpless rid up an' hollered:

"'Yer I is, ole man. I done been done in de great bean country what dey calls Clarke, and what I dunno' hit aint wuth knowin'.'

"'What does you know 'bout beans?' my ole moster says.

"'I knows a heap,' Mr. Rumpless says; says he, 'I knows folks down in Clarke don't raise none.'

"'How's dat?' my ole moster says, says he. 'I'm sho dey brings 'em up yer to sell.'

"'Dat's so,' Mr. Rumpless says, 'but dey don't raise 'em,' says he. 'You know when anybody raise anything dey lifts hit up, but Clarke folks de don't lift up no beans; all dey has to do dey pulls de beans down.'

"'I don't see into dat,' my ole moster says.

"'I don't reckon you does,' Mr. Rumpless says. 'But what ud you say ef I was to tell you dem beans what we buys f 'om Clarke folks grows up in de tops o' trees?' says he.

"'Dat ain't no[t]hin',' ole moster says, says he, 'bean vines runs up in trees constant,' says he, 'an' ef you was to go out yander by my garden fence now, I wouldn't be surprise ef you didn't see my bean vine done clam up in dat oak tree.'

"'Dat's so,' Mr. Rumpless says, 'I done been out dar and seed it, an' dat's what make I says I knows a heap 'bout dem beans what dem Clarke folks gethers to sell to we all in de winter time.'

"Wid dat he up an' narrate all 'bout his trip to Clarke. De folks was des gethin' beans when he got dar. Ever' which a way he look he seed folks up in de trees wid cotton sacks on 'em, des a pullin' beans. He was 'stonish', case dem beans was right in de middle o' de big woods.

"He looked an' he looked, case he warnt willin' to b'lieve his own eyes at fust. But atter w'ile he foun' out dey warnt but one bean vine, an' hit run f 'om one tree to an'er. He looked at one o' dem trees an' he knowed whar hit come f 'ome time he seed hit, caze dey warnt but one man what had dem sort.

"When he foun' dat out he des turn his horse 'roun' an' foll[e]red dat bean vine back all de way to my ole moster's garden in M'ringer.

"Dat was de las' winter dem Clarke folks ever sole any dry beans in M'ringer, 'caze ole moster had dat oat tree cut down, an' we never let dat bean vine git off 'n' de garden fence no mo'. I cut de tree down myse'f.

"Moss Jimmie, ef you don't b'lieve what I tell you you go

down dar in M'ringer an' look right side o' ole moster's garden fence an' you'll see de stump o' dat tree, an' hit's got my handwrite on it whar I put dar wid my ax."

(The [Birmingham] *Weekly Age-Herald,* May 14, 1890)

Underground Farming

"I say, Jake, do the crawfishes ever destroy the cotton crops down in Marengo?"

"What make you ax dat question, boss?"

"Because I saw something like it in the Birmingham paper not long ago. A man wrote from Faunsdale that the crawfishes were ruining the cotton in the bottom lands. He said they pulled the young stalks down into their holes and eat 'em up."

"Right dar dat ar man was mistooken. Crawfishes don't 'stroy cotton stalks. Dey're to smart for dat. Yah! yah! yah! Crawfish sorter like a nigger. If you hire a nigger to hoe out yo' bean patch and tell him to 'stroy everything c[e]ptin' de bean vines, I say he'll go for de weeds and de crab grass, but if he find air watermillion vine er cotton stalk he'll sho leave 'em right dar. You can't make a nigger 'stroy dem two things, case he thinks hit 'ud be bad luck.

"Well, a crawfish he's nigh 'bout es smart es a nigger—I

mean des yer common niggers like we has 'roun' Aubu'n, scusin' dem sort down dar in M'ringer. Crawfish kin walk backuds sames es fowuds, an' hit don't make no diffunce wid dem which een's up. Whatever a nigger kin do on top o' de ground' a crawfish kin do under de dirt[.] I wouldn't be s'prised ef dey aint some mighty rich crawfishes down dar in M'ringer by dis time. I most know dey is.

"No, sah, dat man whar writ dat letter f 'om Fonsdale, he don't know dem M'ringer crawfishes like I does. Wonst 'pon a time I thought des like him, but I done foun' out better, I done seed wid my own eyes, an' I knows.

"Dey use to been a man down dar name or Mr. Rumpless, an' he had a big slipe o' bottom lan' an' ever year he [']lowed de crawfishes eat up all his cotton. He come to ole moster one spring, he did, an' he [']lowed he be dad burn ef de crawfishes warnt 'bout to ruin him, pulling de cotton stalks down in dey holes an' eaten' up, an' he ax my ole moster what mus' he do 'bout it.

"My old moster he scratch his haid aw'ile an' toreckly he up and [']low:

"'I got a mighty smart nigger name o' Jake; I'll loan him to you dis spring, an' maybe he kin fine some way to stop de rabbidges[.]'

"Dem was de very words ole moster said.

"Well, I went over dar to Mr. Rumpless' plantation, I did, an' I tuck my stan' in his bottom lan' to watch how de crawfish was gwine to do.

"I hide myself in a deep ditch, caze I knowed de crawfishes ud be sorter bashful if dey seed me.

"Well, I never hatter wait long. Time I got down in de ditch dey mence, an' man, sah! I never is seed sich fast work in a cotton patch befo'. I staid dar tell I done foun' out all dey ways, an' den I went back an' I tole Mr. Rumpless he neenter be no ways oneasy, caze ef he des lef de case to me I'd sho git ahead o' dem crawfishes fore hit was time to go to market.

"Mr[.] Rumpless he warnt zackly satisfy, but my ole moster he up an' [']lowed:

"'You kin pen' 'pon anything Jake say, case smart aint no name for dat nigger. He's de peartes boy in M'ringer!'

"Wen Mr. Rumpless yeared dat he never had nair nother word to say; he des turn his bottom lan' over to me, and dat how come Mr. Rumpless got so eberlastin' rich[.] I'm de casion o' him a savin 'bout a thousan' bales o' cotton ever year."

"How did you do i[t]?"

"I s'rrounded dem crawfish. I did dat. I made em work for me des like dey was niggers, an' I was Mr. Rumpless' overseer. Yas, sah; I fooled dem crawfish.

"Whilst I was a stannin' dar in dat ditch I seed de cotton stalks des a drappin, des like sump[i]n' was a pullin' 'em down in crawfish holes. I says to myself, 'Hayo!' Says I: 'I speck hits des like Mr. Rumpless say; de crawfishes is a eatin' up all o' his cotton!'

"I walk on down de ditch toreckly to see ef hit was gwine on de same way all over de plantation. Man, sah! hit was wusser an' wusser de furder I went. Some places dey warn't nair stalk lef' a stannin'.

"Well, sah, I rooted roun' dar tell de fust thing you know I foun' a big hole in de bank. I looked in dat hole, an' man, sah! I never is seed sich a sight befo'. Hit warn't a blessed thing but des a cave 'bout two time es big es Aubu'n. Hit was a reg'lar crawfish plantation. Hit look des zackly like a big coal mine—only I ain't never seed nair'n, but I've yeared deze yer niggers whar been convick talk 'bout coal mines.

"I des squatted dar an' look an' look, I was scared to go in dar at fust, caze dey was crawfishes 'nough in dar to eat up a man boddaciously. An dey was a hustlin too, mon. Dey never eat no idle bread. Ever' little ole baby crawfish was busy, yit. I've seed niggers work tolerable peart wen de overseer was straight behine em wid a big whup, but man, sah! I never seed no niggers work like dem crawfishes.

"Dey was vide off in gangs, an ever gang hit had a fo'man, same es niggers fo' freedom come out. Dat fo'man he kep' em gwine. Wen dey got anywhars an want to come b[a]ck, dey never stop to turn roun'; dey des run backuds."

"What were they doing?"

"Dey was farmin'."

"Farming?"

"Dey was dat. Dey was pitchin' dey crap. Some was boin' holes thoo de top o' de groun', an' some was a clammin' up dem holes an' a pullin' de cotton stalks down thoo de holes. An' dar de cotton stalks was, des es natchel, only dey wus upside down. Day was a good stan' o' cotton dar, too, mon. Dey warn't nair stalk missin' hardly.

"D'you see dem crawfishes; dey laid right still tell atter Mr. Rumpless done chop his cotton to a stan', den dey start to pullin' it thoo. Dey was sharp. D[e]y didn't want de trouble o' choppin' cotton out. Dey 'lowed dey'd let folks whar warn't es smart es dey was do all de hard work.

"De cotton hit was stannin' in dar bottom up, but hit was growin' des like hit been usen to stannin' on hit's haid all hit's born days.

"I watch dat cave all de year, but I never tole Mr. Rumpless what I was gwine to do, caze dat warn't none o' his business.

"In de fall o' de year I seed de crawfishes pickin' cotton. You never seed such a sight es dat, is you, boss?"

"I should say not."

"Well, sah, you aint never seed no fast pickin' den. A

crawfish kin pick cotton wid his claws dat fast hit make a nigger shame to look at him.

"I 'mence to study 'bout how dey was gwine to gin dat cotton, caze I never seed no gin house nowhars 'bout. But dat never pester de crawfishes, caze dey knowed a thing or two I ain't dreamed 'bout yit. I seed 'em gatherin' lots o' grass, but I never knowed what dey gwine to do wid it. I found out, dough, bimeby. I seed 'em weavin baggin' out'n hit. Yas, sah, dey weave des es good a baggin' as air 'liance in dis country 'ud want. Pine straw ain't nowhar. An' please gracious, dey wropped up de cotton in dat baggin' and hit ain't seed nair gin yit. I was stonished. Sholey dem crawfish ought to a had mo sense'n dat. Nobody ain't gwine to buy seed cotton packed dat way. De crawfishes dey never pestered deysef 'bout dat. Hit warn't de fust cotton crap dey ever made.

"I done study out how dey gwine to take de cotton to market. Dey was a right smart river runnin' under dar, an' de crawfishes dey had plenty o' flatboats.

"W'en dey mense to load up dem flat boats wid cotton bales I slipped off up home an' tole all my folks good-bye. I tole ole moster not to grieve atter me, caze law knows dey warn't no tellin' whar I was a gwine. I might be gwine to heben, but hit was a mighty downud cose to git dar.

"I wrop myse'f up in a blanket, an' I laid down mongst de cotton bales on one o' dem flat boats, an' atter w'ile dey start. I had me some grub 'long an' a little o' dat stuff what always go on a flat boats to cyo snake bites. Sides dat I had de all-firedest bigges' seine anybody ever seed. Hit was big 'nough to have kivered Vaughn's mill pond.

"Well, we went on, we did, down dat roover. We kep on a gwine, we kep on a gwine, an' hit look like we never was a gwine to git to a stoppin' place. Dem crawfish dey sung an' dey talk an' dey drink liquor same es anybody else on a flat boat. I larn how to talk crawfish good es anybody fo' we got whar we was gwine.

"Bimeby all de flat boats stop right agin one aner, an' I knowed hit was time for me to be a doin' sumpin, 'sides layin' dar sleepin'.

"I got up, I did, an' I was des es easy es I could be. I spread dat seine all over dem flat boats, an' I fasten her down.

"Toreckly I yeared somebody holler:

"'Hello, down dar.'

"De crawfishes dey hollered back at him.

"'What you got down dar?' says he.

"'A thousan' bale o' cotton,' says de crawfi[s]hes. 'What's hit gwine to fetch?'

"'Twenty cent a poun',' says he.

"'What you givin' for crawfish meat?' says I.

"'Crawfishes is worth a cent apiece,' says he.

"'All right,' says I, 'I'll sell you a thousan' bale o' cotton an' 'bout fo' million crawfishes I got down yer,' says I.

"When de crawfishes yeared dat you never seed sich a scramlin' to git way in all yo' bo'n days. But dey was dar to stay. I had 'em all dar safe in dat seine.

"Hit turn out we was done got to Mobile and I sole out all dat cotton an' all dem crawfishes, an' when I got on de cars to go home I was dat loaden down wid money I couldn't hardly walk, let 'lone de groceries I had to tote. But I tuck all dat money to Mr. Rumpless, an' dat's how come him so rich."

"And now you have wound yourself up. You said that cotton wasn't ginned."

"Did I say dat, boss?"

"Yes, you did, and you needn't try to deny it."

"Well, bless gracious! I b'lieve I did for a fack."

"You forgot that time."

"Y[a]s, sah, I did. I forgot to tell you when cotton grew upside down hit don't never make no seed, an' dat's de reason dem crawfishes never had to gin it.

"Boss, if you study up anything else whar Jake forgit, don't you be bashful 'bout it. You up an' ax me, an' I'll more'n ap to tell you all 'bout it[.]"

(The [Birmingham] *Weekly Age-Herald,* June 25, 1890)

Jake's Senses

"I des now made out what Mr. Winston's atter. I been a seein' him bruisin' round wid a big bag hangin' on his neck, but I never knowed what he was up to. I 'lowed maybe he done got pinted marshal agin. He is been marshal wonst. Last Jinnerwerry we 'lected a new mayor and council, and I yeared some say we was gwine to have a new set of audiences fo' long. Mr. Borrikin he was de ole marshal, he kept on a totin de club and pirootin' 'roun town of a night des like he been a doin'—an' he's marshal yit. Ef you don't believe me you des git up a row whar he can see you.

"But when I seed Mr. Winston gwine 'bout and poking his nose in all de nigger cabins, I say to myself, says I:

"'Jake, you better keep one eye skint on Mr. Winston, caze he aint a totin' dat bag for nothin'. He's a huntin' for sump'n' whar somebody stole, an' if he luck to fine hit, he'll be mo'n ap to clap hit in dat bag he got dar hangin' roun' his neck.'

"I warn't oneasy, fur es I was consarn, caze d'is two things I never does do: I never steals an' I never tells no lies. I never 'spicion' Mr. Winston was gwine to come to my house. Dey warn't nothin' dar for him to come atter. I tole Ma'jane so. But he come, dough. Yas, sah, he did dat. 'An he brung dat bag long, too. I sot dar in de do', an' I watched him a comin'. I says to myse'f:

"'Dat ar white man's a runnin' on a mighty cole trail. If he's a huntin' for watermillion whar somebody done tuck, he wont fine nair' piece o' rime yer, yit, an' es for fryin' size chickens, he aint gwine to fine nair' f[e]ather 'cep'n dem whar come off 'n de chickens Ma'jane raise, 'an she never raise 'em off 'n nobody's roos', neither[.]'

"De nigher he come de wusser I was pestered[.] Seem like all de devilment ever I done in my born days ris up right dar in my mine.

"I never is seed de eenside o' dat ole calaboose, an' I'm hopes I never will. I aint done nuthin' to be put in dar fur. Some folks thinks I talks a leetle too much, an' some says I tells lies 'bout M'ringer, but dey can't prove it. A white lady come to see me not long ago, an' she 'lowed she want me to quit tellin' dem big lies to Moss Wilbur Burton, caze Moss Wilbur ain't got no better sense 'n to put 'em in de Burnin'ham paper, an' dat way ever'body what read 'em is 'ceived in dey mines. I promised her I warn't gwine to tell him nair 'nother lie, an' I aint, nei[t]her. Ef you see anything in de paper what Jake tole, you kin des set it down hit's de rummunt truth.

"Dat was all I could study bout es I sot dar and watch Mr. Winston clammin up de hill todes my new house, an' I made sho dat lady sent him dar to rest me for lyin.' But dat never pester me much, caze dat was de truth I tole 'bout d[e]m crawfish raisin' cotton, an' ef anybody don't b'lieve it, des let him come to my house an' I'll show 'em one o' de crawfish laigs.

"Mr. Winston he kep a comi[n]', he did, an' toreckly he put one foot on my do' step, an he lowed:

"'Jak[e], I'm a takin' de fo[l]kes senses.'

"Man, sah! dat like to a scared me out o' ten year growth. Long es I stays yer dat's one thing I [']lows to keep ef I kin. I sees a right smart o' folks knockin' 'bout dout any sense, but I don't want to try my han' at it. Es for me, when I loses my senses I want somebody to sen' me to de 'sylum an' let 'em doctor on my haid[.] D'aint no use o' livin' ef you aint got no sense.

"Mr. Winston he never wait for me to say nair word. He look like he come atter my senses, an' he boun' to git 'em. He retch down in dat bag an' he pull out 'bout de biges' book ever I seed outside o' M'ringer, an' he [']lowed:

"'I'm gwine to take down you' senses in dis yer book.'

"Des den I see how de lan' lay. Mr. Winston speck to write a book, an' he want to put in dat book all de sense o' de smartes' folks in Aubu'n. Man, sah! dat'll be de sensibles book ever anybody seed in dis country.

"Mr. Winston [']lowed:

"'What you' name?'

"I says: 'Law! Mr. Winston, you been a knowin' me all dis time an' you ax me what my entitle?'

"'I knows yo' name,' says he, 'but I want to year you state hit[.]'

"'All right,' says I, 'ef dat what you want, hit's state o' Lee county, Alabama, used to be M'ringer, an' folks call me M'ringer Jake, an' when I gits a letter hit's corrected to Jake Mitchell.'

"He writ all dat down on a big piece o' paper, an den he says:

"'Is you white or colored?'

"Dat sorter stump me. Hit got plum away wid me[.] I've went head many a time answ'in hard queshuns, but dat'n was a huckleberry over my 'simmon.

"I studied awhile, an' toreckly I up an' says:

"'Is you talkin' 'bout how I was down dar in M'ringer, or is you talkin' 'bout how I is now?'

"'Talkin' bout how you is now,' says he.

"'Well, den,' says I, 'w'en I was down dar in M'ringer I was migh[t]y nigh a w'ite man,' says I, 'but sence I been up yer de sun's bleach me dat bad I'm bleege to go for a nigger,' says I, 'an' mo'n dat,' says I, 'I use to been over 6 foot high, an' now des but look how I'm swunk[.]'

"Mr[.] Winston writ all dat down des like I tole him, an den he says:

"'Whar was you born at?'

"Dem queshuns was a comin' harder an harder, Mr. Winston's a mighty smart man, an ef he des had a been raise down dar in M'ringer I wouldn't be supprise ef he hadn't a been de jedge o' de cote right now. He kin ax queshuns wusser'n air Opelacker lawyer.

"'Is I got to answer dat queshun?' says I.

"'Yes,' says he. 'Ef you don't you'll be put in jail.'

"'Well, den,' says I, 'I don't zactly recolleck back to de t[i]me wen' I was born, caze dat happen wen I was tolerable young. D'is always been a spute bout it,' says I. 'De fust time I was born hit was in ole Virginny,' says I. 'I knows dat case Gen'l Lee said so wid his own mouf. But atter I went to M'ringer I was born again same es a chile o' grace at a stracted meetin,' says I.

"No sooner Mr. Winston got all dat put down he up and says:

"'I spose you's de head boss o' dis house?'

"I leave it to anybody ef dat was a fair queshun.

"I dassent turn roun' an' look in de house to see what was

gwine on in dar; but Ma'jane she been a sweepin', an' de minute she yeared dat queshun I yeared de broom stop. I knowed des zackly how she was a stanin' holdin' dat heavy broom stick an' lisnin' to see what I was gwine to say, I was right smart dashed, I was.

"'I say,' says I.

"'I've yeared tell de one whar rock de cradle most, in ginnerly rule de roos'.'

"Mr. Winston he writ dat down an' den he come at me agin.

"'What's yo' perfession?' says he.

"'I done been turned out'n de church,' says I.

"'What do you do for a livin'?' says he.

"'You aint got room to put all I does in dat book,' says I.

"'Aint you des a common lab'rer?' says he.

"'Naw, sah,' says I. 'I'm de oncommones' han' to cut grass an' set out tater slips an' dig graves ever you see. You kin put it down ef anybody want to die dey kin git dey grave dug cheap ef dey'll des call on M'ringer Jake.'

"Down dat went.

"'Is you got any kine o' zease?' says he.

"'I got a right smart o' mis'ry in my lef' knee,' says I. 'Dat's how come I'm a layin' up today. But I done rubbed hit wid cassene ile, an' I reckon hit'll be all right gin anybody want a grave dig.'

"'Who own dis house?' says he.

"'M'ringer Jake,' says I.

"'Is hit got air cumb'ance on hit?' says he.

"'Naw, sah,' says I, 'but dey aint no danger o' hit blowin' 'way, caze hit got a morgin on hit to hole hit down.'

"'What yo' wife name?' says he.

"'Ma'jane,' says I.

"'What kin is she to you?' says he.

"Look like he was termed to pin me down cloast.

"'Me an' her warnt no kin 'fore we was spliced,' says I; 'we was des sorter camilious. We taken sich a likin' to one aner de preacher jined us, an' we been gittin' 'long mighty well ever sence, cep'n sometimes I goes off on a 'scurgion, an' you know de gals bleege to look at a likely man wid his Sunday cloes on, an' impartic'lar ef dey don't know he's got a wife at home. But Ma'jane neenter pester herse'f 'bout de gals an' me. I knows ef me an' her was to git revoce dis yer house 'ud be her'n.'

"'Is yo' wife white or colored?'" says he.

"W'en dat queshun come out I cotch sight o' Ma'jane out in de cornder o' my left e[y]e and I knowed sump'n warnt gwine on like she want hit to. Anybody kin tell w'en Ma'jane's flustrate, c[a]ze she looks like one o' dese yer slycoon clouds, an' de lightnin' flashes outer her eyes. If sump'n aint done tolerble quick, d' is mo'n ap' to be a dust raise ef de top of somebody's house don't git blowed off.

"'My wife's plum white,' says I. 'You see h[e]r dar, she look like a ginger-cake complected lady, but dat's caze de winder curtains in my house is red,' says I, 'but you ought to see her diked,' says I, 'an' you'd be ashame you ax me dat queshun.'

"'What's yo' chillun's name?' says he.

"Bout dat time Ma'jane she up an' went out in de garden to gether beans for dinner, an' I want sorry. You know a man don't like to answer all sorts o' queshuns fo' his wife[.] Women is mighty cuis critters.

"M[a]'jane she was done los' interest in dat talk, an' she done gone in de garden. I says, says I:

"'Is you talkin' 'bout dem what was born down dar in M'ringer, or does you des mean dem whar was born in Aubu'n?'

"'I means all ob 'em,' says he.

"'Well, den,' says I, 'you put 'em down toler'ble peert,'

says I, "caze dey was a right smart chance o' chillun call me pappy down dar in M'ringer. Dar was black Tobe an' yaller Tobe an' ginger-cake Tobe an' lef' han' Tobe an' big Tobe an' little Tobe an' twin Tobe—'

"Man, sah, Mr. Winston stop me 'fo' I got ha'f thoo wid de Tobes.

"'Call some yuther name sides Tobe,' says he, 'dat make me giddy,' says he.

"'All right,' says I, 'but you mights es well let me git thoo,' says I, 'caze dey want but seben mo' Tobes.'

"'What you name so many Tobe fer?' says he.

"'I never named 'em,' says I, 'dey mammies named 'em. I d[o]n't never spute wid a 'oman 'bout namin' a baby,' says I. 'Dey ginnerly knows who's de mammy o' de babies, an' dey ought to name 'em,' says I.

"'Call over some different names,' says he.

"'All right,' says I, 'I'll call some gal names,' says I[.] 'Dar's Tildy an' Tiny, an' Tip an' Tup, an' Coot an' Plum, an' F[li]rtin' Ann Repoleon—'

"'Name o' sense,' says he, 'was you de daddy o' de whole county of M'ringer?'

"'Naw sah,' says I, 'des lots of niggers down dar in M'ringer 'sides mine, but ef you go down dar 'bout Mr. Rumpless' plantation, I wouldn't be supprise ef you didn't see a right smart chance o' likely boys an' gals whar favor Jake, an' I never go back on my favor. Mr. Rumpless had 'bout the likeliest gals in de settlement, an' ever time I married one o' dem gals, ef me an' her didn't gee haw, I'd quit her an' marry another'n. I ain't a braggin',' says I, 'but folks says dat how come Mr. Rumpless got so everlastin' rich.

"'You kin jedge for yo'self,' says I, 'ef I'm a male or a shemale.'"

(The *Birmingham Age-Herald*, July 6, 1890)

Jake Heard From

Marengo Melons and How They Made Mr. Humphrey's Fortune

 "Dis yer's watermillion time o' year agin," remarked Jake, halting at the corner and surveying a street blockaded with wagons.

"Hit sho' is," assented a bystander, named Johnson.

It may be remarked parenthetically that Mr. Johnson is always unanimous on the subject of watermelons, and the very slightest prospect of a treat is sufficient to divert him from the never very serious business with which he happens to be occupied.

"Hit'll be my time to set me up next time," continued Mr. Johnson. "Right now at dis present time I'm like I yeared a caydet say he was wonst."

"How was dat?" inquired Jake.

"He lowed he was firanchilly imbarrass," and by way of illustrating his meaning, Mr. Johnson turned his trouser pockets wrong side out.

"Dey tells me watermillions is pizen sickly dis year," remarked Jake.

"I'm willin' to resk 'em ef anybody willin' to furnish de scads," said Mr. Johnson.

"You aint usened to watermillions like dis," said Jake.

"What de reason I aint?" inquired Johnson.

"Caze you aint never lived in M'ringer, whar watermillions grows in bunnance," said Jake.

"Don't care ef I aint, I've lived in Flurridy," said Mr[.] Johnson, indignantly.

"Flurridy is Flurridy," said Jake sententiously, "but M'ringer hit's a different thing. I've yeared tell dey was a right smart chance o' some things in Flurridy, sich es alligators an' pine trees an' frogs, but wen hit come to watermillions, Flurridy aint no whar side o' M'ringer."

Mr. Johnson uttered a prolonged grunt.

"H-u-m-ph! Dat what you say. Dat's all you knows about Flurridy. You aint never been dar. You aint never seed waggins an cyarts an wheelborrers haulin' watermillions and mushmillions to de depot all day an part o' de night. You aint never seed whole trains wid sebenteen cyars all [l]oaded up wid nothin' but watermillions f'om one een to de yuther, and hit got hit's haid pinted up north to take em to de big cities."

"How come I aint?" inquired Jake.

"Caze you aint never been in Flurridy."

"Dat's right," admitted Jake. "You plumped the middle man out dat time, but you aint got de game yit. To taw hit de groun on de wrong side o' de dead line. He! Haw! Haw! De folks down in Flurridy day be dat po' dey hatter sell all de watermillions dey raises to git money to buy bread. Dey dassent to keep a little ole similin to eat yit[.] Down dar in Mringer, de onlies reason dey don't ship train loads o' watermillions off hit's caze dey aint got no casion to. Dey got money nough. Dey aint no po' crackers."

"Is all de M'ringer folks got money?"

"Cose dey is."

"I'm sho glad to year dat, caze I knowed you was a M'ringer man an I was scared you never had de scads to buy us one o' dem in dis yander waggin."

"If ever you sees a M'ringer man whar ain't got bunnance money, you des fetch him to me. He'll be des es good a show es I want to see, an' I'll give you a quarter des to let me look at him[.] You ain't gwine to fine nair'n, dough. An' more'n dat, you ain't never gwine to fine nair M'ringer man whar pay money for watermillions. Shucks! Hit ain't down dar like hit is up yer. I've seed dese yere country folks come five mile up yer to Aubu'n des to buy a fi' cent watermillion, and de grass runnin' way wid dey craps. Ef you was down dar in M'ringer a plowin', an' you was to git watermillion hongry, all you'd hatter do, you'd des hatter tell yo' mule to wo, an' stoop down an' pick up one off'n de groun'. I've seed de cotton rows packed dat tight wid wa[t]ermillions tell you couldn't plow 'em. Hit's a fact, sah, des like I tells you. My ole moster lost seben mules dat way in one day wonst."

"How?"

"Dey was plowin' cotton, an' dey stumbled 'gin watermillions an' fell down."

"Ef dem had a been fine mules hit wouldn't a killed 'em des to fall down," shrewdly observed Mr[.] Johnson. "Dey warn't no 'count."

"Yes, dey was, too. Hit warn't de fallin' down whar killed 'em[.] Ef dey des had a fell down on de dirt dey wouldn't a hardly grunted. But dey fell on a big watermi[l]lion an' de rime broke thoo' an' dey got drownded in watermillion juice."

"Dat must a been a sho' juicy watermillion."

"All de M'ringer watermi[l]lions is juicy. Dey ain't like

dese yer watermi[ll]ions roun' yer whar got so many seeds in 'em dey breaks yo' teeth out to eat 'em. Dat's how come I ain't no mo' teeth an I is right now. I ain't gwine to eat no mo' of 'em, caze I'm scared I'll break out my gums."

"I'm willin' to resk my gums on 'em."

"Ef M'r[i]nger watermillions had a been like dese up yer my ole moster ud a got busted one year."

"How come?"

"'Case dey was a dry drout dat summer, an' de corn an' de cotton hit like to a got burnt up off 'n de face o' de yeth[.] De groun' was des like a bank o' ashes, an' a big win' come long an' blowed off a right smart o' M'ringer dirt down in Clarke, an' ef you'll fine de spot whar dat dirt lit at, you'll see de riches lan' in Clarke."

Jake paused a moment, and Mr[.] Johnson as if awakening from a brown study, remarked:

"I reckon I sees how dat was. Dat was one year M'ringer folks warnt too proud to peddle watermillions. Yo ole moster never made no corn an' cotton, but he sole his watermillions, an' dat kept him f 'om starvin'."

"Dat'll do toler'ble well for a Fluridy nigger," said Jake, contemptuously. "Nobody neent'n to speck no better[.]"

"How did he do, den?"

"How did my ole moster do? He des turned all his niggers in de fiel's an' tole 'em to pull out dey knives an' go to slashin' watermillions open. We slashed 'em, too, an' wen we got done de groun' was dat boggy we couldn't hardly git out o' dar. De watermillion juice wet de groun' two feet deep."

Mr[.] Johnson scratched his head in a perplexed way. He seemed to have had a very beautiful [B]armecide feast, but neither the region encircled by his rope belt nor his hungry eyes and watering mouth expressed satiety. He staid awhile longer, r[e]sting first on one foot and then on the other, pondering the situation, and then as Jake made a motion as if to go, he arrested him with the remark:

"Looks like ef dem M'ringer folks was es smart es you makes out like dey was, dey would a got big rich on watermillions."

"Dey was one man whar did, an' he never sole nair' watermillion, neithe[r]."

"Well, I like to know how he done it, den."

"Well, dat man was name' Mr[.] Rumpless, an' he had 'bout a hundred niggers to start on. We'n he got done wid his watermillion crap, he had two hundred."

"Sole watermillions an' bought an'er hundred?"

"I tole you he never sole nair' watermillion."

"Swapped watermillions for niggers eben steben?"

"Naw; he des made his niggers eat watermillions, an' de wotermillions was 'prizen sickly dat year, an' dey doubled de niggers up."

(The *Birmingham Age-Herald*, July 27, 1890)

A Lesson in Natural History

 Marengo Jake appeared in the street the other day holding in his hand an oblong pasteboard box, in the lid of which three slots had been cut. Without saying a word, he held out the box toward a group of men standing in front of a store. The act was suggestive, the expression of Jake's countenance quizzical, and nobody seemed disposed to take the proffered box. It looked too much like one of those put a nickel-in-the-slot devices, and if it had been in the hands of any other man of equal rank and color, a church collection would have been immediately suggested to every beholder. But Jake's religion, if any he has, is not of so practical a turn, and as his fame in another direction is well established, it was easier to believe that he was bent upon practicing some innocent deceit on his white friends.

He stood perfectly still for several minutes and nobody dared to say a word. Finally, seeing that the white men were determined not to risk anything in exploring the mystery, he gently lifted the lid of the box and disclosed to view a Texas horned frog. Everybody was astonished. It is well known that east Alabama is not the habitation of that animal, though frogs of divers sorts abound.

The group of men gathered closely around Jake and viewed the frog with wonder and curiosity.

"Where did you get it?"

"Is it alive?"

"What are you going to do with it?"

"What is it?"

"How long have you had it?"

These and other questions were propounded with confusing rapid[it]y. But the Marengo sage never lost his head.

"Dis yer's a M'ringer frog," he said. "Hit's 'live. Ef you don't b'lieve it, you des tech him on his horns. He'll hook you in a minute. I cotch him in de grass. Dey ain't nair' 'nother'n like him in dis country. I dunno how come dis'n yer, 'cep'n he come up f 'om M'ringer wid some o' dese yer caydets. Ef Mr. Watlin'ton had a been yer, I'd a made sho he fotch him in his pocket, but Mr. Watlin'ton done got his eddication an' I wouldn't be supprise' ef he ain't done married an' raisin' up a fambly by dis time. Anyhow, hit's a M'ringer frog, only hit mus' be a mighty young un, 'cep'n hit swunk sence hit got yer. Down dar in M'ringer dey grows es big es de common run o' [s]teers, an' folks has to stan' out'n de way when dey comes 'long, don't dey'll git hooked. De cows is scared ob 'em yit.

"Look how flat dis'n's a squattin' in de box. I don't blame him for being scared. I'd be scared too ef I was in his fix. Ef anybody was to shet me up in a box wid des some little holes for me to draw my bref thoo, I'd mence to study bout all de devilment I been a doin all my life, caze hit'd look mighty like my een was done come. Dis yer frog dunno what I'm gwine to do wid him. I speck I'm gwine to sell him to Mr. Fessor Mell, but hit wouldn't hep his feelins none ef I was to tell him so, caze he wouldn't know but what Mr. Fessor Mell was gwine to eat him. Some folks does eat frogs. Ef I was to tell him I was gwine to turn him loose, he wouldn't be hope up much, caze more'n ap he'd starve to death cepin he kin eat rocks. Down dar in Mringer dey eats grass, but dey don't fool long wid no little [o]ommooda like dat whar grows in folkses' yards up yer. Hit's too short. Dey'd break off dey horns tryin to root hit up out'n de groun. I'm talkin bout a big frog like dey is down in Mringer. Dis little feller might could git a few mouffuls wonst in a wile, but he never would grow no bigger'n he is now.

"I knows what he's studyin'. He's got M'ringer sense ef he is little. He speck me to sell him to Mr. Fessor Mell, an' he low he'll be kep' in de college for folks to look at. Atter wile he speck to git quainted wid de caydets, an he know in reason he'll git a chance to go home long o' some boy whar live in M'ringer. I'm hopes he will, but I want to git my money out'n him fust.

"I reckon you-all thinks hit's mighty cuis I'm de onliest one whar ever cotch a frog like dis up yer. But I knows de reason o' dat. Dis yer frog let me ketch him purpozely. He been a layin' dar in dat grass I dunno how long, waitin' for somebody to come long whar smelt like M'ringer folks. Time he smelt me he come hoppin' to me. He warn't no ways bashful. I speck he yeared tell o' me fo' ever he lef' M'ringer, an' he knowed me time he seed me. I was tolerbly well quainted wid de horny frogs wen' I lived down dar in M'ringer. Me an' dem use to have big times long o' one an'er. I never is tole nobody how me an' dese yer sort o' frogs hope a man down dar to git rich. I kep' dat to myse'f, caze my ole moster would a got ashy wid me ef he had a knowed 'bout it. He'd a lowed I b'long to him, an' all de money I made, ef I make hit wid my han's or wid my smartness, hit was his'n. But ole moster he's dead now, an' I don't care who know it.

"Down dar in M'ringer dey was a man name' Mr. Rumpless. He warnt so mighty rich like dem yuther M'ringer folks, but he own one gingercake gal whar look like she was made out'n poun'cake an' candy. Man, sah, dat was de likeles gal ever I seed, but y'all neenter tell Ma'jane I said so. When she walk she bounce same es a Injy-rubber ball. Her lips was 2 inches thick, an' dey was dat red dey look like one o' dem big roses in Mr. Lupkin's yard.

"I laid off to have dat gal ef she'd have me, an' she warnt no ways contrady 'bout it. She 'lowed I was de peertes' young man she seed. But Mr. Rumpless he up an' 'lowed no nigger shouldn't have dat gal cep'n he done sumpn' mighty smart.

"Dat was de way de lan' laid.

"Well, I studied, I did, an' toreckly I had de thing all fixed up. I knowed whar' de horny frogs had dey trompin' groun' at. Hit was in a big bottom whar' de grass growed 'bout 15 foot high. I went down dar', I did, an' I tuck a good look at 'em. I seed dey'd do for what I wanted wid 'em. All dey need was a little 'tention. I counted 'em. Dey was 400 big an' little. De grown uns was des 'bout es big es dese yer steers you sees Gill Finley han'lin' lumber wid. De young uns was all sizes. Some warn't no bigger'n dis'n. But, man sah! you never is seed nothin' grow es fast es dem things does down dar in M'ringer. A little un like dis'n ull git es big es a fice in a week.

"I went to work, I did. I cotch de young uns, an' I fooled wid 'em tell I got 'em plum gentle. W'en dey got a little bigger I yoked 'em up same es steers, an' I driv' 'em all over dat bottom.

"Des bout dat time aner nigger mence to set up to dat ar gal. He was a right peert nigger too. He pick haf a bale o' cotton in a day. He made him a lather to get up on dat high wringer cotton, an he des stick to one stalk tell he got her picked clean. Dat's de way he pick so much in a day. He didn't have to move his lather more'n two or three times a day.

"One day Mr. Rumpless [']lowed: 'Jake, ef you don't stir yo' stumps, Cudjo 'll be more'n ap to git yo gal. He's a smart man,' says he, 'you see wilst you been foolin roun he's done a smart trick.'

"I tole him des to hole on a wile an ef I didn't do sumpin smarter'n Cudjo he was plum welcome to let Cudjo have de gal.

"He [']lowed he'd gimme tell Christmas, an he would'nt wait no longer.

"Dey warn't no wil'er' 'n sho 'nough steers, but dey was one thing 'bout 'em pestered me mighty bad: Dey didn't know how to walk; dey des jump. I know if dat was de way dey was gwine to go along dey'd juck a waggin all to pieces. Dat wouldn't do, you know, caze I was layin' off to take de whole drove down to Clarke an sell 'em to dem Clarke folks for sho 'nough steers; but if dey was gwine down dar jumpin' my cake was all dough.

"I studied. I kes kep' on a studyin'. I never slep' none for forty-nine nights. But the mo' I studied de bigger de confusement in my mine.

"I talked tolerable big, but I was feelin' mighty poly. I couldn't see no way to make dem frogs walk stid o' jumpin'. I was bad pestered. I hooped dem frogs, but dat never done no good. Dat des made 'em jump wusser an' wusser.

"Hit went on dat way tell plum chrismus eve night, un den hit popped in my haid what to do to dem frogs.

"I run over to Mr. Rumpless' house an' tole him ef he'd des wait on me 'bout one week mo' I'd do de smartes' thing anybody is done, an' hit'd more'n ap make him de riches man in M'ringer.

"But Mr. Rumpless wouldn't year to me. He 'lowed his promise was out, an' he was gwine to let Cudjo take de gal nex' day.

"He did, too.

"Looks like I wouldn't a done dat smartness atter dat. But I did. I done it des to make Mr. Rumpless sorry he didn't gimme dat [g]al. I cut de leaders in dem frogs' laigs so dey couldn straighten 'em. Dat's all what was de matter wid 'em all de time. Dey want to walk, but dey couldn't walk, caze dey laigs was too crooked.

"Me an' Mr. Rumpless drive 'em down to Clarke an' sole 'em, an' dem's de onlies kine o' steers dey got down in Clarke to dis day.

"Hit made Mr. Rumpless mighty rich, but he was so punish in his mine on de 'count o' not lettin' me have dat gal, he druthier staid po' all his life.

"Ef I had dis yer frog down dar in M'ringer, he'd be wuth $50, but long's he's yer, I'll let him go for ha'f a dollar."

"Here's your money," said a cadet, and walked away with the prize.

(The *Birmingham Age-Herald*, September 21, 1890)

Miss Mary; or,
The Value of Education

 "De likelies' white lady whar ever made a track in M'ringer was my young mistis," remarked Jake, confidently. "Her name was Miss Mary. I rickolleck her des like I seed her yistiddy. When she was a little gal, she was dat full o' fun an' devilment; she couldn't keep still save her life. Her ha'r was de color o' de remmunt gole, an' time she was grown, hit retch de groun'. Her face use to mine me o' one o' deze yer sugar peaches. Hit was right white, cepin on her cheeks, an' dem was red same es a rose. When she opened her mouf, she showed a row o' teeth so white hit hurt yo' eys to look at 'em. Nobody never looked at de diamon' rings on her han'. She had 'em dar, dough. But her han's was so pooty nobody couldn't take dey eys off 'n 'em to look at rings. Dey was a sight pootier 'an rings. She had a leetle teenchy weenchy foot, wasn't much bigger'n my big toe.

"Atter wile she growed up, an' ole moster sont her off to

college. Man, sah! w'en she come back f 'om dat college hit look like de sun done bust out'n de clouds an' light up de worl' like hit never is been lit befo'. An' she knowed it all, too, mon. She could talk outlandish talk good es I kin talk M'ringer. She could play on anything anybody brung her, cep'n a fiddle. She could des everlastingly knock a piano. Hit make you plum giddy to watch her little han's runnin' over de keys. Dey look sorter like de water in a branch whar hit runnin' mighty fas over de little rocks.

"Ole miss gin her a party soon atter she got back f 'om college. De word was sont out all over Perry an' Wilcox an' everwhar, an' mighty nigh all de quality folks in de worl' got a invite to dat party. Dey come, too, mon. Old moster had 'bout two hunderd likely young men like me des to take de horses w'en folks come, an' we had much es we could do, too.

"Dey aint no use o' me tryin' to tell you how she look dat night. You aint never seed nobody look like she did, cepin' you been to heaben an seed de angels walkin' de golden streets.

"Dat was her fust party, but atter dat ef she got any sleep she hatter git it in de day time. Dey kep her gwine ever night o' dis worl'. Dey warnt nair night de year roun' she didn't git a invite somewhars, an es for beaux, well I never tried to count em. I druther try to count de stairs. Dey des swarmed same es bees roun' ole moster's house. I des hatter quit workin' in de fiel'. Ole moster made me take my stan' by de gate an stay dar all de time des to take de young gempmen's horses wen dey come to cote Miss Mary. I got tolerable well quainted wid 'em all. Dey drapt many a quarter in my han'. I never shot my han' w'en I seed a quarter comin'.

"Well, sah, twarnt so mighty long 'fo' I know which a way de lan' laid, an' whar de win' was blowin' f 'om. I knowed dey was 'bout fo' hundred o' dem young w'ite men was gwine to git disappinted in dey mines. I knowed dey warnt but two stan' any chance to be my ole moster's son-law, and I made sho I knowed which one o' dem two was gwine to walk off wid Miss Mary. I watch dem two mighty close. I watched 'em 'fo' dey got to de house, an' I watched 'em atter dey lef' it. Sometimes I follered 'em down de road a piece to see ef dey look happy or nonplushed. I knowed ef Miss Mary said 'yes' to air one of 'em his face 'ud shine des like de sun; an' ef she happen to say 'no' to him he'd look like he was huntin' some place to hide hissef at an' die.

"One o' dem fellers lived in Perry, up dar 'bout Uniontown. His name was Mr. Petty. His daddy owned two hunderd niggers. He was des es likely a lookin' chap es ever I laid my eyes on. He des match Miss Mary, too, caze his ha'r an' eyes was des 'bout de same color o' her'n. Man, sah! I was always glad to year Mr. Petty's horse's huffs. He most in ginnerly come in a gallop. His horse was plum black, cep'n a white stair in his forward, an' he was de best horse ever I seed come f'om Perry. When he run he scarcely toch de groun'; he des skim 'long same es a rock skeet crost a mill pon'. Mr. Petty love to show off how he could ride. An' he could ride, too, mon. Wen he laid his laig crost a horse hit staid dar tell he purpozely tuck hit off. Look like he des growed to a horse. De horse mought jump and he mought rar, but Mr. Petty was dar. Him and Miss Mary dey use to go to ride sometimes. Dey rid right side by side. Miss Mary knowed what to do wid a horse. She warn't scared. She'd run a race wid him yit. Mr. Petty he tried to out-do her, but he never done it. She 'lowed she could go anywhars he could. I yeared her tell him so. Den he up an' axed her ef she would go wid him thoo life. She tole him she'd hatter study bout dat aw'ile. She 'lowed she was too young to marry yit aw'ile.

"One day dey went out to take a ride, an' I dunno whar all

dey went, but I know in reason he been a tryin' to outride her all de time, an' he couldn't do it. Es dey was comin' up todes de house all of a sudden, Mr. Petty wheeled his horse an' made him jump de fence into de paster. Es he went he hollered out:

"'Come on ef you kin.'

"Man, sah! hit made me trimble in my boots w'en I seed Miss Mary turn her horse to foller Mr. Petty. I hollered to her to stop for de Lord's sake, but she aint payin' no 'tention to me. She went over dat fence same es a sky rocket. She never stop den. She hollered to Mr. Petty to foller her ef he could, an' way she went, clippity-clippity, crost dat paster, over gulleys an' rocks an' briers an' ever'thing else. Mr. Petty, he follered her. I tuck my stan' in de fence cornder to see what was gwine to happen, caze I was oneasy in my mine. But dey come back atter w'ile. Nair one warnt hurt a bit, but all de ribbins was done come off 'n Miss Mary's ha'r an' her horse look like he was plum wrop in a net made out'n silk and gole stran's. Man, sah! ef she warn't a pooty sight wid her ha'r streamin' all roun' her!

"Des es dey passed me Mr. Petty leaned over todes her, an' he 'low:

"'Angel! speak de word an' make me happy. Say you'll be mine.'

"Miss Mary she tossed her head an' laffed. She 'low:

"'I never is gwine to have no man what can't beat me a-ridin'.'

"De yuther young man what I tole you 'bout I dunno whar he come f'om. Hit must a been a fur ways, 'caze dey warn't no signs o M'ringer blood 'bout him. He was a dark complected man. He look like he war always sorry 'bout sump'n he done some time or other. He rid his nag in a walk all de time. Ef she had trotted, I wouldn't be supprise' ef he hadn't a-fell off, 'caze I never is b'lieved he could ride much.

Dey say his daddy never did own nair huff of a nigger, an' dat was one thing set me 'gin him. I didn't want no po' w'ite trash comin' dar to cote my young mist'is. Dey said he had a heap of sense, but he never showed it. Dey 'lowed he could tell you 'zackly how fur hit was to de moon. I dunno how he find dat out. Ef he 'pen 'pon ridin' dat ole sorrel up dar he'd hat ter live a mighty long time fo' ever he'd fine out how fur hit war. He never had no rings on his fingers like Mr. Petty, an' ef he ever had air quarter 'bout his britches he aint never showed it to me. I tole him one day 'twarn't no use o' me hitchin' his critter, 'caze ef de critter was to go off he could walk an' ketch up wid him. He never said nair word; he des kep on lookin' sorry.

"One day bofe o' dem fellers come dar to see Miss Mary onbeknownst to one aner. I dunno what dey done in de house, hit warnt so mighty long fo' Mr. Middleton an' my ole moster got to scoursin 'bout what kine o' folks lives in de moon, an' Miss Mary an' Mr. Petty went out to ride.

"Dey warnt gone long. When dey got back dey bofe look sorter nonplush. Mr. Petty look bad pestered.

"Dey rid up to de gate, an' Mr. Petty, he lit, but Miss Mary, she des sot dar on her horse. Toreckly she [']low:

"'Come on Mr. Middleton, and les us [take] a ride.'

["I] never seed dat man move quick befo'. Hit 'stonish everybody how quick he got hisself on dat ole sorrel.

"Him an' Miss Mary, dey rid off, dey did, an' I tuck my stan' down de abnue to wait for 'em to come back.

"Dey was gone a right smart while. Dey was ridin' mighty slow w'en dey pass me. Look like Mr. Middleton want to say sump'n' mighty partic'lar, but he couldn't git it out. Toreckly he drapt a word or two, dough. He 'lowed he speck dey warn't no o' him a comin' back caze he 'lowed Miss Mary druther have de comp'ny o' Mr. Petty. He axed her what he mus' do.

"Look like Miss Mary was 'bout to cry, de way her voice soun'. She tole him he was cruel to her, an' he ought not make her say sich a think, but she want him to keep on comin' tell he git tired.

"Dat was all I yeared dat time. 'Twarn't long, dough, 'fo' some o' us niggers foun' out how de lan' laid. Ole moster an' ole miss dey wanted Miss Mary to have Mr. Petty, but she 'lowed she druther die. She loved Mr. Middleton. Gracious knows what she see 'bout him to love.

"Well, at las' one day I yeared Mr. Middleton ax Miss Mary to run 'way wid him, but she 'lowed ef dey done dat ole moster wouldn't give 'em no prop'ty.

"Wen dat man yeared dat he ris up straight in his stirrups, an he lowed:

"'I aint cotin yo niggers. I dont want dem, I wants you.'

"But dey never run way. I dunno how come dey never.

"De war come on, and bofe dem young men jine de army. Dey was bofe cap'ns, an dey bofe writ letters to Miss Mary. But Mr. Middleton dassent correct his letters to Miss Mary, caze ole moster would a seed em, and he would a kicked up de bigges sort o' row. We had de plans all fixed up, dough. He corrected his letters to me, an I tuck em to Miss Mary. I done dat for de sake o' my young mistis, not becaze I like Mr. Middleton.

"Hit went on dat way plum till de war een. Den bofe dem young mens come home. Dey was change bout mightly gin dat time. Mr. Petty's niggers was all sot free, an he never had nothin to go pon. Mr. Middleton never lost nothin, caze he never had nothin to lose, cep'n dat ole sorrel horse. But he had a mighty good eddication, and hit warnt long fo' he was makin' money han' over fist.

"Man sah! I aint yer dis minute ef ole moster warnt plum willin' for him to come to see Miss Mary den.

"I yeared em talk once mo'. I yeared Miss Mary tell Mr.

Middleton dey'd hatter break off dey gagement, caze she done lost all her prop'ty. But Mr. Middleton lowed he had 'nough for bofe, an' he was glad she never had nothin', an' es for breakin' off dat gagement, he wouldn't hear to it.

"De nex news I knowed dey was fixin' up de big house for a weddin'. I never staid dar to see it. I hit de grit. I got clean way f'om dar. I warnt gwine to stay dar an' see my young mistis marry a man whar aint never owned nair huff of a nigger.

"Miss Mary's ol'est boy's been yer to college. He's des like his mammy. Oh, he's a likely young man! W'en he fust come yer he 'lowed he was gwine to git a eddication, caze he done yeared his daddy say you could lose any kine o' prop'ty cep'n dat.

"Eddication do stick to a man. I got a right smart myse'f, an' ef I was to lose my new house up de railroad, I speck I could make a livin' teachin' school. I could l'arn Ben White an' Jim Bailey a heap o' things dey dunno."

(The *Birmingham Age-Herald,* September 28, 1890)

A Model School

 It is Jake's boast that he never turns back. He occasionally gets into a bog and flounders somewhat, but he keeps going in some sort of fashion till he reaches firm ground. It is this indomitable spirit that has carried him over many difficulties, which would have been insuperable to more timid souls.

His recent boast that he had "a right smart o' eddication" and if adversity should overtake him he could earn a livelihood by teaching, made a stir among the colored population. His claims were regarded as preposterous, and especially his assertion that he could teach those veteran schoolmasters, Jim Bailey and Ben White. Some of the colored people were indignant. They resolved to form themselves into an examining board and put the braggart to the test the first time they met him. Fortune favored them, for while they were yet in conference along came Jake, scythe in hand.

"We all des been a talkin' 'bout you," was the way they greeted him.

"You is?" said Jake, not the least abashed. "Well, I'm hopes y'all ain't said nothin' bad 'bout me."

"We was talkin' 'bout dem big brags you been a makin'. We des now yeered you was a school teacher."

"Is y'all des now yeered dat sho 'nough? Y'all's hine de times."

"We wants to know whar you got dat edication at whar you been a braggin' 'bout. Some o' us got some edication ourse'f, an' we gwine to fine out how much you knows. Yer, take dis yer book, an' lemme year you read some in hit."

Jake took the proffered volume, and for a moment it seemed that he was caught in the snare that had been laid for his unwary feet. An audible smile ran round as he opened the book and held it upside down before his face. But Jake was equal to the occasion.

"Y'all ought to be shame to laugh at a man 'caze he lef' his specks at home. Dat's de onlies reason I can't read dis book. Take yo' ole book. I got to go and cut Gin'al Lane's grass."

"Yaw! yaw! yaw!" laughed the chorus. "Po' excuse better'n none. You can't fool us. You dunno B f'om bullfoot, yit. Talk about taachin' school! You never is been eenside a school-house."

"I is, too. I teached school two years down dar in M'ringer atter freedom come out. I did dat. I had de bigges' school ever been in dis country. I had three hunderd grown gals and fo' hunderd big boys in my school, 'sides de little chillun. Y'all don't b'lieve it, maybe, but hit's a sho' fack. I ain't gwine to tell you no lie. Ef you-all wants to year all 'bout it, I'll up an tell you."

"Well, we wants to year all 'bout dat school, 'caze hit must a been a mighty cuis school what you teached."

"Hit was a cuis school. Hit warn't no ways like de whi' folks college. Hit warn't like nair nother school in dis country, caze hit had de ables' body teacher whar any school ever had.

"How come me to teach school? Me an' ole moster was bofe broke w'en de war come to a een, specially me, caze my ole moster had his lan lef', an' I never had nothin'. I never even had no moster to 'vide for me. De edication I got lis'nin' at my young mistis an' my young mosters gittin' dey lessons was all I had to go 'pon. No wonder I went to school-teachin'.

"Well, sah, I axed my ole moster ef he thought I could larn' dem young niggers roun' dar anything, an' he 'lowed I was de very sort o' teacher dey need, caze I had de strenk to do de work. He tole me all how I mus' do, an' I tuck an sont word out in de settlement I was gwine to teach school. I laid off to do des like my ole moster tole me to, an' I knowed I was gwine to give satisfaction.

"I went down to de school-house one Monday mornin', an lo an behole! de house was plum full o' little niggers, an dem whar couldn't git een some ob 'em was stannin' roun' outside, an some was done clum up on de roof. De niggers was mighty anxious atter edication dem days, an' I was de poplist teacher ever been in M'ringer.

"I went on in de house, I did, an' I tuck a cow bell out'n my shut, an' rung it. Atter dat I tuck an' called all dem chillun to me, one by one, an' axed what dey names was.

"I done tole you dey was a right smart passel ob 'em, an' gin I got thoo axin names de sun was down. Man, sah! hit was plum dark yit. Den I said:

"'School's 'smissed!'

"Dat was des like ole moster tole me to do, an' I knowed hit was plum right. Ef anybody do like my ole moster tole em, dey couldn't go wrong saves dey lives.

"De next mornin', atter I dun tuck in school, I up an' call a boy name o' Jim Bailey—"

"Yaw! Yaw!" interrupted the chorus.

"I did dat," continued Jake. "I called up Jim Bailey, an' I tole him to spell baker. Ef you b'lieve me, dat ign'ant nigger didn't know de fust word how to spell hit.

"I tole him to take his stan' dar by my dest an' wait dar tell I could 'ten' to him. Den I called up a boy name' Ben White."

"Yaw! yaw!" again broke in the chorus.

"Yas, sah," continued Jake, "I called up Ben White, an' I tole him to spell baker.

"Well, sah, dat nigger was scared. Ben was one o' deze yer white-eyed niggers, you know. His eyes was mighty white anyhow, but dat time dey was whiter'n ever. He sorter stutter, too. He des natchelly stutter, but dat day he stutter wusser'n ever. He stutter so bad I was scared he was gwine to shake all his teeth out'n his mouf.

"I tole him to take his stan' dar by Jim Bailey, an' bofe ob 'em be good boys tell dey year f'om me agin,' an' impartic'lar not to move nair foot nor bat nair eye.

"Den I called up a boy name o' Jess Jackson."

"Yaw! yaw!"

"Jess was a yaller complected nigger. He was toler'ble peert, an' I made sho' he was gwine to know how to spell de word, but ef he did I laid off to loosen up his hide wid a fo' foot hick'ry for bein' too smart.

"But he never done it. He spelt at her, but he never spelt her right.

"I tole him to take his stan' right by de yuthers.

"I called for Green Watkins nex', an' he come a rackin' up."

"Yaw! yaw! yaw!"

"Green was de greenes' one yit. He never is yeard nobody spell nothin' yit. I dunno whar he been raise' at, he was dat ignant.

"I made him stan' in the row wid de yuthers, an' I called Sarann an' Cindy an' Becky an' Florann an' a whole passel mo' o' de bigges' gals, an' I tried dem. Dey couldn't spell no better'n de boys, an' I made 'em stan' in a row by deyse'f.

"Well, sah, fust an' last, I called up all de niggers in dat house. Some ob 'em could spell a little, but couldn't none ob 'em spell baker right. One feller, he spelt her lef-handed an' another'n spelt her bottom up'ards. Hit's a sho' fack. Ef dat boy had a went to air nother teacher, he never would a larnt him nothin', caze dat boy's eyes was natchelly set in his haid upsided down. But I fixed him. I made him stan' on his haid when he was a studyin' his lessons, an' I tuck an' nailed his years to de flo' so he couldn't git up tell he knowed ever' word. W'en I got ready for him to git up, I ginnerly pulled dem nails out wid my teeth—y'all neenter laf; I use to have teeth an' dey was strong, too, mon.

"Man, sah, dat nigger's in Congress now, an' he wars year-ring in dem nailholes.

"Well, sah, gin I got all dem niggers stannin' up in two rows I went ahead an' done des like ole moster 'vise me to. I got me a waggin load o' fo' foot hickries, an' I went t work on 'em. I tuck Jim Baily fust, and I loosened up his hide so good Jim growed to be a big fat man."

"Yaw! yaw! yaw! Ef you ain't a sight in dis worl'!"

"Hit's a fack," remarked Jake. "Ef hit hadn't a been foor dat hoopin' Jim ud a always been a runt.

"After I got done wid Jim I tuck holt o' Ben White. I gin Ben such a hoopin hit stunted him, an' he never did grow much atter dat.

"Next I tuck holt o' Jess Jackson. When I lit on to Jess he

opened his mouf so big he aint never got it shot to dis day."

"Yaw! Yaw."

"But I larnt Jess a right smart o' sense, caze he's a 'fessor in a college somewhars now."

"Speck he is. Yaw! Yaw!"

"Yas, soh, he's de 'fessor o' drummin.' Green Wadkins he's a 'fessor, too. He's de fessor o' boot-blackin.'

"Well, sah, w'en my arm got tired hoopin' dem boys I des thowed hit roun' one o' dem gals' wais an' let hit res' a'wile. Dat's de way ole moster vise me to do: an' den dey'd all go home happy. An' I done it, mon.

"Cose I never got done dat day, but I cyad it on next day, an' wen I got thoo wid baker I gin 'em aner word. I gin 'em pony, des like my ole moster tole me to.

"Dey couldn't spell pony no bettern dey could spell Baker, case dey wus pizen ignant.

"I went on dat way two years, and I made lots o' money."

"How come you to quit ef you made so much money? Look like you'd a kep on."

"How come me to quit? Well, ef you want to know de truth, hit was caze some o' dem chilluns' daddies an' mammies warnt satify, an' dey tuck an' kick up a rucus wid me."

"Aha! Hit was caze you never larn dey chillun nothin'."

"No, hit warnt neither. Nobody never had nair word to say 'bout dat. Everybody 'lowed I was de bes' teacher dey ever seed."

"Well, hit was caze you hooped some o' dem boys too much."

"You done gone wrong agin. Dem boys' daddies and mammies dey knowed I couldn't git nothin' in em' 'cep'n' I loosen dey hides so dey could hole it. Dey was all plum satisfy.

"Hit was de gals' mammies whar kick up. Dey was plum hot. Dey [']lowed I hug some o' dem yuther gals harder an' mo' oftener'n I did deyrn.

"I wouldn't be supprise ef dat warnt a fack, too, caze you know hit take mo' huggin to do a likely gal dan a right down ugly un. Hit was de ugly gals' mammies whar raise de rucus.

"I got to be knockin long, but des fo I go I'll larn y'all how to spell baker—bay-ba-key-r-ker-baker."

(The *Birmingham Age-Herald,* October 5, 1890)

Mosquitoes of Marengo

"I years folks talk lots 'bout skeeters," said Jake to a group of his friends and admirers, "but I aint never seed nairn 'bout Aubun yit. Sometimes of a night I've yeared some little ole thing a zoonin' 'roun my years, but I never pay no 'tention to dem. Ef dem's skeeters dey're mighty po' little ole weakly things. Dey don't pester me; dey des sings me to sleep. Dey aint got de strenk to bo' thoo my hide. Dey aint got de weight yit. Ef somebody was to tie a fo' poun' rock on de back o' one ob em, he might could git a drap o' blood out'n a thin skin feller, but es for me, dey're plum welcome to work on me tell dey gits tired. Dey won't make seed corn off 'n me, not dem little ole gnats whar dey calls skeeters up yer.

"Down dar in M'ringo dey was some sho' 'nough skeeters. Dey was right smart o'em in some places. Late in de evenin' I've seed em rise up like a big black cloud out'n one o' dem sloos down dar. Dey make folks think hit was gwine to rain. Hit more'n ap to rain, too. Hit rain blood whar dey

gwine. I dunno what y'all 'ud do up yer ef you had dem many
skeeters. Yo' skins so thin dey'd punch you to de holler de
first time dey hit you, an' den dey'd be a nigger funal."

"Hit look like a plum wonder dey never kill dem folks
down day," remarked one of the audience.

"Dey did kill folks sometimes, but dey never is killed
nobody whar was born 'an raise in M'ringer. Hit was des de
newcomers whar come f 'om a po' country whar got killed.
Dem reg'lar M'ringer folks dey was raised up wid plenty to
eat all de time, 'an dey hides done growed thick same es a
steer's hide. Dey warn't no po' white trash down dar
nowhars. De 'skeeters cleaned 'em up fast es dey come. But
de quality folks dey warn't scared o' 'skeeters. Dey skin was
too thick. All a 'skeeter could do to dem he could tickle 'em
a little 'an make 'em eachy. Dat was de onlies' way a 'skeeter
could pester dem."

"I wouldn't want to live whar dey was so many skeeters,"
said one of Jake's hearers. "I'd be scared I might be tickle' to
death."

"You needn't be no ways oneasy 'bout dat," replied Jake,
"'cep'n' you was born an' raise up yer, 'caze ef you was born
down dar dey wouldn't pester you a bit more'n dese yer red
bugs does. Dey did tickle one man to death down dar,
dough, 'case he warn't born dar. He come dar when he was
a little boy, an' his mammy kep' de skeeters off 'n him tell his
skin got toler'ble thick. By dat time he was done growed up
a big boy, an' he 'lowed he was a man. Dey couldn't keep dat
feller in de house of a night no mo'. He was 'bleeged to go
to see de gals, an' he went to ever party an' ever meetin' dey
was. Well, sah, dey was a 'stracted meetin' a gwine on in de
settlement, an' dat boy he was dar ever night de worl' sen'.

"One night, es de preacher was a callin' up mo'ners, dat
boy laffed out loud. Nobody never knowed who done it dat
time, caze dey was so much fuss an' confusement gwine on

'bout den, nobody couldn't tell which way de laf come fr'om. But toreckly he laffed agin, and de preacher seed him. De preacher axed him ef he warnt 'shame to laf in de meetin' house. De boy he 'lowed he couldn't hep hissef caze dat yuther boy settin' by him tickled him. Dat yuther boy 'lowed he never done no sich a thing. Wid dat one word brung on aner, an' dey kep a sputin tell atter wile dey got to fightin, an' dey fit all over dat meetin' house.

"Well, sah, es dey was goin' over an' under de benches an' gougin' at onean'er's eyes de folks yeared a mighty laffin' gwine on all de time. Atter w'ile somebody up an' low:—

"'He's a laffin' so he cain't fight. I speck he's got de laffin zease, or either a skeeter's got him. Les us part 'em.'

"Hit turn out des zackly dat way. Dat feller done got to laffin' an' he couldn't stop, and' de yuther'n was a hoopin' him caze he couldn't fight for laffin'.

"De preacher [']lowed dat mus' be sump'n mighty funny he was a laffin' at, caze he ain't never yeard o' nobody a laffin' w'en dey was a fightin' befo'.

"Dey parted 'em, dem folks did, an' dat feller sot down on a bench, but he never stop a laffin'. He kep on a laffin' wusser an' laf till he drap dead off'n de bench on de flo'.

"Dey never did fine out what was de matter wid him till de crowner came dar an' sat on him. De crowner had on a tolerbly thin par o' britches, an' de minute he tuck his seat he bounced up again like sump'n done stuck him. Sump'n did stick him, too. Hit was a skeeter whar stuck his swode in him. Hit warn't no wonder he jumped.

"Dey foun' dat skeeter right on dat dead boy's short ribs. He done sot dar an' tickle dat boy to death. W'en de crowner sot down on him he up and gin him a stob, an' de crowner never sot down dar no mo' till dey got dat skeeter out'n de way.

"Cose dat was a little skeeter, but ef y'all had a seed him you'd a called him a gallinipper, I speck. But sho' 'nough M'ringer gallinippers is big es a grasshopper, an' when dey sings hit don't soun' like ole aint Susan Miller a singin' de trible up in de meetin' house. Hit soun' like one o' dese yer calliropers whar goes roun' wid de shows an plays de pie-anner wid steam. Dem little skeeters is heap bigger 'n any o' dese yer starve things 'bout yer. Dey're right smart o' use deysef down in M'ringer. Sometimes folks gits sick down dar f'om livin' too rich. Dey has too much blood in 'em, an' hit's got to be drawed off. Dats what dey uses dem little skeeters fur. De doctors scrapes off some o' dat thick M'ringer hide an puts de skeeters on an tells 'em to root hog or die. I've seed 'em bleed folks many a time dat way down dar in M'ringer.

"Cose de big gallinippers is a heap mo usefuller 'an de little uns. De folks couldn't git long widout em down dar. I knowed a man down dar whar got rich des raisin gallinip-pers."

"Law!"

"Hit's a sho fack. His name was Mr. Rumpless. He never had hardly victuals an clo'es for his fambly tell he foun out how to work gallinippers. But he made money han over fis' atter dat. Wen freedom come out he turn loose bout fo' hundred niggers, an he made em all workin' gallinippers. Dey pestered him mighty bad awhile, but twarnt so mighty long fo' he was glad dey did, caze dat was de casion o' him makin money out'n em.

"Dey use to kill right smart o' his hogs. Dat's how come he tuck to watchin' 'em. He watched 'em wid his double barrel shot gun, an' he laid off to shoot de lights out'n all he could fine.

"Twarnt long fo' he found out gallinippers was in de

habits o' stayin' up all night an' sleepin' all day des like some Aubu'n folks. Atter he l'arn dat twarnt no trouble 'tall to fine 'em, he des hatter go to some sloo 'bout dar.

"He nodis wen dey roostes dey sticks dey bills down in de groun'—an' dey got mighty long bills, too, mon. Dey kin stick you thoo fo' blankets an' two quilts easy 'nough. Dey bills is de longes' part 'bout 'em.

"Another thing, he nodis whar lots o' 'em was in de habits o' roostin' de groun' 'ud mo'n ap to be dry.

"On his place dey was a mighty rich sloo, but hit was dat wet nobody couldn't plant nothin' in hit. But dey was one little spot whar right smart o' gallinippers roosted, an hit was dry.

"Dat was nough for Mr. Rumpless. Stid o' shootin' dem skeeters, he cotch em an' penned em up an' fed em and went reglar in de business o' raisin em.

"Dey raises mighty fast, gallinippers does. De one whar was born las night he'll have great gran-chillun tomorrow.

"Hit was a fast way to make money."

"How?" somebody interrupted. "You ain't never tole us how he was gwine to make money yit."

"Yes, I is, too."

"How, den? Did he make middlin meat outen dem skeeters?"

"Naw: dar aint no meat 'bout a skeeter. Dey're des a leather bag set up on a steel wire frame wid a sharp spear runnin' out befo' 'em. Dey aint made out'n meat.

"W'en Mr. Rumpless got a big pile o' dem gallinippers he tuck 'em roun' de country an' let 'em dry off folkses' lan' for 'em, an' dey paid him a pile o' money for it, too, caze dey was lots o' rich lan' down dar what was too wet to plant.

"He never done nothin' but des let his skeeters roos' on de wet lan' one day, an' man, sah, dey'd dry it off ever' time.

Dey'd stick dey bills down so deep dey'd go plum to whar de worl's holler, an' w'en dem bills was pulled out, de water 'ud run down thoo de holes.

"Dat's de way Mr. Rumpless got so rich."

(The *Birmingham Age-Herald*, October 12, 1890)

Lightning

 A gentleman was performing the menial task of currying his own horse the other day, when he was espied by Jake, who happened to be at work in a neighboring garden. Spade and hoe were dropped with that promptness which is characteristic of Jake when there is a dime in immediate prospect, and the next moment the same hands that had been turning the "stubborn glebe" were vigorously wielding the curry-comb, equine protests to the contrary notwithstanding.

"Moss Jimmie, hit goes gin my aligion to see a nice, likely gent'man like you scrubbin' a hoss," Jake began. "Down dar in Mringer de white men dey never hardly stirred dey coffee, dey was dat scared dey make corns on dey han's. But dey was a right smart chance o' niggers down dar, dat was de reason. Wo, sah! You better lef dat foot on de groun right whar hit's at; caze ef you was to kick me on de haid you'd be more'n ap to split yo' huff ha'f in two. I'm got a Mringer haid, an not one o' des yer Aubu'n simlins. Yas, sah, Moss Jimmie, I speck you've yeared tell de groun was black down dar in Mringer. Well, de reason dat's caze dey's so many black Afkins down dar. Hit's all dem niggers' shadders what done turn de dirt black.

"Wo, pony, keep still, sah. I ain't gwine to hurt you. I knows how to curry a hoss. I ain't staid a whole year in a lib'ty stable for nothin'."

"Where did you ever stay in a livery stable?" inquired the gentleman, taking a cigar out of his pocket and lighting it.

"Down dar in Uniontown," replied Jake. "Soon atter freedom come out I went up to Uniontown an' hired to a lib'ty stable. Dat's how come I knows so much 'bout hosses.

"Moss Jimmie, dat seegar smell mighty nice. Hit smell same es gals gwine to meeting wid cin'mon draps on 'em. I wonder whar de mate o' hit's at."

"It got burnt, I reckon," the gentleman replied, after a futile search of his pockets, "but never mind, here's a dime for you. Now go on with your yarn about the livery stable."

"Thanky, sah. You's a plum gent'man, an' I ain't des now foun' it out. I been tellin' Ma'jane all de time you mine me o' dem M'ringer gent'man whar use come to hire hosses down dar in Uniontown."

"Why, Uniontown is not in Marengo."

"No, sah, not 'zactly. Uniontown hit's in Perry, but hit's a toler'ble good town. Hit's so close to de aidge o' M'ringer some o' de M'ringer richness slops over on it. But I wouldn't a staid in dat Uniontown stable ef all dem hosses had a been Perry hosses."

"So some of them were not Perry horses, eh?"

"One o' em wasn't. Dey was one M'ringer hoss in dar, an' man, sah! he was a sooner. Dat hoss was name Lightnin', an' he was lightnin, too, man. Nobody never had nothin' to do

wid dat hoss but des me. He wouldn't let no Perry nigger
tech him, let lone curry him. All dem young gent'men roun'
dar use to drive Lightnin', caze he could trot so fas'. De fust
one spoke for him was ginnerly de one what got him, an' den
all de yuthers was mad. Dey fit 'bout him sometimes, too—
dey did, dat. An' I've knowed 'em to play a game o' seben-
up to see who could have him. Oh, he was a traveler. He
runned a race wid a 'spatch wonst, an' he beat it, too, mon.
A man put a 'spatch on de telegraph wire at Moplis de same
time Moss Tom Rumpless started f'om dar drivin' Lightnin'
(an' I ain't gwine to tell you no lie). Fo' ever dat 'spatch got
to de nex station Moss Tom was dar an' done onhitch
Lightnin' f'om de buggy. Fack, sah.

"One night de whi' folks dey made up to have a big party
out in de country 'bout ten miles, an' all de young gentman
in Uniontown went. Well, sah, dey come 'roun' to de libly
stable in a crowd, an' ever' one want to drive Lightnin'. De
boss man he was sorter confuse in his mine which one to
'commodate, caze ever' one 'mence to talk at wonst. Ever'
man 'lowed he spoke for Lightnin' fust, an' dey was a right
smart chance o' confusement. I reckon dey'd a been de
bigges' fight ever you seed hadn't a been for me. I come up,
I did, an' I 'lowed I could settle dat difficulty, ef dey'd let me.
De boss man 'lowed: 'All right, go ahead.'

"Well, sah, dey was a nigger boy name o' Bill hope us in de
stable. He was a right peert boy, too, caze he was born an'
raise in Mringer. I tole Bill to take all de horses out in de lot
hine de stable an' put 'em in a row. He done it. Es he was a
gwine I hilt up two o' my fingers dis way so he could see 'em,
an' he nod his haid same es to say he onnerstan. I did't let
dem gentmen see me do it, dough. I didn't know what was
gwine to happen.

"Well, after Bill done got dem hosses in a row hine de

stable, I tole dem gentmen to go back dar an' see ef ever thing was fa'r an' squar. Dey went, an' dey come back an' [']lowed it was all right.

"Es dey comin' back thoo de stable I was a stannin' dar 'gin de wall wid my han's hine my back. I didn't know what might drap in 'em. Sho 'nough, toreckly I felt sump'n. I slipt my han' roun' whar I could see it onbeknownst, an' lo an' behole! dar was a bran' new silver dollar. I knowed who put it dar.

"Atter dat I tole de boss man to ax me who was to have de fust hoss an' who was to have de next un, an' so on, same as boys 'vides out fishes w'en dey goes a seinin.' Nobody couldn't 'spute but what dat was fa'r an' squar, caze I ain't seen de hosses.

"De boss man, he up'n says: 'Who de fust hoss for?'

"I says: 'Dat'n's for Moss Cad Bolin.'

"'Who de second un for?' says he.

"'Dat'n's for Moss Tom Rumpless,' says I.

"Wid dat Moss Tom, he flung up his hat an' hollered, caze he done got Lightnin'. Dem yuthers, dey was right smart nonplush, but day dassent kick up no row, caze hit was all done fair an' squar."

"All but your part; you got Tom Humphrey's dollar," said the gentleman.

"Law, Moss Jimmie, what a good han' you is to guess," said Jake, laughing.

"Well, es I was a sayin', dem fellers dey dassent raise no rucus, but dey let in an' made out like dey was glad dey never got Lightnin'. Dey lowed dem yuther hosses wes des es fast es him.

"'No, dey aint, neither,' Moss Tom says, says he, 'Lightnin' kin trot backuds fastern any dem yuthers kin trot forruds,' says he.

"'Well, we'll see 'bout dat,' dey says.

"I reckon dey was a right smart o' red liquor at dat party. Leasways, dem yuther gent'man got on a mighty big tare. Dey tuck an' unhitched Lightnin' f 'om dat buggy an' dey 'versed de hamen—"

"Versed it?"

"Yas, sah, turned hit een for een. An dey hitched up dat horse backuds. De put his haid right whar his tail ought to a been. De britchin hit fit roun his shoulders, an de Dutch collar work right gin his hams.

"Well, sah, I aint yer dis minute ef Moss Tom Rumpless didn't drive dat hoss home des zackly dat way. Hit was a tolerble dark [n]ight, an Moss Tom couldn't see how his hoss was hitched, imparticular caze he been a knockin red liquor tolerble heavy.

"All de same, he beat ever one o' dem yuther fellows home. He lef em on de road. Dey made sho' dey was gwine to beat him, caze dey never studied bout no hoss trottin backuds.

"W'en I stepped out'n de stable, me an' Bill, to take Moss Tom's horse, I [']lowed:

"'Hayo! Moss Tom, how is you got dis hoss hitched?'

"'Dat hoss all right,' Moss Tom says, says he, 'I beat em ever one,' says he.

"'Ef you did,' says I, 'you got him hitched up hine part befo,' says I.

"'No I aint,' says he. 'You're drunk,' says he, 'whar you git yo liqua at?'

"'Ef you b'lieve you got Lightnin hitched up right,' says I, 'you dess git out an zamine him,' says I.

"He got out, he did, but no sooner he done it de groun' flew up and hit him in de face. I hope him up, but de nex' news I knowed he was a layin' on de groun' right under

Lightnin'. I pulled him out f 'om dar, an atter dat I hilt him
up tell he could feel dat hoss all over f 'om een to een. But he
warn't satisfy den. He warn't satisfy tell he slipped his han's
long de lines and foun' out whar de bit was at. Den he gin in.
He couldn't spute no mo'. He des up an [']low:

"'I thought ole Lightnin's mouf was mighty hard.'"

(The *Birmingham Age-Herald,* April 26, 1891)

An Abridged
Nar[r]ative

 Three little white boys were setting out [to] spend Christmas rabbit hunting. At their heels trotted a bob-tailed cur, upon whose swiftness and keenness of scent depended their most enthusiastic expectations. Anticipation had lent them a delicious foretaste of the excitement of the chase and the triumphal return with such rich trophies as would make all their acquaintances green with envy.

"Won't old Jim Brown be 'stonished when he sees us comin' back?" cried one bubbling over with enthusiasm.

"He will that! He'll wisht he had a went," said another.

"I'm glad he never. He's so biggety, he'd a said the reason we caught so many was 'cause he was 'long."

"I wisht I had a took his bet. He said he'd bet his two stone glasses 'ginst my white alley we wouldn't ketch a thing."

"Whyn't you take him up, you goose you?"

"'Cause."

"I know the reason. You always so everlastin' scared you'll lose that old white alley."

"You would a been too if it had a been your'n. Ole White's the best marvel in this town. I've had her so long she knows zactly what I want. If I'm playin' ring, she goes for the middler every pop, an' if I'm playin' sweeps, she jest lays close till I knock 'em all out."

"You reckon Jim would a bet if he had a knowed we was goin' to have old Bob?"

"Naw. He thought we was jest goin' to have a little fice. He never knowed we could git old Bob, had, he'd a went with us."

"Lemme tell you somethin'. Le's give old Jim four or five rabbits jest to make him shamed o' hisself."

And thus they rattled and prattled, as they ran rather than walked, till they had cleared the town, when a gruff voice from the corner of a fence arrested their attention.

"Hayo!"

The salute was so unexpected that all the boys stopped simultaneously from sheer surprise.

"Whar y'all little boys gwine?"

It was the voice of Jake, and through the interstices of the fence partial views of his grotesque figure and grinning face confirmed his identity.

"Whar y'all gwine?" repeated Jake.

"Huntin'," was the answer.

"What y'all speck to ketch wid dat ole bob-tail dog?"

"Rabbits. That's the best rabbit dog in this country."

"Don't y'all know a bob-tail dog can't run? W'en y'all makes a kite you don't never speck hit to fly 'cep'n you puts a tail on it, does you?"

"Course not."

"Same thing I done tole you. Ef you was to try to fly a kite 'dout a tail, hit'd des turn over an' flop down on de groun'. Y'all knows dat, an' you got sense 'nough to put a tail on ever' kite you makes. Well, de good man whar makes de dogs he's got mo' sense 'n you all is, an' ef dogs didn't need no tails, he wouldn't put none on 'em."

"Bob ain't got none."

"I know he ain't got none now, but he been had one. W'en he was a pup he had a tail, but somebody done cut hit off 'n him. He can't run fast save his life, 'caze he ain't got no tail to balance his haid, an' he'll turn a summerset. His behime parts dey'll fly up sho'. Maybe he might could run ef y'all was to tie a rock to his stump."

"Rabbits can run, an' they ain't got no tails," said one of the little boys, shrewdly.

"Dat's so, honey," returned Jake, "dey kin run same 'es de win'. Dey'll everlastin'ly git way f 'om dat ole dog y'all got. Dey won't study 'bout gwine in no holler, 'caze dat ole dog can't push 'em cloast 'nough. De one whar made rabbits never gin 'em no tails caze he knowed dey never need none. Dey hine laigs is so much heavier 'n dey fo' shoulders dey aint no danger o' dey turnin' a summerset. Ef he had a built dogs de same way, he wouldn't a gin dem no tails neither. But dat aint de onlies' reason I wouldn't go huntin' wid a bob-tail dog. I'm dis sort o' man: I'm sort o' partec'lar what sort o' comp'ny I keeps, I is. I ain't gwine to soshate long o' no bob-tail dogs an' no bob-tail niggers neither, caze I dunno how come dey tails bobbed off 'n 'em. Dey're des de same 'es a man whar got a bran' on him. Dey been in some devilment some time or other, an' dey won't do to trus'. Dey done it wonst, an' dey'll more'n ap do it ag'in. You can't 'pen on 'em for nothin'. I reckon y'all specks to beat all de yuther boys ketchin rabbits today, don't you?"

"Yes, we do. I know we'll beat Tommie Wood, cause he ain't got nothin' but a fice."

"Is dat a 'spectable fice he got?"

"Dunno what you mean."

"Is he ever been 'scused o' suckin' aigs or stealin' sheep?"

"Dunno."

"Well, is he got air tail a hangin' on de hine een o' him?"

"Yes; he's got a long tail, an' he curls it up over his back."

"Dat's a good sign den, caze ef he was bobbed hit'd be a sho sign he been a doin' sump'n wrong, an' folks bobbed him for it. An' he quoils dat tail up over his back—dat's 'nother good sign, caze w'en you sees a dog do dat hit show he ain't done nothin' what he's shame o' hisse'f 'bout. Dese yer dogs what you see gwine 'bout wid dey tails draggin' on de groun' or tuck twix' dey laigs, dey'se dat shame an' feared dey ain't no 'count. Dey ain't 'spectable dogs, an' more'n 'at de tail what dey totes don't belong to 'em. I'm scared Tommie Wood gwine to beat y'all ketchin' rabbits today."

"What you mean by a dog totin' a tail that don't belong to him?"

"I means des what I says, honey. Down dar in M'ringer whar I use to live de whi' folks made it up to have a big dog race one Chris'mus wonst. Dey was gwine to turn loose a fox whar dey done cotch, an' see whose dog cold outrun.

"Dey was a man down dar name o' Mr. Rumpless, an' he never had no race dog, but he was more'n ap to be into ever'thing whar dey was any bettin' gwine on. So he sont out word he want to buy a fas' dog, an' no sooner he done it yer come de dog sellers f'om all over de lan'. Dey brung ever' kine of dog you ever seed, an' Mr. Rumpless he scacely knowed which un to buy, dey was so many. But atter while he th'owed all de dogs to one side, cep'n two, an' he was right smart pestered in his mine which one o' dem two to take. One o' 'em was a long, keen dog, des built right to run same es a streak o' lightnin' thoo a crabapple orchard, but dat dog had a mean look like he been a suckin' aigs, an' look like he never had de strenk to lif' his tail off 'n de groun'. De yuthern was a mighty peart dog, an' he quoil his tail mighty tight over his back, but he was little, an' his laigs was mighty short for a race dog. De big dog was name Major, an' de little 'un was name Dandy. Atter w'ile Mr. Rumpless made up his mine, an' he 'cide de question. He 'low:

"'I b'lieve I'll take Maj'e, do' he do look like he been a stealin' [s]heep or doin' sump'n mean.'

"No sooner he said dat aver man, by name o' Grimes, he up an' 'low:

"'Ef dat's yo' han',' says he, 'I'll take de little dog whar quoil his tail over his back, caze dat dog ain't gwine to 'ceive nobody, an' w'en dat fox is cotch Dandy 'll be somewhars cloast about.'

"Everybody in de crowd hollered, 'You mighty right, Mr. Grimes.'

"Wen Chrismus come de folks gethered f 'om de fo' eens o' de yeth. Look like de whole worl' was dar to see dat race. Dey tuck dat fox out in de open perarer whar dey speck to turn him aloose. Den de bettin begin. I never see sich bettin in my life. Every man showed his dog an' his pocket-book. Dey was more'n ten thousan' dollars bet on that race. Some bet on one dog an' some on an'er. A right smart chance o' money was put up on ole Major, but some folks was skeer'd o' him, caze hit look like he never had de strenk in his backbone to hole up his tail. But Mr. Rumpless planked down everything he had in dis worl' on Maje, an' dat how come he broke.

"Dey turn de fox loose, dey did, and dey sicked all de dogs on him. At fus hit look sorter like old Maje was gwine to beat, caze he kep up sich a racket barkin nobody never seed nor yeared no dog but him. Dem what bet on him dey gin to crow, an' dey lowed Dandy was dat busy holin up his tail he couldn't run.

"Ole Maje he tuck de lead, sah, an' he made mo' fuss'n two trains. But Mr. Grimes never look bad. He kep a stiff upper lip, an' he 'lowed he had mo' money to put up on Dandy ef anybody want to win it.

"Dandy was de nex' dog behine ole Maje. De race was twixt dem two. Some yuther dogs was lopin' on behine, but dey was lef so fur behine dey was shame to open dey mouf.

"Dey kep on, dey did, dey kep on, tell after while dey come to a brier patch. De fox he never stop for dat, an' neither the dogs. De folks watch to see how dey gwine to come out on de yuther side. Toreckly dey seed ole Maje come out, but lo an' behole! he never had nair sine o' tail. He was a plum bob-tail dog, an' de fus jump he made he turn a double summerset. Ole Dandy des run right over him, an' de nex' news anybody knowed Dandy had dat fox in his mouf chawin' him."

"What become o' ole Major's tail?" inquired one of the little boys.

"Dat's des what I'm gwine to tell you 'bout now," said Jake. "Dat dog never had no tail. He been cotch in a steel trap or sumpn, an' his tail war cut off for suckin' aigs or stealin' sheep. Dat ar dog seller tuck an' sewed a black snake on dat dog's stump, an' fool Mr. Rumpless. Wen ole Maje was a runnin' thoo dat brier patch de briers cotch holt o' dat snake an' pull hit off.

"Y'all come by yer dis evenin', an' lemme see what you cotch with yo' bob-tail dog."

⟡ ⟡ ⟡

Late in the afternoon three tired bed-raggled and dejected little boys were making their way homeward empty-handed. They skulked through lanes and by-ways as if to avoid observation, and so it came about that they accidentally ran upon Tommie Wood, who had one solitary hare to show for his day's work. Almost at the same instant they espied Jimmie Brown posted at a commanding position immediately on their way home, and apparently waiting for them.

Something must be done, and that quickly. A hasty consultation was held, and it was decided that Tommie Wood's rabbit must be bought at any price.

Tommie was approached. He was willing to sell his game, but when he named his price one of our little friends stood aghast—nothing less than the far-famed white alley would buy his rabbit. Two of the boys were willing to make the exchange and by some process of reasoning or persuasion they induced the third, who was the owner of the marble, to consent.

Tommie having the long coveted marble, sped on home, while our three friends trudged on slowly, making as great a display of the hare as possible.

"He promised not to tell anybody he sold us this rabbit, didn't he?"

"Yes, he did. Course he ain't goin' to tell on us, now he's got my white alley."

Reaching the top of the hill they were suddenly confronted by Jim Brown, who had been hidden behind a bush.

"See here!" said Jim, holding aloft the white alley. "You all got a rabbit for it, an' I give my two stone glasses for it."

The next moment Jake rose from a crouching position behind the same bush.

"I reckon y'all willin to gimme dat rabbit now, caze y'all ull be shame tote him thoo town. Everbody 'll know y'all never cotch him wid a bob-tail dog. Twarnt y'all's fau't you never cotch nothin. Y'all's des es likely a hunters es ever I seed ef you des had a had a good dog. I'll save y'all de trouble o' totin dat ole dead rabbit home. I kin make a stew out'n him, but he wont do y'all no good. He'll des make folks laf at you," and he laid his hand on the game. A gentle pull and it was his.

(The *Birmingham Age-Herald,* December 27, 1891)